A HEROIC COMBAT NOVEL OF THE INCREDIBLE
COURAGE AND HEROISM OF AMERICAN GIs
AT WAR IN GERMANY!

THE WATCH ON THE BRIDGE

"Recommended." (Library Journal)

". . . a rich, swiftly flowing story . . . David Garth has a sure hand on the soldier idiom and is equally at home in high-level staff meetings. His book is a good thing." (The Boston Sunday Herald)

"Even knowing the outcome does not prevent a mounting curiosity as to how such a rich prize was left intact. . . . This is easily one of the better adventure tales of the year." (Utica Daily Press)

"IMPELLING FORCE." (Austin American Statesman)

Also by David Garth

MANILA MASQUERADE
NEVER MIND THE LADY
ANGELS ARE COWARDS
FOUR MEN AND A PRAYER
A LOVE LIKE THAT
CHALLENGE FOR THREE
EASTWARD IN EDEN
ROAD TO GLENFAIRLIE
TIGER MILK
THUNDERBIRD
BERMUDA CALLING
GRAY CANAAN
THE TORTURED ANGEL
FIRE ON THE WIND
THREE ROADS TO A STAR

THE WATCH ON THE BRIDGE

David Garth

WARNER PAPERBACK LIBRARY EDITION

First Printing: April, 1965
Second Printing: December, 1967
Third Printing: October, 1972

Library of Congress Catalog Card No. 59-5681

This Warner Paperback Library Edition was published by arrangement with G. P. Putnam's Sons.

Warner Paperback Library is a division of Warner Books, Inc., 315 Park Avenue South, New York, N.Y. 10010.

ACKNOWLEDGMENTS

The author acknowledges with deep appreciation the information and assistance of The Office of the Chief of Military History; The Departmental Records Branch, U. S. Army; the Book and Magazine Branch, U. S. Army; *The Bridge at Remagen* by Ken Hechler.

WATCH ON THE BRIDGE

FOREWORD

SOMEONE ONCE said, a book reviewer, I think, that almost every intelligent foreign correspondent eventually reaches the point where he finds himself so moved and so fascinated by the events he has observed that he is driven beyond the short stint into the realm of the sustained effort of book writing. The majority of these books die half written, especially the attempts at novels. Reminiscence and report do not necessarily constitute a novel, nor can symbols replace human beings, or ideological conflict emotional conflict.

I am sure that this must be true, because in the course of my thirty-two years as a foreign correspondent I have failed in several attempts at the sustained effort of book writing. And the only reason I have succeeded now is because of something a man once told me that I did not believe and that he himself later denied.

I would like to explain that. During a recent winter my wife and I settled down in our New Hampshire home, happily snowbound, for my first real American vacation in several years. I frankly nourished some thought of being stimulated to a sustained job of original writing, but I remained as dead center as a stalled pendulum. I suppose that I may have dimly realized that from all my experience there was nothing I desired to write about on my own time. I was either lazy or tired or, most likely, I had nothing I wanted to say.

Then one wintry evening I was sorting out a file of old dispatches and came across one on that Rhine bridge. My attention was caught primarily by my lead, which referred to "ten minutes of flaming action that immediately became historic and upset the entire Western front." I must have been somewhat excited, because I do not generally write that way. However, as I reviewed that dispatch, I remembered clearly the action at the doomed bridge that brought on the most spectacular development of the entire World War II.

I knew a great deal about that event and the old dispatch was like a spotlight that searched out several memories for me in sharp clear focus.

First, of course, was the bridge itself, that country cousin bridge, that doomed country cousin bridge, a four-hundred-yard steel ribbon over a river that flowed deep and swift between the cliffs.

And there were the words of Winston Churchill summing it all up, like a great organ diapason, in the stirring way he could express a thought: "The greatest fortune of war that fell to our arms."

And there was an officer talking to me in the kitchen of a farmhouse in the nearby town of Gelsdorf the day after the astounding events at the bridge. This memory was the sharpest of all.

He was in the combat-observer section assigned to First U.S. Army, a major, and I had met him several times before. I had reached Gelsdorf after a fast dash from III Corps' headquarters at Zulpich and by that time the bridge was already becoming the most important bridge in the world and hell was breaking loose at the river. The sky was full of swooping planes and tracer fire and explosions like great balls of reddish-yellow flame. The roads through Gelsdorf were jammed with artillery and anti-aircraft units, with lines of combat troops strung out along the muddy shoulders, all pushing pell-mell for the river, while the MPs had established a control center in town and were organizing the jumbled traffic into route interval. In all that mess I had been stalled, and while waiting for my jeep to be given its place in the traffic pattern, I encountered this major. He had come from the river, and as soon as he recognized me it was apparent he had something he wanted to tell me. He had something he wanted to say. *He had something he simply had to say.*

I can see him very clearly even now, after all this time, as he talked in that Gelsdorf kitchen, a lean man in a stained trench coat buttoned tight around his throat, his face unshaven and his eyes hooded with fatigue under his steel helmet. He lay back in a wooden chair with his muddy combat boots stuck out before him, without any apparent strength except in his voice and whatever was in him that kept the words coming. He did not make sense to me and I kept listening, waiting for some nugget I could use for a dispatch, something worth putting on the wires, and he talked and talked, pouring it out, and I finally found myself believing him not at all. When my driver came in to tell me that the MPs would give us a break if I came quickly, I went quickly. I left that officer there in the kitchen still trying to talk it out, beginning to repeat himself, trying to set up in words something he could not seem to handle mentally.

But I had listened carefully, an occupational trait, and, strangely enough, I did not forget what he had told me. I did not believe it, but I did not forget it. Several months later, after the end of the war, I ran into him again at the Mayflower Red Cross Club in Paris, as I was preparing to wind up my European assignment. He looked and acted completely different—easy, poised, trim in green blouse and pinks. In a mood to cut up old touches, I tried to discuss with him the story he had given me in Gelsdorf. To my surprise he denied it immediately.

"Look," I told him, "I don't care about the story. I'm not going to print it. But don't tell me you didn't tell me. I was there in that farmhouse kitchen. Remember?"

Well, he said casually, if that was the way I wanted it, then he must have been drunk. I did not think he had been drunk. Emotionally surcharged and physically exhausted, I had thought, but not drunk. However, I did not argue the point and I never saw him again. Nor, as I happen to know now, will ever see him again.

But, again, I could never have really forgotten what he told me. Because, when it stirred again in my memory during that New Hampshire winter, time seemed to have etched it in clear sharp lines. Suddenly I wanted to write the story of the bridge.

Please understand that I have not meddled with the events of that day at the doomed bridge. That is history, amazing and almost unbelievable but authentic and documented, and I could not, if I would, meddle with it.

But without that Gelsdorf story, unbelieved and even denied, I could not have written the story of the bridge. It was like trying to put bricks together without mortar. It had to be included and the only way it could be included was to write the book as a novel. I have had to use some speculation and imagination to flesh out the framework of the story voiced once, and never again, in that Gelsdorf kitchen, but the end result is the same.

So I have explained why something I did not believe came to drive me to write the story of the bridge as a novel. Those who will not believe my embellishment will find sufficiently absorbing, I think, the actual events that swirled about the bridge. But those who do believe it will realize what I mean, and this Foreword is mainly for them.

As to whether I have come to believe it myself, that remains my own business. It is enough that I shall always be glad I wrote the story as I honestly felt convinced it should be written and gave it the only title possible for such a story.

ROBERT B. WHITTING

Hanover, New Hampshire
May, 1958

THE APPROACH

1.

Robert Berkham had been a correspondent for many years and life was beginning to wear on him by February, 1945. He was a big man, with a rather peering expression from behind horn-rimmed glasses, slow of speech and deliberate in movement. He was liked well enough in the press camps, although many of his colleagues remembered him as more sociable in other days. Berk, they thought, was tired, as who the hell wasn't, but he still was an extremely astute newspaperman.

Berkham was tired, of course. He had been in the Pacific, at Kwajalein, he had lived in the ETO press camps at Oran and Malta, he had followed the European invasion in the battles for Cherbourg and Saint-Lô and he had nearly been killed in July, 1944, when he got too far down front and just missed being caught by a premature drop from a flight of American bombers.

But what bothered Berkham was not physical fatigue so much as disenchantment with the routine aspects of his job. He was bored with mass briefings and news handouts and censorship that made him refer to "Allied troops" when he damn well meant "American troops." His real interest lay in analyses of high-command decisions and personalities, which were translatable in their effects upon human beings occupying ditches and foxholes and log-roofed bunkers and ridges and valleys and shelled farmhouses and cellars and pup tents from the North Sea to the Swiss border. Obviously he could not get this kind of material past the censor, so Berkham put most of it down in his personal war diary.

A hit-or-miss affair, this war diary of Berkham's, which he used to blow off steam or hazard guesses, and periodically he destroyed his notes because he was afraid he might take them along with him on his visits to the fighting front and Berkham risked no mischance that would allow them to be seen by other eyes than his own.

On September 23, 1944, he had written in his diary: "Yesterday there was a SAC conference at Versailles. Ike and Bradley, of course, but Monty didn't show up. He sent his chief of staff, Freddy de Guingand. I'd guess Montgomery knew what Ike had in mind and he did not want to be bound by it. So De Guingand came along to keep Monty informed, but at no risk to Monty's own inclinations. The truth is that the British are out to take over the entire operational command and relegate Eisenhower to administration and greeting VIPs. Montgomery wants to run the battle along the whole Allied front and Eisenhower is engaged in his own grim battle to be Supreme Commander in fact as well as in name."

On October 20, Berkham renewed his acrid introspection on the British field marshal. "Stars fell on Brussels on the 18th. Ike had to go to Montgomery's headquarters to be sure Monty attended this SAC conference. Why? Monty still hasn't cleared Antwerp, but there must be more to it than that, because otherwise Bradley would not have gone to Brussels, too. No, Ike wanted his two top field commanders there because he wants to be sure the British definitely understand something. This must have something to do with The Plan."

That was the first mention of The Plan. Berkham referred to it again in January, 1945. "Ike has been away on some hush-hush rarefied meeting. Probably wrestling with the British Chiefs about The Plan. Around SHAEF The Plan has been a mysterious thing since last September, but, of course, it's the coming battle for the Rhine. The big deal. The blue chips. The Plan is like some veiled work of art in a public park, but when they pull the string it will be a life-size statue of Montgomery, beret and all. The Americans are spear carriers in this production.

"This is the kind of operation Monty loves. The set piece, with his own sweet time to get ready and all support concentrated behind him, all he wants in artillery, air, supplies, and, of course, all the American troops he can get. The Germans are perfectly aware of this and they'll be concentrated heavily to defend the Ruhr. That's going to be a bloody battle up there when Monty tries his single envelopment of the Ruhr."

Berkham mused about this. "But something is going on," he wrote. "The SHAEF planners have given everything to Montgomery and the British Chiefs want to be sure that nothing interferes with that. The Americans are to give flank protection to Monty and that's their part in The Plan. Now, it's pretty sure that Ike agrees with Monty's big show in the north, but he and Bradley would like a double envelopment. They would like to mount a secondary drive across the upper

Rhine somewhere—probably through the Frankfurt Gap. But the SHAEF planners and the British Chiefs won't stand for a secondary offensive. That might draw off too much support from Monty and that's against The Plan. So I'm guessing Ike will veto a major American effort. Too bad. I think Ike's heart is with the American idea of a double envelopment of the Ruhr, but The Plan has him committed to Monty like handcuffs."

In February Berkham explored the struggle in the Allied High Command once again. By this time he was in a press billet in Namur at the Army Group headquarters of the tall, drawling Missourian, Bradley. A winter rain had turned to thin sleet and drove against the windows like a rattling obbligato of birdshot. Berkham crouched over a folding table, his Eisenhower jacket filmy with the dampness of the room, and took occasional sips from a mess cup of whisky as he made his last notation on The Plan.

"Ike," he wrote, "is still making his bid to be Supreme Commander in actual fact. He has overruled the SHAEF planners in one respect to The Plan. Montgomery's big attack into the Westphalian plains remains the main Allied effort. But Ike is insisting that the Americans close up to the west bank of the Rhine before the big show starts. He is giving Bradley permission to make an attack to clear out the enemy west of the Rhine. It has to be done fast, though, because if the American attack bogs down Ike can't risk the appearance of delaying Montgomery's spectacle in center stage. The spear carriers will have to move fast." Berkham gave a rumbling chuckle at that.

"So the Americans are to attack as far as the Rhine," he penned. "A minor amendment to The Plan, but I think they'll use this opportunity with speed and imagination and, if they catch the Germans off balance, who knows what might happen."

He added a final introspective comment. "The command decision is done. Now the human beings up front take over. A lot of guys moving toward a river. *Die Wacht am Rhein.*"

He glanced into his mess cup after he had written that and thought what a great help a touch of whisky could be to personal journalism.

2.

FIELD MARSHALL Walther von Model, commander of Army Group B for the Führer and the German Reich, had visited the small castle on the Rhine only briefly, but the impact of his presence lingered among the small group of officers like the clanging echo of a hammer stroke on an anvil.

Model was not dangerous in speech or manner. The German Feldmarschall was icy, in fact, calm and reserved, with his monocle lending him a glittering opaque quality. His face was clean-shaven, strongly boned, and expressionless.

But his words and his bloodless reserve made him the embodiment of those fearful orders from Berlin. The Westwall was to be defended to the last man. They were to give up no ground. They were to stand and fight. They were to stand and die.

Model seldom visited the town of Remagen and it was plain that he had little time to spend here and that he did not like the small castle that had been selected for his conference. It could be called a castle only by courtesy, a large square house of yellow brick with a pair of turrets and a commanding view of the Rhine giving it the grander appellation. It had served several times as a headquarters, for an Army security detachment, a Volksturm regimental command post, and a military communications center. It showed the wear and tear of this occupation, and its present deteriorated grandeur was further sullied by the bitter cold of the late February wind that blew down the Ahr valley. The stone walls of the rectangular great hall were etched with streaks of rime and the fire that glinted in the massive fireplace looked pallid in the shadowy onslaught of late afternoon. Beams of dull dark wood and hangings of blackout drapes gave the room a mournful ponderosity, keynoted by a boar's head hanging somewhat askew over the fireplace.

Field Marshal Model had seemed to address his remarks to the dilapidated boar's head. He had walked slowly up and down, flicking at the skirts of his overcoat with his baton, glancing briefly from time to time at the boar's head, as if it were a symbol of his detached and impersonal attitude toward the small group of officers clustered around the fireplace. He had fought some notable battles in Russia, this

Model, and the Knight's Cross with Diamonds hung at his throat and his voice was like some measured precise instrument of cold exact analysis.

"You will not think of anything but your own front," he said dispassionately. "You will not think about the Englishman to the north. We took care of him at Arnhem last fall and we will take care of him in the Ruhr. We are ready for him. We have known for weeks what he is up to. You will think of the Westwall. The Westwall is to be held at all costs."

He wheeled in his stride and the crisp slow beat of his heels on the scuffed parquet floor accentuated his remarks.

"The Americans make limited objective attacks. Then they stop to consolidate their gains. They are sparing of the lives of their troops. The Americans are making their move. Their main effort will be toward Bonn. That would anchor their flank. Then they would try to close gradually to the Rhine. That will be their plan of attack. They will be denied every inch of ground. If you lose ground, you will counterattack and regain your position. You will not withdraw without orders. The front is to be held. That is understood."

He paused and glanced up briefly at the boar's head. The firelight gleamed momentarily in his monocle.

"Tenacious defense everywhere on your front. If the Americans pay the price in blood and time to overrun the Westwall, they will, of course, pause to regroup. And then they will face the Rhine. It took them four weeks to cross the Roer. A man can almost jump across the Roer. How long would they take for the Rhine? Any river crossing is the most complex operation of military science. And the Rhine is the legendary defense of the Fatherland. Always this has been so. Your most worthless Volksturm battalion will fight like madmen on the Rhine front. What will our rested and refitted veteran divisions do? Will the Anglo-Americans pay the price for the battle of the Ruhr and the battle of the Rhine?

"Time is what we shall gain. Time is what the Führer needs. The longer the Anglo-Americans are kept from the heartland of the Reich the more they will think of a negotiated peace. How true this is. The Americans think only in military terms, but the English think in political terms, too, and the longer they are forced to battle the more they will fear the Russians. The Anglo-Americans will be amazed at the staying powers of the Reich. Our new jet aircraft will soon be in the air. Already Luftwaffe men are being called back from other units. The Americans will have to drop their terror bombing raids and fight for control of the air again. You will stand your ground and make the Americans pay a terrible price in time. That is clear?"

He stopped then and regarded the silent group of officers around the fireplace. At last, the Field Marshal looked at them in his measured way, his hands clasped behind him. There was Von Zangen, commander of the 15th Army defending the Rhineland from Cologne to Coblenz. It was Von Zangen who had fought the bitter battle of the Scheldt against the Canadians and delayed the use of Antwerp to the Allied forces for three months. There was General Botsch, capable tough Kampfgruppe commander. And Hitzfeld, commander of the 67th Corps whose lines fifty miles west held the center of the army front. Model glanced at these men. The other officers he gave no notice whatever—Major Scheller, the tall young aide to General Hitzfeld, and the fat red-faced Colonel Blum, chief of the local Wehrkreis headquarters.

Model spoke suddenly.

"I am appointing Lieutenant General Botsch to the defense of the bridgehead area here and in Bonn. He will be responsible to me. There has been," the Field Marshal continued, his voice sharpening, "some confusion in command. This is the end of it. Botsch, your headquarters will be in Bonn."

"I suggest," said General Botsch, "that my headquarters be between here and Bonn. I will be in better communication here, Herr Feldmarschall."

"Here?" said Model, and sauntered over to a window. He looked down from the castle window and surveyed with cool introspection the bridge below—a long graceful steel span across the fast gray river—its three symmetrical links resting on four stone piers and sentineled by two heavy stone towers at each approach. He could see the railroad tunnel across the river and the high forbidding bluffs of the Erpeler Ley.

"The old Ludendorff," Model said, musing. "That one."

He sounded as though he were recalling some minor acquaintance. If, or when, American troops reached certain strategic points, that bridge would be blown. He had no worry about the demolition plan; that was clear and thorough and ready. The only worry was premature demolition. That would infuriate the Führer. There must be no confusion about this. That was why he had selected Botsch.

He gave a last glance at the graceful bridge below and turned away.

"The main American attack will be in the Cologne plains between Cologne and Bonn," he said. "Make your headquarters in Bonn. Establish your bridgehead defenses west and northwest. I see no difficulty here. What else, Botsch?"

"Sir," said Botsch, "I request a full division for the defense positions at Bonn and a reinforced regiment here."

Model gently rubbed his right cheek with his baton and surveyed the boar's head over the fireplace.

"I have heard you before," he said. "Those troops are not available." He stood, thinking, and suddenly there was noticeable a slight tic in his right cheek. "I shall do what I can for you," he said, and glanced toward his adjutant. There was an immediate click of heels.

"Now," said the Field Marshal, "let us have no more talk of the rearward areas. The combat commanders will look to the front. That is their only concern. I shall hold them responsible. Heil Hitler."

He touched his baton briefly to the burnished visor of his high-peaked military cap and strode toward the door to the courtyard, his adjutant striding ahead and barking a brusque command to attention. The senior officers left the fireplace and followed the Feldmarschall out into the courtyard to salute the departure of his car.

For a few moments there was silence between the two officers left behind. The staff conference had broken up like a boat hitting a submerged rock. Major Scheller glanced at Colonel Blum and then studied the small glow of the fire against the great blackened cave of the fireplace. Colonel Blum grunted and heaved his bulk to his feet. He pressed a bell in the wainscoting beside the fireplace and then stood with his back to the hearth, his overcoat hanging open, rubbing his pudgy hands together.

"Not so bad," he commented. "The orders are quite clear. Give up no ground. If ground is lost, attack and regain position. No withdrawal except on order. And any concern over the rear area is defeatism and cowardice. Of course. What else, eh?"

Tall young Major Scheller glanced at him sharply. This shapeless hulking administrative officer, what did he know of holding a front where your divisions were becoming remnants and spreading themselves thinner and thinner to patch the sagging defenses of the Westwall? Didn't the High Command remember what happened to the German 7th Army when it was forced to hold on too long in Normandy last summer? The Americans would remember. And here was the 15th Army being set up in the same blind, rigid way.

"What else?" he repeated. "Why, that is not for me to say. But," he said, with restless anxiety, "I know that stand and die orders are like this." He picked up a small stick of firewood and held it rigidly at the ends in his two fists. "And something might happen—" His hands tightened and suddenly the stick snapped off near his left fist. "Like that—somewhere—"

Colonel Blum's little eyes were on him, cold and attentive. "And if something like that happens," he said, "somebody will be shot."

Major Scheller looked at the two pieces of wood in his hands and then quickly threw them on the fire.

The fat colonel was eying him, but before he could say anything his attention was drawn to a girl approaching with a bottle and glasses on a tray. She was a thin blond girl, her hair braided about her head, wearing a black dress and a gray sweater. She set the tray down on a small table near the fireplace and turned as quietly as she had entered.

"*Danke,* Fräulein," said Blum. He rubbed his hands again. "A bit of brandy, eh, Major? Not good enough to offer the Herr Feldmarschall. *Gott, nein!* He would have had us before one of the court-martial boards. But good enough for us in a place like this."

He bent over, pouring out the drinks. Major Scheller glanced after the withdrawing girl. She seemed to limp slightly, as though her left foot were heavier than her right.

"Who is she?" he asked.

Blum looked over his shoulder. "Eh? Oh, the Fräulein. She goes with the place. Looking after things for Von Rimburg. Or, perhaps, she likes troops." He laughed. "But, no. She's a leftover dish, that one."

He spoke in somewhat the same way as the Field Marshal had spoken about the bridge below over the Rhine.

3.

NEARLY the whole day the American truck convoy had been moving through a mesh of sleety rain that in some places had turned to snow and lay in tattered patches across the iron-gray fields. The replacements all had numbers chalked on their steel helmets and that was the one sign of any individuality, however tenuous. Under the cavernous canvas hoods of the trucks they were crowded so tightly among their bedding rolls, rifles, packs, and packages that their faces seemed part of the baggage load.

In Doke Stanton's truck someone's tooth paste had burst and flowed all over a bedding roll like a sticky antiseptic pool. Doke did not care particularly. He was fortunate enough to have a seat by the tail gate. He would not have cared particularly anyhow. The words of the stumpy little captain back at the Army Depot, the last stop before a combat unit, occupied his mind as the swaying truck bumped remorselessly toward his rendezvous with combat.

"Why do I have to go back to fight?" the captain had asked rhetorically. "You're a casual. You've been wounded, hospitalized, and now are being returned to your unit. From that U.K. hospital, to the Staging Depot, to the Processing Depot, and now here at the Army Depot, you've probably asked yourself that question. Right, Sergeant?"

"Right," Sergeant Doke Stanton had said evenly.

"Okay," the captain had said. "You've been up there and done your share, so why can't somebody else do it? Okay. Take the trouble to think such questions through. The whole story is that because you've been up there before you know plenty of the answers, which new men have to learn the hard way. A wise old hand to help the green guys."

Good Lord Almighty, thought Doke, remembering. Was that supposed to be an answer? That pap? A wise old hand —a jeep sergeant in a divisional reconnaissance troop whose luck had run out on him. They had handed him a little printed card, titled THE REPLACEMENT. There was more about a casual on the card: *The casual has an ace you don't —experience. Maybe somebody back home did fire live ammunition at you, but then it was only part of a training problem. The casual has had live ammunition fired at him too, but not from fixed mounts. He's a good guy to latch onto.*

Well, that might be, but as far as Doke Stanton was concerned he was not a good guy to latch onto, by any stretch of the imagination. For his preoccupation was not to survive in combat, but to avoid combat altogether. That required an angle. He'd had an angle, he had thought, a very good angle, and that was why he had not fought the medical classification board tooth and nail before he allowed them to start the machinery that returned him to his combat unit. His angle that had looked so good had betrayed him and he might have known it would, because when your luck ran out it was gone and he should never have taken the slightest chance.

Doke, braced against the tail gate with one foot, moodily surveyed the muddy truck following at route interval. The trick, he thought, was to survive with credit even though you hated every minute of it and were frozen sick with fear. To be secretly what they called a psychoneurotic and yet go back home with credit for having been a real brave guy. Now he could see that was wrong. The trick was to survive, period. What the hell difference would it have made if they had given him a CDD as a psychoneurotic or a combat fatigue case or anything else in the book? Nobody remembered that kind of thing after the war was over or gave a damn one way or the other. And, besides, he had his wound to fall back on. My God, when his jeep had struck that mine, he had been tossed twenty feet into the air and he landed right on his head. When he had staggered to his feet he had been spitting blood and he could not hear anything. Afterward, pieces of the jeep had been found scattered for a hundred yards around. There it was. It was all he had needed. Surviving had been his last bit of luck and he had squandered it by playing an angle. Because when you had fought with fear so long, you did not want to betray yourself if you could help it. How damned stupid! And the damned impersonal Army had taken advantage of you and slammed you right back to combat. The son-of-a-bitching Army with its son-of-a-bitching war. He was a body with a Spec number. God, how stupid!

He discovered that his left hand was tightly gripping his knee. He clasped his left wrist in his right hand and squeezed it. He could feel the bumps in the road coming right up into his stomach.

So he was a casual and they had told him at the Army Replacement Depot, "On your way back you are going to be close to a lot of new men going up for the first time, who will look to you as an expert able to give them the lowdown. When they ask you what it is all about, you can be the right guy in their careers as soldiers by handing out honest advice on how to get the job done. You can share all those practical answers which you learned the hard way."

Another of those printed cards. The Army Replacement Depots had them for every occasion. It was a wonder they did not advise a soldier on his dreams. *Now, look, soldier, when you think of your wife, don't think of her in a black lace nightgown. That won't help you be a part of the team. Think of her sitting quietly at home of an evening reading your letters over and over again and feeling a pride that you are doing your job with the rest of the Joes.* Yes, it sure was a wonder.

He jabbed the brim of his helmet with a thumb and pushed it back on his forehead. He was a recon sergeant and these replacements were mostly infantry and they would have to get their honest advice from some infantry Joe who had learned it the hard way, but Doke Stanton could tell them about fear, the great cold fear that they would know.

Still even that was unnecessary, because they were beginning to feel it now. The horseplay of the depot, the easy profane attitudes, the discussions on chow, women, and rumors, the obscenity that was adverb, noun, adjective, and verb and so much a part of the language that it became meaningless and canceled out altogether, the dog-eared copies of *Stars and Stripes,* all these had vanished with the miles left behind by the swaying trucks.

As long as they were in the Replacement Depots, it was sufficient unto the day. There was always that one last step before the fighting lines. But that step had nearly vanished now at the end of a long ride through a winter rain. The combat zone seemed to be encircling them and drawing them close.

Some of the towns had obviously been taken only recently. Limp white flags hung occasionally from windows and in one town square a bronze statue did duty as a telephone pole amid blasted heaps of rubble. In muddy streets were the unmistakable marks of tank treads and there were clusters of military signs with their code names and stretcher jeeps outside aid stations. Along the sides of roads ran the strands of military wire, with here and there an abandoned jeep in a ditch, or a tank retriever in a nearby field, a steel monster with blinking red eyes, and sometimes in adjoining fields were the signs of recent artillery emplacements, a sea of sandbags around a deep crater and littered with steel casings and empty boxes and huge gouged ruts. Occasionally the truck wobbled across a treadway bridge with the combat engineers still working at some foaming little creek, or lurched over shell holes in the road that had been too recent to fill. Why, Doke Stanton thought, this area had probably been held by the Germans as recently as the last couple of days.

Suddenly the truck stopped and the drawling Southern voice of an MP was heard talking to the driver. "Drop your chickens here, Jack, and get movin'."

The white helmet appeared around the back of the truck and dropped the tail gate. "This is it, chums. Shake it up."

Doke dropped to the ground and felt the jar all through his numbness. He shouldered his bedroll, held his musette bag and carbine in his free hand, and moved away from the truck. All along the road men were spilling awkwardly out of the trucks and looking vaguely around them, like arrivals on a new planet. And now that the trucks were silent you could hear the artillery, somewhere off to the west, and they were really there now with the wings of death and combat over them all.

They seemed to be on the outskirts of a small town. There was a half-demolished shell of what appeared to have been a warehouse and parked along a side road were several waiting trucks, the drivers lounging near a depot piled with jerricans.

"Come on," an MP was urging someone. "You hang around this road, Joe, and you're askin' for it. The Jerries drop stuff around here pretty reg'lar."

They were herded over to the wall of the warehouse like some grudging brown flock, and they stood there with their rolls and equipment and weapons and the numbers on their helmets, while officers and men of the divisional personnel unit ran a tally. They picked off Doke Stanton.

"Name, Sergeant."

"Stanton."

They caught it on the list. "Stanton, Douglas K. Casual? You're recon, huh? Well, stand over there and we'll send you down to the recon troop pretty quick. Okay, next."

They stood there and heard the sound of the guns and the sputter of jeeps and the roar of trucks and realized they were in Germany with the fighting units not far ahead of them—the little lines on war maps were just ahead; where those Joes were, there were those little red lozenges that majors and lieutenant colonels put on acetate coverings on war maps for generals. It was easy to rub those red lozenges off the acetate. You just took a cloth and gave a wipe and it was done. It was not that easy for the Germans, but they tried.

Doke Stanton waited to be sent down to the divisional reconnaissance troop, his carbine slung over one shoulder, his bedroll propped against a leg, and his gray eyes staring ahead into the mesh of rain. If the regiments weren't busy, the replacements might get a short talk from a colonel. If the regiments were engaged, they would go right into foxholes and chances were that some of them would be killed before they got there. Even during this wait they were cemented together by fear, for fear was the greatest factor in war. It would affect everything they did from now on. Nor, no matter how long they lasted, would they find the fear subsiding. They would have no cockiness. They would pretend nothing. They would have no memories and no future. They would live wholly and completely in the present. Never waking with any hope beyond the hour, spirits reduced to the same bare bones as their bodies, awake only to peril or to animal comforts. Combat wounded all men, even those unscathed, for it set them a little apart ever afterward from their own lives.

Stanton felt himself shivering, as though the dankness of the day had worked through his overcoat and combat boots. The tremors ran through his body and would not stop. Now he got the shakes, he reflected bitterly. Why couldn't he have developed the shakes back at that hospital in the U.K.? They would have given him a CDD for sure. Now he had to try either for a Section Eight or else cling to the last desperate hope that the angle he had trusted would yet pay off for him. What was his brother doing?

He thought of Major Clay Stanton, Headquarters First U.S. Army, and his lips moved almost imperceptibly.

"Come on, Clay," he muttered. "Move, for God's sake. For God's sake, make it fast."

For Doke Stanton realized better than any medical board that he had no war left in him, no war and no luck.

THE BRIDGE

1.

IT STOOD on four stone piers, with three graceful spans, and was sentineled by two blunt stone towers at either end that were nearly medieval in appearance.

Where it spanned the famous river, the water ran swift and dark and deep, and, as with its four sentinel stone towers, it seemed protected by the steep bluffs on either bank. The bluff on the east bank was the more forbidding. It towered six hundred feet of black basalt, grim and unassailable, so that the bridge itself emptied its traffic into a railroad tunnel close to the river.

On the west bank the bluff was not as severe, softened further by the little town that grew away from the bridge to the north. As the forbidding east bank breathed the harsh realities of Götterdämmerung and the steel-shod legends of Siegfried, so the west bank countered with a breath of the Meistersinger and Gemütlichkeit in its town of winding cobbled streets, its gray homes with gabled roofs and chimney pots, and its St. Apollinaris Church that looked over the town like a benevolent patriarch and shared dominance with the yellow brick, twin-turreted little castle of Rimburg-Clewes.

It had been built during World War I and named after the general who had ordered its construction as a military necessity. The townspeople had not liked the idea because the construction in their opinion had spoiled the picturesque view, but after a while they had accepted it. However, the bridge had never become popular or well known. It never carried the tourists, for example, of the greater bridges on the river. It became mainly a railroad bridge with a pedestrian crossing a yard wide on either side of the tracks and the only reason for its existence was the freight trains of wine and mineral waters from the Ahr valley. Otherwise it remained remote and ignored, a country cousin bridge on the great river, a four-hundred-yard span that loomed suddenly for river steamers as they plowed around the bend upstream that the townspeople thought so picturesque.

Yet, in a way, the obscure bridge held a tradition more graphic than the greater bridges on the river. Near its site Julius Caesar had built his bridge two thousand years before, and where he had sent the standards of his legions had been a grim and forbidding frontier. It still was. The basalt cliff that frowned down at the slim steel bridge was the most eloquent possible witness that the river marked both the true and legendary frontier of the German Reich. What lay west of the river could be lost and the Reich could survive—but east of the river was the great industrial Ruhr, the Saar, the underground war plants, the laboratories, the Autobahns, the spirit of the nation and the sinews of its war machine and the grip of the leaders. Tenuous indeed was the life of anything that attempted to link that final national bastion to whatever might endanger it.

And because the front west of the river was in danger, the bridge was doomed. It simply waited for its appointed time.

No one understood that better than the carpenter, August Kleinert. He had lived in the town all his life and had worked on the original construction of the bridge. He had worked in the past few months for horse- and motor-drawn military traffic.

August had bitter memories associated with the bridge. He could remember the end of the last war and the American troops of Occupation tramping across to the Vaterland as free and unchallenged as birds. He could remember those French—how they had swarmed all over the town and how they had filled the demolition chambers of the four stone piers with cement. *Ach,* those French! They had really fixed those stone piers for good.

But the carpenter knew there had been a new demolition plan ever since 1939. Not that in those great days of 1939 and 1940 there had seemed to be any need for it, but the military were thorough. They had not only devised a complete demolition plan but made systematic tests, what they called the "dry runs." August Keinert, working frequently on the bridge to repair bombing damage from those *verdammt Amerikaner,* was well aware of the demolition plan. He knew that the main cable of the electric fuse was encased in a thick steel pipe that ran along beneath one of the railroad tracks. There were sixty zinc-lined boxes set at vulnerable points and when they were loaded with explosives and the sixty charges detonated, the bridge would become unhinged in matter of seconds and collapse into the river. The ignition switch for the fuse and the generator that supplied the current were securely guarded inside the railroad tunnel on the east bank. The engineers used a circuit tester to check the electric ignition system, but they left nothing to chance. The most efficient and hard-bitten troops in the Wehrmacht, they also maintained a primer cord that could be lighted by hand to set off the charges if the electric ignition failed.

August Kleinert, the carpenter, had known of this demolition plan for a long time, but only recently had he begun to sense that the plan for this bridge was more than merely good military operating procedure; it was an actual and imminent probability. The bridge engineers set up a new charge that would blow a hole thirty feet wide and twelve feet deep in the approach to the bridge and that could only mean an added safety factor to block off any enemy force and give the time needed to detonate the main charges on the bridge. To August Kleinert that looked as though the situation was becoming tense.

And then there was the arrival of that lieutenant general from Bonn—Botsch. August Kleinert was working out on the bridge with some new planking when the general drove up in his Opel staff car and both the combat commander and the bridge commander hurried to confer with him.

The carpenter watched the little group of officers with interest as they stood at the western approach to the bridge, the snapping cold wind swirling the skirts of their military overcoats. Kleinert tucked his reddened hands in his armpits and tried to catch snatches of their conversation. When one of those top officers from Bonn came here, it was an event, and this was Botsch, who had responsibility for the bridge.

The general was questioning each commandant in turn. With the combat commander he reviewed security measures in a terse but friendly way. Emplacements? Observation posts? Road blocks? He turned to the engineer commander and his voice had the same quick staccato inquiry. Under what conditions could the demolition of the bridge be guaranteed? The engineering officer talked quickly and eagerly, his voice indistinct in the wind.

The carpenter blew on his numbed hands and knelt down on the planking to resume his work. The bridge was doomed then, really kaput. He hammered mechanically for some moments, digesting this realization, then glanced up again. The officers had driven off in the staff car toward the town. Probably to inspect defense positions of the Volksturm. He thought of the Volksturm and spat expressively through a gap in the planking. The Volksturm might be some good on the east bank, but they were no damned good with the river at their back. And anyhow everyone around here was sick of the bombing.

He cast a glance at the sky as the thought struck him, on one knee with his hammer poised. It was clear today. Good hunting for those American fighter bombers that swept in over the Eifel, flying fast and low so that the bombs were on you before you knew it. The past few days of rain and fog had been better protection than the flak batteries. The bridge had been hit several times in recent months, but there had always been the time to repair the damage. Now, if the bridge should be bombed, it might be kaput before its time. Any bridge over this river took special care. There were thousands of men in the Westwall defenses who might have to find their way back to the great defense line of this river.

He fell to working with feverish haste, hammering at the new planking, but still uneasy about that clear sky over the Eifel, glancing up from time to time, listening. The slave laborers under the rifles of their guards were digging new emplacements on the west bank below the bridge for the new anti-aircraft battalion that was expected; and above the bridge, engineers were marking a mined area. *Achtung Minen!* There were so many of those signs. Some of them meant nothing, but no one could be sure, especially the slave laborers.

He was crowded to one side as a military column crossed the bridge to the east bank. It was a limp, tired formation of battalion strength, apparently supply or maintenace troops. The carpenter watched them, glowering. Very little came from the east bank nowadays. Most of the military traffic seemed to flow from the west—ambulances, walking wounded, occasional anti-aircraft and artillery units—the carpenter spat again expressively. Well, let them go. Those troops were no good. There was nothing left in them. Just as long as they kept a few of those parachute battalions up at the front, the Americans would have the devil's own time reaching the river.

He picked up a piece of planking and sighted expertly down its length, and it was then he heard the sound. He stiffened, still grasping the end of the plank, sifting the sound in his consciousness as though it were something he had heard in his sleep. And, even as he jerked his head around to scan the sky, the sudden shrill blast of the whistle in the nearby plywood factory split the air and he knew he had heard aright. Those *verdammt* American bombers were winging in over the Eifel again and in an instant he had dropped the planking and was racing madly toward the tunnel on the east bank. He pushed his way in with a group of shouldering guards and engineers and flung himself flat, panting, by the side of the tracks near the big generator. He could hear them now, the drone of the bombers, and, *lieber Gott,* they were all going to catch it today, the bridge would be blasted, and the town would catch it, too, and why did not this goddamned war end someday, and why didn't that 20 mm flak battalion open up and those 88s along the river, and that unit of rocket launchers? He waited for the first whine of the bombs and the shuddering shock as they exploded, but nothing happened. He could hear the American planes but not their dreaded bombing runs.

He took his arms from around his head and cautiously crawled over some prostrate forms to the tunnel entrance. On hands and knees he glanced up at the sky over the river. For a moment he stared uncomprehending, his sharp little blue eyes contracted under his shaggy sandy brows. Something was different. And then he realized what it was—the sky that he had remembered as clear had suddenly, miraculously clouded over. That whipping east wind had brought up some scudding clouds and piled them in a tossing gray welter over the Eifel and the river and the bridge— and the bridge —August Kleinert let out a yell and shook his fist at the sky.

"Yah!" he yelled. "Yah, you Yankee *dummköpfe!* Yah—"

They were buzzing around up there like hornets, those American planes, but they could not find a hole in the overcast and they could not get off their bombing runs and, by God, maybe they weren't going to catch it today after all, unless they just dumped their bomb loads. But the Americans were more likely to head for a secondary target, if they would give up on this one. That blessed cloud cover, that was what had blunted those sharp striking planes with the big stars on their wings. He felt like putting his thumb to his nose and waggling his fingers at that exasperated droning overhead beyond the cottony cumulus, but he was afraid he might be daring fate. The Americans might dump their bombs yet.

But, no, suddenly they were gone. The roar of their motors simply was no longer there. The sergeants were barking commands at the security troops and the slave laborers across the river were being herded back to their work. The Americans had gone.

The carpenter returned to his work out on the bridge. He still was breathing hard, as though he had been running hard, but today had been a real bit of luck. He found the plank he had dropped when the alarm whistle had sounded and again knelt to begin his work. This bridge was not for the Yankees. They had much money and planes and tanks, but all their money meant nothing to a cloud cover. He chuckled harshly. How much the Americans would pay for this bridge—and there was not enough American money in the world to buy it. But of course, the Americans knew themselves there was no chance of any kind to get this bridge. Their bombing attempt showed that. And even there they had been fooled.

His exhilaration included the bridge itself, as though it had been a part of a conspiracy to fool the Americans. It had taken several beatings from the air and it was still standing and serviceable, but it needed a little help like that cloud cover today.

As he was tapping a plank into place with a hammer, he hit his thumb and the pain abruptly dissipated his exhilaration. He gingerly flexed his bruised thumb and reflected bitterly that none of this mattered in the end. The way things were looking the bridge was finished, unless the Americans took it and that was simply impossible, even if they'd had any wild idea of it.

But he reviewed the thought, still nursing his wounded thumb, his eyes narrowed against the frosty bite in the air. He looked up at the Erpeler Ley, east of the bridge, with its flak battalions and its dominating height from which observers could see ten miles in every direction. He looked at the twin towers of the bridge on the east bank with those machine-gun emplacements and the railroad tunnel with the big generator that gave power to the electric ignition system. He could remember the whole masterly demolition plan and the mined approach to the bridge on the west bank. And all through the town and in a defense perimeter beyond were observation posts, roadblocks, mines, automatic weapons emplacements, and carefully planned strategic check points beyond which no American troops could penetrate without causing the demolition plan to be put into immediate effect. No, that World War I memory of December, 1918, when the American Occupation troops had crossed the bridge, could never be repeated. There would be no American foot set on this bridge— *Donnerwetter,* but there would not!

A man's thoughts might wander when he was exhilarated or drunk, but as he reached for a handful of nails and started hammering again, August Kleinert reflected that he was dealing with realities now, like a sore thumb, and the plank under his knee, and the conviction that this bridge and all the work he did on it would soon be at the bottom of the river.

2.

THE BRIDGE was on the military maps of the Americans, of course. All the Rhine bridges were, like the railroads, the rivers, the road systems, the contour lines, and the towns. But that did not mean the Americans were thinking of the bridge, or any bridge on the Rhine, in their operational plans, particularly at the headquarters of Twelfth Army Group which commanded the slogging dependable First U.S. Army and the ebullient and spectacular Third.

Robert Berkham had closely followed the progress of the American attack at the big headquarters and then piled his bedding roll in his jeep and driven to the headquarters of First U.S. Army. Driving from Namur to Spa, his hands jammed deep in the pockets of his trench coat and his head hunched in the turned-up collar, he reviewed Bradley's attack plan and particularly the new Letter of Instructions that was being sent to the two army commanders. The tall Missourian, Bradley, who looked like the principal of a country school, had really rigged something there and it must have appealed to Ike, because the Supreme Commander's great aim was to destroy all the enemy possible and this was the second time he'd had the chance. The first was when the German 7th Army had been caught in Normandy last summer. And the second time was now—west of the Rhine.

All Ike and Bradley had needed for their design was the knowledge that the Germans were going to stand and fight. And evidently Hitler had obliged. There was to be no retreat west of the Rhine and Bradley had designed his attack to bag every last German this side of the river. Then he would sit down and wait for Monty, but, in the meantime, for a spear carrier he was honing a mighty sharp spear.

Of course, the attack plan was one thing and its execution was another. What was it Robert E. Lee had once said?—"I try to get the commanders at the right place on the field." There was probably more to generalship than that, but even that simple thesis implied speed and flexibility. Bradley's attack depended on exactly those factors. Instead of moving toward the Rhine in a concentrated push along the whole front, he was going to drive hard with his left toward the river, anchor it at Cologne, then turn the First

Army southeast and attack in a pincer drive with the Third Army slamming northerly to Coblenz. If it went off as Bradley hoped, the whole Rhineland between Cologne and Coblenz might be swept up like a gigantic scoop of earth in the twin jaws of a steam shovel.

So Bradley had devised it and now it was a matter of the men who had to make it work. Berkham drove to headquarters of First Army, because it was near Namur and because he knew it better than Patton's Third, to get a line on the human side of a big attack order, something that would give life to the words that were directing men at a river fifty miles away.

Words, mused Berkham, meant to surprise with a fast slanting attack instead of a broad frontal push. "Letter of Instructions 16—Clearing of area north of the Moselle and west of the Rhine—Hodges (First Army) to invest Cologne from the northwest and then to attack southeast converging with Patton (Third Army) drive to the Coblenz-Mayen area."

Well, there it was. The kickoff. And so the veteran correspondent moved down closer toward where the world of men and battle began. He wanted to follow the attack with some division eventually. He did not feel so tired today. There was always something quickening about an attack that had imagination and drive and purpose. "Letter of Instructions 16—clearing the area west of the Rhine—" Berkham grinned slightly as he drove into Spa and followed the "Master" code signs.

He checked in at the press billets and then made his way to the big square building that housed First Army's command post. In the cobbled courtyard he came across an officer sitting in a jeep, evidently waiting for his driver. Berkham paused as he recognized him as Clay Stanton, one of the officers of the Combat Observer Section that made specialized reports from the combat zone to the commanding general.

"Hello, Major," said Berkham.

The officer had been staring at the spattered windshield of his jeep. He turned his head slowly. "Oh," he said, "hi, Mr. Berkham."

"Things moving around here?" inquired Berkham pleasantly, nodding at the headquarters building. "Should be plenty shaping up."

"I guess there is," said Major Stanton.

He sounded curiously detached. Berkham glanced at him again. He was a West Pointer, this Stanton, working right up here under the brass. Berkham had never known him well, but in their few contacts he had found him pleasant and articulate. Now he seemed curiously withdrawn.

"Going toward the shooting, Major?" Berkham inquired. "Or shouldn't I ask?"

"Why not?" said Major Stanton. His mouth curved slightly in a thin smile. "Yes, I'm going down with the combat guys."

"Something big jumping off today?" Berkham said. "Where?"

"I don't know," said the officer. The shoulders of his trench coat moved in a barely perceptible shrug. "I have personal business." His gray eyes under the brim of his steel helmet looked right past the correspondent.

Berkham rubbed his chin with a thumb. Real strange and nothing for him to bother about, except that all during his newspaper career he had been attracted by the offbeat. This sure was a good example of it. Fourteen divisions ready to attack on the First Army front and this major was going down there somewhere on personal business. It sounded like leaving a calling card on a Sherman tank.

Major Stanton's driver came hurrying up, a trip ticket in one hand and a carbine in the other. He got in behind the wheel, slid the carbine into a rack on the dashboard, and started up the engine.

"My best to them all," said Berkham.

Major Stanton nodded and flirted a gloved hand in farewell. The jeep burst through the gates of the courtyard and swung off down the muddy street.

Berkham walked on toward the headquarters building. He had thought there might be a string to coming events somewhere in that officer's departure for the fighting front. Obviously that was a big jump for anyone at Army to make.

He could have had no reason to know that it was a string to one of the greatest stories of the war.

The two Stanton brothers had begun their lives as so-called "army brats," that opprobrious term for the children who were brought up in garrisons and ferried about in transports and generally regarded as noisy, rootless, and spoiled.

What cleaved the Stanton brothers from this status was the fact that their mother, early in their lives, could no longer stand their father or his life or his personality. He was a professional officer, of course, althought not a West Pointer. He had become commissioned after a private military academy and requisite examinations around the turn of the century. He had plodded along through the years gradually and finally achieved the rank of lieutenant colonel where he stuck immovably and bitterly and retired just before World War II. Even the tremendous need for officers found no niche for him. He was left retired.

Strangely enough his lack of achievement in the Army seemed to have given him a passionate attachment to the Army as a career and he began to look to his two sons with a dedicated zeal.

Colonel Stanton experienced some difficulty in his design, due to the fact that his wife had won custody of his two sons and his main efforts had to be confined to two months in every year. But he made prodigious attempts during those times, and after he retired he added to these attempts a strain of nebulous family tradition which had no genesis beyond himself, but rather adopted the entire American army heritage like buying an old Revolutionary scimitar in an antique store.

He was sure that the root of any successful Army career was a West Point diploma and in this he very likely was entirely correct. What he simply and conveniently overlooked was the fact that neither of his sons was drawn to Army life. With this convenient blind spot Colonel Stanton was formidable indeed.

He was a spare straight man with a freshly shaved air about him that was almost ascetic. He had keen gray eyes behind steel-rimmed glasses that lent a riveted intensity to his glance and had made him the administrative terror of the units he had commanded in garrison. It was too much for his elder son, Clay. Clay Stanton went to West Point without any great inclination and busted out once, because of a history deficiency. Under his father's stern tutelage he spent all one summer committing an entire history textbook to memory, regained the Point and graduated in time to be caught in the updraft of rapid promotion in the breaking years of the war.

But the younger son refused point-blank. He was Douglas Kendall Stanton, called by his mother "Doke," and for the Army he had no inclination at all. Colonel Stanton, perforce, was content with one chance at a new Army name and let Doke alone. Doke, of course, became a civilian soldier after Pearl Harbor left no choice for anyone.

It was funny about that in a way, Doke's enlistment. He was working on a Connecticut newspaper and thought that as long as he was sure to be drafted he might as well enlist while he could still select his branch of service. Accordingly, he applied for Intelligence and by the time the Army wheels had ceased turning he was being trained for combat reconnaissance, a far cry from the kind of Intelligence Doke Stanton had in mind. His father, of course, began to pull all kinds of strings to get Doke admitted to Officer Candidate School and was finally deterred only by Doke's subborn refusal to accept.

"I don't know beans about the Army," he said, "but I figure my luck is better as an enlisted man."

That was the first time Doke mentioned that theme of luck. Where he picked it up, there was no telling. He considered that he was starting out in the war with a certain amount of luck to his credit in some ethereal bank and any waste of that luck meant he would run out of it when he needed it. It was like some kind of nebulous currency. To become an officer, Doke considered, would be a wasted check. It was as though he imagined an officer charging out ahead of troops with a sword. Colonel Stanton could not understand this attitude. It could have been that Doke was ridiculing him, but the Colonel was not able to grasp such an eventuality.

As it turned out, the Colonel had the last laugh, for the commanding officer of the divisional reconnaissance troop was cast in the same mold as Colonel Stanton. He was Captain Jeffrey Cummings Baker, called inelegantly "The Book" by the recon men, a replacement who had taken over command the previous October when big, friendly Captain Ellison had been killed during that awful period when the recon troop had spent fifteen days in the line near Aachen. Ellison had been a friend of Doke Stanton, a jovial officer who would speak his mind at Division and bed down among his men, and his brilliant reconnaissance ability had been thrown away with his life, killed by a sniper while trying to do an infantry job he did not know. The Book was sent by Division to take over the troop and it was like a junior edition of Colonel Stanton arriving on the scene.

He was a man with plenty of courage, but lacking in both judgment and humanity. He went completely by the book, his shrine was the field manual and the directive and the dotting of the "i." He had been an insurance adjuster in civilian life, which certainly did not disqualify him either as a competent leader and a human being, but perhaps accentuated the narow limits of legalism by which he lived. He was not popular at division headquarters, but his thorough devotion to orders and his tight faultless administration gave a stronger impression of competence than he really possessed. He was like someone who had learned a language phonetically—all The Book's ability was superimposed by dogged study of the fine print. He had no feeling or instinct for his job and the reconnaissance troop had never functioned with as much dash and effectiveness as when Ellison had led it.

Sergeant Doke Stanton, Casual, reported back to The Book on that wintry evening after his long numbing truck ride through the rain from the replacement depot.

Nick Halsema, the big first sergeant, brought him down to the command post from the division area. Halsema stowed the jeep in a small vehicle park in a copse of woods and then led the way through the darkness by engineer tape strung along a narrow, rutty road, gave the countersign to a challenge from the recon outpost, and came out into a field. He paused a moment, dangling Doke's musette bag in one hand, and Doke waited at his shoulder, bedroll poised on one shoulder and his carbine slung across the other.

Scudding clouds whipped in opaque fluffiness across the night sky and the ground was hard and churned underfoot. There was no light, nor any sound beyond the hum of a nearby generator and the distant sporadic bark of small-arms fire vaguely to the east. Doke Stanton stood there, breathing slowly and deeply, waiting and listening. This was his little patch of home in the Army, briefly his place of waking, eating, talking, waiting, fearing, like a postage stamp on an endless stretch of railroad track, a little place to live on yet awhile in the miles of front and the millions of men from the North Sea to the Swiss border. It was a little spot in Germany on a dark wintry night and he stood here by the side of a steel worker's helper from Cleveland, the two of them in this patch of field, because men behind big desks in big chanceries thought this way or that, and so now behind them was the assembly line, the replacement depots, the ports, the great industrial plants and the long freight trains and the war bonds and the ration stamps and the V-mail letters, and where he and Halsema stood was the place where all this huge effort had managed to push them. Nothing much ahead but the rest of Germany.

"Quiet," said Halsema. "Don't like it. Our arty has been moving up, but the Krauts generally throw some stuff over. Could be they're saving up for a shoot. We've got lots of armor and arty up close."

"Things been rough?" asked Doke. He forced himself to speak evenly, conversationally.

"Rough enough," said Halsema. "Though we don't have it as bad as the infantry Joes, God knows. Remember Aachen?" He was silent a moment. "Everything seems busting wide open," he said, musing. "I hear we're goin' to screen the left flank of an armor push. Don't sound like no picnic, hightailin' it along with them tanks, but you never know."

Again he was silent momentarily, then shrugged. "The CP's over here," he said. "In an old mill. Let's go."

Doke became aware of a steady creaking noise as they approached a formless black shape at the end of the rough stretch of road. He could see vaguely the ponderous slow swing of the arms. They were challenged again. Halsema spoke a terse word and swept aside a hanging tarpulin. A blade of light was unsheathed.

"Okay, kid," said Halsema. "I'll see you later."

He dropped his bedroll and ducked under Halsema's hand holding back the blackout entrance. The captain was writing a V-mail letter on a clipboard under a kerosene lamp hanging on a nail in a beam. His armored car was parked in the square brick room and his radio operator was in the M-8, monitoring his set.

"Sergeant Stanton reporting," said Doke, and only then did the captain look up.

"At ease, Sergeant," he said, and went back to his letter.

Doke studied him, thumb hooked in his carbine strap, and knew that he would get no help from this man. He was tall and thin and liked to wear leggings instead of the combat boot, which further accentuated his somewhat bowed legs. He was rather good-looking, with thick black hair that had an unruliness to it and black-lashed gray eyes. His face was angular and his mouth wide; when he laughed he showed every tooth he had and they were square white teeth. Doke had never liked him.

The Book put his clipboard aside and reached inside his combat jacket to stow away his ballpoint pen.

"Well, Sergeant Stanton," he said in his even, dispassionate voice, "I'm glad you're back. We need experienced men. There's a mission coming up very soon. Are you all ready?"

"No," said Doke Stanton. "Of course, I'm not ready." In that instant he wished he could have talked to someone, not just anyone, but someone. Perhaps he might have been all right, he thought, perhaps not; but it would have helped.

The captain rubbed the back of his head and regarded him in a detached way. "You have been certified fit for duty, I understand, Sergeant," he said in that soft restrained voice.

"I passed a physical," said Doke Stanton. "But just because I didn't get the shakes when anyone mentioned combat duty, they thought I was all right mentally. And the only reason I didn't get the shakes when they mentioned combat was because I thought I was all through with it—" He broke off suddenly and looked at the captain intensely. "Are there any orders here for me?"

"Orders, Sergeant? Why, no, what orders—?"

"Any word, any letters, anything? This is important to me, Captain. Are you sure?"

The captain shook his head. "Nothing."

"Look, sir," said Doke, "I've been snafued long enough. I want to be damned sure I'm not getting snafued now. For God's sake, are you sure?"

"At ease, Sergeant," said the officer. Doke fell silent, not so much because of the command, but because he knew it was useless. He had been trying to fan a dead fire into life. Of course, there was nothing here for him.

"All right," the captain said, after a long disciplinary pause. "Now," he resumed. "None of us want to be here, I imagine. You have been sent back and reported fit for active duty. If you could have arranged something else, that was your business. You are back here now and I expect you to pull with us. You're going to depend on your fellow troopers and they are going to depend on you."

"Captain," said Doke Stanton, "I've had all that kind of stuff in the repple depple."

"It did not impress you, I see," said the captain. "But you are an experienced man and you know I'm right. When we pull out I expect you to do what you're trained to do. At least, you've been out of this for a while." He stood up and walked to a door in the brick room. "Bosky," he called. A sleepy-looking enlisted man appeared, putting on his helmet. "Take Sergeant Stanton over to the First Platoon," said the captain. "You'll be under Lieutenant Milroy, Sergeant. You can sack in tonight and report to him in the morning. Good night."

Doke followed his guide out of the CP and accompanied him along the perimeter of the field. The Book was still the same and yet you could not reasonably blame him. He was impersonal like the whole Army. The war was handy for impersonal people. Don't think of Douglas Kendall Stanton as himself or someone. It was nothing to anyone else but Doke Stanton that he liked certain things and disliked others, that he hated pain and loved to read, that he was responsive and passionate, that he was five feet eleven with crew-cut brown hair and bluish-gray eyes and all his senses and all his limbs and these represented his own intact being and once you were shot or torn open by a shell or blown up by a mine, what made you laugh or what made you indignant or what kind of food, books, people you liked, or what you wanted to be and what you wanted to do, vanished immediately from only one person and that was Doke Stanton. You were so important to yourself and so unimportant to the Army.

He realized he was very tired. He stumbled as he followed his taciturn guide, Bosky, to a log-roofed dugout built at the base of a shapeless mass that might have been a farmhouse. "Here's one of the First Platoon's billets," grunted Bosky, and knelt down, extending a torch into the dugout. "You got room in here?" he demanded. "Hey, snap out of it. Here's a new guy for your platoon. Wake up, for Christ's sake, the captain wants that—"

Doke suddenly heard it, with a sense of incredulity that he was actually hearing the often remembered, always feared, the rending of the night with a high thin unearthly shriek and then a shattering concussion that hurled him off his feet and slammed him to the ground as though the ground itself had risen to meet him. Even as he lay gasping in the dark, his whole chest pounding, there was another of those terrible screams that anticipated the exploding shell and he dug at the frozen earth with his fingers, twisting himself at the ground like an animal trying to get away from a rifle, clawing, his face tight against the earth. There was a sudden streak of red that flashed through his eyelids and his whole body left the ground and came back hard, his helmet fell off, and there was a rending crash and shattering of glass as the roof of the nearby farmhouse fell in with a din of plaster and tile. The entire earth seemed writhing and seething and he screamed as another high thin shriek burst around his ears and his fierce grip at the earth was shaken loose. He came to his hands and knees as someone yanked at him, his voice bubbling in his throat and his breath stifled by the weight on his heart. His ears were ringing and there was a greasy smoke in his face and a smell of burned powder.

Somebody yanked at him again and he tried to twist away, tried to fling himself to the earth and dig himself a hole out of the iron-hard ground. He was being pushed and dragged and a scream finally tore itself from his throat as he staggered drunkenly. Then as another of those long thin shrieks of the incoming shells split the night he was hurled bodily into a hole, grabbed at by hands and yanked down into darkness among a group of men and he lay there shaking all over, sobbing, and his voice coming in gasps jerked from him as though his stomach were being pounded by an iron fist. "God," he managed, strangled. "God, God—"

Then he simply whimpered down in the darkness of the log-roofed dugout, feeling more like an animal than a human being and not caring, quivering uncontrollably, not caring, still clawing at the muddy earth, not caring.

3.

THE CORPS commander referred to it briefly at First Army headquarters the following morning. "Jerry hit us with some artillery last night," he said. "Trying to hit the tank assembly areas. Didn't do much damage." He flirted a hand. "Poked here and there for a while and then quit when our stuff began going over."

He had mentioned it casually, as a bit of information, in the War Room where the First Army staff was meeting with the Corps commanders. Two correspondents had been allowed to attend: Joe Cloughen, of one of the press syndicates, and Berkham.

Berkham, sitting off in one corner of the War Room, twisting a pencil around in his fingers, thought that Corps was still the Big Picture and a long way removed from the Little Picture. There was an air of imperturbability at Corps level, just as there was at Army and Army Group. At Corps they could talk of being hit by a little artillery in a negative way. Or they could say, "We caught ourselves a counterattack, but it was beaten off," or "Some fanatic paratroopers moved up behind the barrage and jumped with knives into the holes with our troops." Simple impersonal statements of fact that did not reflect the grim pressure on human beings who were hit with "a little artillery" or fought off the counterattack or wrestled hand to hand in their holes with Nazi paratroopers armed with knives.

Of course, there was no real reason why this could be otherwise. These commanders at Army and Corps level had to think in terms of those red lozenges on the maps. But below Corps the Little Picture began to be more discernible at combat headquarters, like Division, and the picture became smaller and smaller down through regiment and battalion until it became as small as a man's foxhole or the inside of his tank.

Berkham studied the three Corps commanders who were to carry First Army's attack—Collins of the VII Corps, Huebner of the V, and Millikin of the III. Each commanded three infantry divisions, one armored, and a cavalry group. Collins and Huebner had been fighting since D-Day. Millikin had just recently been moved over from Patton. A lot of this briefing by the Army staff was mainly for him. First Army had a different viewpoint about things from Patton's Third.

Millikin was asking a question. "How about the Rhine bridges?"

There was a momentary silence in the War Room. The Army staff officer who was conducting the briefing took a long deliberate drag at his cigarette and leaned back. He blew out a stream of smoke.

"General," he said, "you don't need to bother about any bridges. The German is thorough about such things. You can bet he'll have any and every bridge blown to smithereens before we get near the river."

Sure, thought Berkham, if you could be sure of anything you could be sure of that. Army certainly could not include anything so remote as grabbing a Rhine bridge in a long-range operational plan. But still he looked at the III Corps commander with interest just for having asked the question. He was a cavalryman and there was something about him of Patton's flair and drive, no doubt about it.

The Army staff officer flicked some ash from the end of his cigarette. "All the same," he said, "we're calling off air attacks on those bridges as we hit Phase One of this attack. We're just playing it by the book." He shrugged. "Doesn't make a hell of a lot of difference, what with the weather we've been having. Anything else?"

There did not seem to be. The three Corps commanders, with their aides and their artillery chiefs, stood up. They knew what they had to do. They had to send in their divisions fast and hard and keep them going that way. Collins, of course, could drive his VII Corps. He had been doing that since he captured Cherbourg last June. And Huebner was the tough hard-boiled commander who had led the 1st Division ashore in Normandy and now had taken over the veteran V Corps. Millikin had a restless energy in his long stride as he moved toward the door.

Berkham sauntered over to the big map with Joe Cloughen as the War Room cleared of all those little silver stars. He stuck his hands in his pockets and studied the map, eyes narrowed.

"Patton's got the job, I think," commented Cloughen. "Attacking through the Eifel. That's rugged country."

"Maybe so," said Berkham. "This country on Hodges' front is Eifel, too, and they've got that swing in direction to southeast. Ever think what it takes to swing a big attack, Joe?"

he mused, leisurely. "Like turning a bull by the rump in the middle of a charge, I shouldn't wonder."

The way Bradley had figured it the Germans did two things that could be relied on. First, they did not build defenses in depth because that might encourage the troops to withdraw. And second, they had those blood-and-iron orders from Hitler to stand and fight. So, reflected Berkham, if the Americans could hit hard enough to smash through the defense crust and then shift fast into an attack diagonally through the German front they might catch themselves a lot of Germans when they linked with Patton and tied the string west of the Rhine. Then the driving momentum would slow and the fiery energies would cool and they would wait, looking at the fabled river with its demolished bridges—wait, listening for Montgomery to blow his trumpets up near Arnhem.

Berkham thought about it, the Big Picture, one last time. His mind was already trying to localize this attack into clearer coverage, something closer to the men who would have to move and fight at the tempo that was to be demanded of them. It was a lot to ask of those guys, thought Berkham. From now on they would be given the spur until they saw that river. Bradley's attack plan would give them no chance to slow up until they had the Rhine at their fingertips.

He regarded Millikin's III Corps front. It was his men who would slice down through the Ahr valley and make the link with Patton's armored spearheads. Looked like an interesting attack. Where was III Corps' command post? Zulpich?

Well, it all looked good, but Model was over there, that chilly Prussian, and Von Zangen with the 15th German Army, and nothing could ever be guaranteed in war. Zulpich might be a good place to see how this big American attack developed.

Berkham was interrupted in his speculations by an indignant explosion from one of the War Room duty officers. "Major Stanton was supposed to be on duty this morning," he was saying. "General Kean has something for him to do at Eagle Tac. I can't find him anywhere and Lord knows we're going to be busy enough around here—"

Stanton. It reminded Berkham of the officer who had rocketed out of the command post in a jeep, headed for personal business down at the front. Apparently he was off on his own at a critical time and First Army brass would not like that. Berkham volunteered nothing about the missing Major Stanton, but he reflected, fleetingly, how odd for that offbeat little occurrence to obtrude itself on the Big Picture.

A spattered jeep nosed joltingly along a rough road, churned into ruts that had frozen hard, and stopped before an old mill with lazily revolving arms. A tall major in trench coat slid stiffly out of the front seat, slung a carbine over his shoulder, and glanced around him in a slow watchful way. A leaden sky arched over a world of stark trees and fields, studded with barns and houses, and hemmed by a distant ridge whose wooded slopes looked like stubble. A flight of P-47 fighter bombers nosed into that recalcitrant sky off to the north.

There was the sound of vehicles being tuned, barking little jeeps and the deeper roar of armored cars and a sudden ripping burst of machine-gun fire as someone apparently tested a gun. And as he stood there, caught in the iron-hard grip of the chill and bristling bivouac, the officer flinched noticeably at the sudden *whoosh-whoosh-whoosh* of shells passing overhead. He steadied himself, listening. American artillery in action, he was pretty sure, although he did not possess the split-second ear of the men here, who would have known instantly.

He drew a breath and walked into the old mill that was the command post of the divisional reconnaissance troop. A big first sergeant was working at a field desk.

"Good morning, Sergeant," said the officer quietly. "Is the commanding officer here?"

"No, sir. He's up at Division. The Exec is out inspecting the area. You want me to send for him, Major?"

"No," said the officer, considering. "I really want to see Sergeant Stanton."

The first sergeant looked at him. "Sergeant Stanton?" he repeated.

"He's here, isn't he?" demanded the officer quickly.

"Oh, sure. He reported in last night. But I—he ain't a sergeant, sir."

"No?" said the officer.

"Lost his stripes this morning. Got busted back to private."

The officer considered this in silence, his mouth compressed tightly. "Okay, okay," he said, then. "I want to see him. I'm his brother. Or do I need permission from someone around here?"

"Brother?" said the first sergeant. "Yes, sir. No, there's

no trouble about seein' him. I'll shoot you over to his platoon area and tell the Exec when he comes in."

A trooper from the CP guided Major Clay Stanton to a small vehicle park in the lee of a farmhouse whose newly shattered roof gleamed like a sheaf of ribs. The glass was shattered in every window and the ground was littered with tile, plaster, and chunks of stone. Men were working among jeeps with raised hoods. Stanton saw his brother reassembling a .50-caliber machine gun.

"All right, I see him," he told his guide. "Thanks, soldier." He called softly, "Doke."

His brother turned. For a moment he simply looked at him, still bending over the machine gun, a cleaning rag in one hand. Then he tossed the rag away, wiped his hands on his trousers, and strode to meet him. "Hi, Clay," he said, smiling.

They shook hands under the interested scrutiny of the jeep detail. "I'm mighty glad to see you," said Doke Stanton. "Mighty damned glad. I'd just about given up." He took a long breath and his voice was a bit unsteady. "I'd given up," he said again.

"I got your letter," said Clay. "The one you wrote just as you were leaving the hospital. I checked with Division and then came right away, Doke." He found he had difficulty with his voice, too. He had not seen Doke since the brief flying visit he had been able to arrange to that U.K. hospital.

"Let's make big talk. We don't have much time," said Doke. "Let's go."

He led the way to a nearby embankment in which a great gouge had been made for earth to fill sandbags. There was a whole pile of them nearby with a shovel stuck in the top, giving it the effect of a cairn. Doke nodded toward the pile but seated himself on his helmet. Clay Stanton sat down on the pile of sandbags and looked up instinctively again as there was another series of those swishing shell passages. That slaty overcast with those steel-jacketed harbingers—what a grim deathly sky it was. A cub plane hung jauntily above the nearby ridge, spotting for the American artillery at work. He forced himself to relax, unslung his carbine and laid it on the ground.

Doke reached inside his jacket and brought out a crumpled K-ration packet of Chelsea cigarettes. He proffered them to Clay and, as his brother shook his head, he stuck one in the corner of his mouth and struck a match. As he lighted his cigarette, his hand was trembling.

"What happened to your stripes, Doke?" Clay spoke so suddenly that he sounded abrupt.

"What?" said Doke vaguely.

"Your stripes? Why did you get busted?"

"Oh," said Doke. "That. What the hell difference does it make?" Then he shrugged and stared down at the cigarette in his fingers. "I got caught in a shelling last night and when I woke up this morning all I could seem to think of was the mortar pastings we used to get at Aachen. I don't know why, but that's all I could think of. My head was buzzing and my mouth kept filling with bile and I lay in that hole thinking of mortars and I couldn't take it. I asked The Book for permission to report to the battalion aid station. I was sure I had concussion."

He spoke dispassionately, still regarding the burning cigarette in his fingers. "The captain said no. So"—again he shrugged—"I just went to the aid station anyhow."

Clay Stanton said nothing. "That's about all," said Doke. "They gave me a quick examination and told me no dice. The Book had found out that I had taken off and sent a platoon sergeant to bring me back. A platoon sergeant, no less. The Book was in his glory. Busted me to private. They can have their stripes along with their whole goddamned war."

He drew on his cigarette and exhaled a long swift stream of smoke. Major Clay Stanton studied him carefully. Everything about Doke seemed different, even the way he looked. He was thin, so thin that his cheekbones stood out like ridges and his eyes were ringed with shadowy smudges. His thick brown hair had been croped short, accenting the bone structure of his face and head. He was unshaven and his hands were greasy, with blackened nails, and his combat boots were crusty with dried clay. It could not be remembered or imagined that Doke liked good clothes and wore them well, and a sudden errant picture flitted through Clay Stanton's mind of his brother in biege doeskin slacks and cashmere sports jacket and suede shoes, listening to records in their mother's Connecticut home on a wintry Sunday afternoon, at ease, relaxed in his easy effortless way, a drink in one hand, his head resting back against the big chair with his eyes closed. He had been through a lot since then. He had fought in Italy and Normandy and Belgium and here he was in the Rhineland, busted to a private after all of it, edged and terse and desperate. Not that Clay Stanton blamed him. It was simply incredible to find this man sitting on a steel helmet near him such a stranger. He tried to adjust himself to the fact that Douglas Kendall Stanton was going, vanishing, beyond the reach of familiar memories and associations.

Doke was looking at him. "So you don't have any news, Clay?" he demanded. "It's no good, huh?"

"You mean those orders, Doke?"

"Yes, Clay," said his brother tightly. "Those orders. Those lovely orders. Those pipe-dream orders."

Clay moved swiftly to stop the gathering momentum of that despair. "Listen, Doke," he said, "those orders were cut. I told you in the U.K. that the Theater Historian in Paris was interested in you for one of the spots in his cartographic section. I told him you weren't a professional cartographer but that you were talented with maps and he liked the idea of your reconnaissance experience and, of course, he's a great newspaper man in civilian life and he liked your own newspaper background. So he requested your transfer to the Historical Section, ETOUSA, and I know for a fact that First Army approved and cut the orders."

"So?" said Doke.

"Doke, I don't know why those orders didn't reach you. All I can guess is that there was some kind of a mixup in channels. They probably were diverted to the U.K. hospital and just missed connections. But they're sure to catch up with you, Doke. All this will be straightened out."

"No," said Doke. "No more time."

"No more time? The hell there isn't more time. Those orders could be down here in the next day or so."

Doke drew on his cigarette again. "We have a mission," he said. "We'll be moving out pretty quick now."

"But, good God, Doke, those orders will last until you finish the mission."

"You sound as though I were going to the movies. I'm heading into a fire fight, can't you understand that? And I won't make it. I've no guts left and no luck."

"Doke—"

"Listen, Clay, I've had it. I know it."

"You can't know it."

"When you've been fighting long enough," said Doke briefly, "you know it."

"You've got to get hold of yourself, boy," said Major

Clay Stanton. "You get those orders and you'll be on your way to Paris. That Historical outfit has a big place on the Avenue Foch—"

Doke did not appear to have heard him. "I'm a coward," he said reflectively. "Always was, I guess. But I've been able to hide it. In this war I was always scared, sure, but I could think and move. I could try to take care of myself. Now when I get scared I go all to pieces. I just become a blubbering hysterical fool." He gazed meditatively at his cigarette, then reached for the battered Chelsea packet and lighted a fresh cigarette from the burning end of the old one. "I act like some kind of an animal."

His brother drew in his breath sharply. "That sounds like combat fatigue, and bad. But—" He stopped suddenly.

Doke looked up at him then. "But I've been out of combat for some time, so how can I have combat fatigue? How can I be Section Eight already?" He shrugged and looked away. "I pass the physicals, but when I got blown out of that jeep whatever made me tick in combat got blown up, too."

He drew slowly, moodily, on his cigarette. "I was so set on riding out this war without letting on I was a coward that I didn't play my hand right at the hospital. I was depending on those orders. So when the Army began sweeping up replacements wherever they could find them to build combat strength for this big attack, I got slung back into the hopper for the front instead of for the Z.I. What a damned fool," he added, as an afterthought. "Couple of years after this war nobody is going to care whether you're a coward or a hero."

Clay Stanton again tried to reach for Douglas Kendall Stanton instead of this dispassionate stranger.

"You're no coward, Doke. You've done your job. You could have had a battlefield commission a couple of times."

"I've seen too many of those second lieutenants get shot. You crowd your luck with a commission." Doke shook his head sagely, like a philosopher expounding a homily. "Traitors and cowards sometimes can't be blamed. Their brakes just don't hold on a steep grade. I'd go over the hill in a minute, but I'm too scared even to desert. So I'll go into this mission without the guts or the morale to stay alive and a guy like that needs luck or he'll get killed."

Clay pinched the bridge of his nose with gloved fingers. The caustic stranger made him feel a little sick and he tried to fight it down by remembering that the substance behind this shadow had several years ago been imaginative and high-strung and sensitive; thin-skinned, really, and maybe something had been jarred loose in him, gone out of adjustment like an electronic part that made the difference between a humming motor and a lump of iron.

"Shut up that talk," he nearly whispered. "Get hold of yourself. Get hold of yourself, Doke—"

"A recon troop goes out and gets shot at," said Doke. "Why kid around? Mostly we have it better than the infantry, but sometimes we have it a hell of a sight worse. We go out to get a bloody nose, so we can report on the strength in the fist that hit us." He flung his cigarette away savagely. "Get hold of myself? Okay, sure. How are things back at Army? How's the latest crop of Red Cross girls? Pretty good officer bait?"

"Yeah," muttered Clay. "Yeah, I know." And he rammed his way through to the memory of that summer when his father had made him commit a whole history textbook to memory so he could get back into the Point and how he had cursed and suffered. And the substance behind this shadow would often drop into his room late at night when he was trying to finish his rigorous daily stint, while the smells and sounds of a warm summer night plagued him along with distressing thoughts of country club dances, and the substance would thank him. "You're taking the heat off me, Clay. Thanks, bud. Otherwise he'd still be working on me. Have some coffee and rest your brain. Plenty of women asking about you tonight. Why worry about the Old Man when you've got all those women?"

Doke's eyes were resting on him in a long even glance. "Go ahead," said Clay quietly. "Say it the way you want to, fella."

"All right," said Doke, "I will." He clasped his hands around one knee, balanced on his helmet. "I never used to let myself think about it, but now it doesn't matter. About how I really had it made. That job in Meriden. Morning and evening papers and a tie-up with a TV station. Real strong in the state and I was moving right along. That was a nice plant we had there."

"I know," said Clay. His brother had always liked to write, but mainly it had been in the line of introspective fiction. He had written a novel which had never been published and had experimented with playwriting, too. One of those plays had been produced by an amateur group in their mother's town and Clay had not enjoyed it much, but Doke was only getting started at the time. It had been a surprise when he went to work for those Meriden newspapers and held his own in the pressure and discipline and realistic limits of newswriting.

"What I really wanted to do," said Doke, "was get in on that course in American Civilization that was shaping up at Princeton. Not in the teaching end, but they were planning a publishing annex, hooked up with courses in American Civilization at Harvard, Yale, Pennsylvania, Minnesota, and other universities. Publish studies like Socialism and American Life, Religion in America, things like that. I wanted the job of running that publishing annex."

He nodded reminiscently. "Eventually I guess I'd have graduated into my own little publishing house. That's what I wanted, I guess, after all was said and done. Run a real good little publishing house of my own. I would have liked to live in Princeton, though. Nice place to live. Live there with a hi-fi and plenty of records and a damned nice girl who was plenty sexy on the side—"

He paused, remembering suddenly. He had known her for some months and she had not seemed too impressed with him, but the day he left to join the Army she had appeared, amazingly, at that dingy little railroad station at five-thirty in the morning, bareheaded, fur coat, sheer stockings, and high heels. The station was overheated and hazy with smoke and when she came in there was a swift eddy of crisp air swirling around her. They had talked banteringly, informally, until the little two-car milk train for Hartford came in, and then she had accompanied him out to the platform. Well, he had said, so long, Jerry, and to his amazement she came into his arms and there was a blurred long moment, like a step on an eternal threshold, pressed tightly to him, a clean fresh smell to her hair and the cool soft smoothness of her cheek and the racing pressure of her mouth. Then swiftly, softly, her lips close to his ear, "Good-by, slowpoke. Come back soon, ready to get down to business." Jerry Hunter. Her father was a big advertising man in New York and lived in New Milford. Jerry Hunter. Little, dynamic, auburn-haired, with an elusive mocking quality about her that was like some piquant and compelling essence. He'd never had a chance to follow up.

"But," he said aloud, "I think I could have made out all

right." He again arched one shoulder in a slight shrug. "I've learned a lot in this war. I think," he said, nodding thoughtfully, "I would have been a lot more tolerant. Kind of a Lost Cause guy." He was silent a moment longer, then looked at his brother. "All right, I've said it. Where were we?"

Clay Stanton shifted restlessly on the pile of sandbags. That had sounded like a last will and testament and it made him uncomfortable. He had the impression that his brother had been reviewing something for himself, like someone taking a last backward look. God Almighty, but Doke was in bad shape. He was like no one Clay Stanton had ever met before.

He looked at his wrist watch, then leaned forward. "Doke, I'm kind of AWOL, coming down here to see you. What can I do? How can I help you?"

"You brought a jeep, didn't you? Well, let's get in it and head back for First Army. Get out of the whole mess and then play it by ear."

"You'd get a court and so would I."

"Maybe we could figure a cover story."

Again Clay Stanton made a restless movement. "You get a court and that Paris assignment will be finished."

"I'd be alive, though. That's plenty for me."

"Damn it, Doke, you can't go AWOL."

"Yes I can. If I get a chance. Take a court, if that's the way it has to be. I've got a Purple Heart to help me. And I know I'm a psychoneurotic. I'll take my chance with a court."

"I can't help you go AWOL," said Clay Stanton tersely. "That's crazy. Steady down, Doke. Now, what else?"

"Get me out of this mission, Clay."

"I'll see if I can get a line on those orders—"

"You don't have time, Clay."

No, he did not have time. He had to get back to that First Army War Room very quickly. Time! Neither of them had time. They were like a couple of chips bobbing below the crest of a great rolling wave.

"Maybe I can swing some TDY for you in a hurry," he muttered. "But I may have to go to Corps to do it. I don't know anyone at Division. How about your commanding officer? Would he weigh in with a recommendation?"

"The Book?" Doke Stanton laughed shortly. "Try it, sure. Try anything, Clay."

Major Stanton looked at his wrist watch again and then

picked up his carbine and rose to his feet. "I'd better get going. Take it easy, Doke. This will straighten out."

"Think so?" said Doke tightly. "Wish I did."

"I'll do everything I can. Every damned thing." They shook hands. "See you, Doke."

"Good-by," said Doke Stanton. He swallowed as he saw his brother turn and walk swiftly around the perimeter of the field in the direction of the CP. A major at First Army headquarters and he probably would not be able to do a thing. You had to know how to cut corners and take chances in this kind of thing and Clay was a channels and endorsement man. Doke rubbed his hands tightly against his thighs. There he went, the last hope, a tall lean guy in helmet and trench coat.

He turned and walked toward the jeeps, where the newly cleaned machine gun pointed errantly toward the German sky.

4.

THAT MORNING, early, the mist had clung to the river in curling wisps and the bridge emerged and faded as the wisps swirled like wind-blown veils and the bridge sometimes looked suspended in nothingness as its four stone piers were hidden, giving it an unearthly quality of something figurative, visualized.

Ilse Margraven stood at the window of her room in the small castle that overlooked the Rhine and watched, fascinated, the shadow play of the mist around the long slender bridge. Looking at it now, she loved the graceful spans that kept their identity in that evanescent film on the river. Like a truth, she found herself thinking, or a principle, or a purpose.

A knock at the door interrupted her preoccupation and she turned, calling an invitation to enter. It was William, as she expected. He shuffled a few steps into the room and stood there, stocky, stooped, grizzled, wearing a battered overcoat against the damp cold of the unheated castle.

"Two officers are downstairs, Fräulein," he reported. "Martha is giving them coffee."

"Who are they, William?"

"The combat commander of the bridge and the captain of the SS Security. I have built a fire."

She nodded. The army used the castle at will. Usually there was some kind of headquarters here. William coughed.

"People are saying that the Americans may capture Bonn."

"It is possible, William."

"We are not far from Bonn. The Americans would come here, too. It would be terrible. The Americans are savages."

"Have you been taken by the Volksturm?" she asked, interrupting. William became panicky at the thought of the Americans.

"Not yet, Fräulein. *Gott sei dank.*"

"Go out as seldom as possible," said the girl.

He bobbed. "*Jawohl,* Fräulein."

She went downstairs to the great hall, her hands balled tight in the pockets of her sweater for warmth. Limping to the big arched door, she met Martha emerging with a tray. "The Herr SS Hauptmann wants brandy," she said. "At this time of day. Well, better to take our bandy than our coffee, poor as it is." She plodded on, grumbling.

The girl walked into the long stone room with its faded grandeur of the huge hearth surmounted by the boar's head. Only a couple of days ago Field Marshal Model had been here briefly, contemptuously. The chill of the room seemed a lingering aftermath of that visit.

The two officers in the room were known to her. Captain Bratge, the bridge commandant, was a wiry intense man, with something of the nervous intensity of a terrier about him. Once, Ilse Margraven had heard, he had been a school-teacher and she could well imagine him as such, didactic, disciplined, thorough, precise. The other officer was Lang-bach, captain of the SS detachment in town, and his occa-sional visits she dreaded. He was big, towering over the slight Bratge, as they stood before the fireplace, deep through the shoulders and chest, and in his black SS uniform and polished black boots he was like some harbinger of judgment and execution.

"Good morning, gentlemen," she greeted.

Captain Bratge gave her a quick polite salute. Captain Langbach surveyed her, his hands behind his back clasped about the stick he habitually carried. "Ah," he said, "the hostess of Castle Rimburg. Countess Rimburg, is it? Good morning, Countess. You have recently returned from Ba-varia?" He laughed.

Captain Bratge made an impatient gesture at the other officer's heavy attempt at humor and set down his coffee cup. "Fräulein Margraven," he said in his crisp way, "we are expecting a battalion of anti-aircraft troops soon. Perhaps it will be necessary to establish their headquarters here."

"Yes, Captain," the girl said quietly.

"The castle, as you know, is still under control of Wehr-kreis IX," Captain Bratge went on. "Captain Langbach, of course, represents the Wehrkreis—"

Langbach broke in. "And the Wehrkreis wished to con-sult the proper authority at the castle. As a courtesy, of course."

The girl made no reply, But Captain Bratge evidently had other things to do besides set the stage for Langbach's heavy-handed mockery. "I do not know when this will be, Fräu-lein Margraven. Soon, I hope," he said fervently. "But," he added, "I hope there will be no trouble for you."

He again gave her a quick salute. "I must go. Are you coming, Langbach?"

"No," said the SS officer leisurely. "I have been promised some brandy."

Captain Bratge nodded, preoccupied, and departed with his quick springy step. The trim, wiry little officer had known the great days of the blitzkrieg in both Poland and France and now he was security commandant at a relatively obscure Rhine bridge, but one thing was sure, he would be as thorough and efficient about its defense and demolition as he had been with his mathematics class in his schoolmaster days. The girl was sorry to see him go. Langbach was regarding her with those icy blue eyes of his.

"Sit down, Fräulein," he said. "While I am checking security arrangements, perhaps it is my duty to ask a few routine questions, eh? One can never be too sure, eh?"

She sat down, poised slightly sideways on the edge of a chair, her cold hands folded on one knee. Captain Langbach studied her with some attention, then. Several times he had thought of establishing his headquarters here instead of over at the Allmang tavern, because there might be sport here. She was cool and reserved and correct and that made him wonder what she would be like with a real man. But she was thin and she limped and only at sudden times, like now, when she sat with an intriguing grace did he feel his curiosity awaken again.

"You are afraid of something, Fräulein," he said bluntly. "I can always tell."

She straightened perceptibly and he smiled. "Why do you stay here?" he demanded.

"It is my place, Captain Langbach."

"Governess to the Rimburg children and you stay on here long after the Rimburgs have gone to Bavaria. You and two old servants."

"I promised the Count that I would look after this place for him."

Langbach laughed. "Look after this place," he repeated. "I could stable my men here and they could spit all over the walls and burn their trash in this damned room. What would you look after, hein?"

She made no reply. He waited while Martha appeared with a bottle of brandy and a glass on a tray. Instantly he poured out a glass and took a swallow. He turned and spat it out in the fireplace. Martha looked startled at the girl, but at her little smile the old woman shrugged and waddled out of the room.

Langbach wiped his mouth with the back of his hand. "What stuff!" he said. "Vile! If you offered that to the Field Marshal the other day, it's a wonder he did not pull this place down brick by brick."

She had never seen him in quite this mood before. He had always been mocking, dangerous, but now there seemed a slackening of all restraint. Captain Bratge's security and engineer troops were disciplined, but among the SS, the Hitler Jugend, the Werewolves, the Volksturm, there was growing that strange lawlessness and irresponsibility.

He was frowning now and she forced herself to look up at him and he came into sharp clear focus, a big man with his black hair slicked back and those sharp blue eyes and the bluish shadow along his powerful jaw.

He drank deliberately and then stood there with his glass poised. " I do not joke with you," he said. "It was only last month that a woman of a noble name was arrested near Düsseldorf. She was sending a beam to Allied bombers through the chimney. These days the Reich is fighting its great battle and there are the frightened ones who begin to break." His mouth flickered. "You are frightened, Fräulein. Of what?"

"I have always been loyal to my country," she said. "I always shall be. Never would I do anything to hurt my Germany."

"Pretty," said Langbach. "Like a child in the schoolroom with the pretty verse. Let us see, eh? Your mother was English?"

"Half English," corrected the girl. "Her mother was English, Herr Captain."

"You have visited England for long periods. You had some of your education there?"

She nodded. Langbach picked up the brandy bottle. "Your father lived near here — Stadt-Meckenheim. A teacher of music, *nicht wahr?"*

Again she nodded. "Answer it out," he barked at her suddenly. "Sit there, nodding like a simpleton."

"Captain Langbach," she said, "I have done nothing to deserve this discourtesy."

"We shall see. Your father—"

"Yes, of course, he taught music — the piano and the

organ, also choral singing. He was also a trained conductor and composer."

"And two years ago he was called to Berlin. He returned when?"

"He did not return," said the girl quietly.

"Because—?"

"Because he was placed under arrest in Augswein."

"So?" said Langbach. "And your mother, eh?"

"She followed him to Berlin, Captain Langbach. She is now living near Augswein." The girl's voice was low, toneless.

"But you stay here, Fräulein. Even after your employers hurry off, you stay here." He sipped his brandy. "There should be nothing," he said. "A thin quiet thing. The lame and the halt are often pitied, not suspected. You were a dancer once, Fräulein?"

"I was studying," said the girl. She seemed to be breathing a little more rapidly. She had gone through this catechism before with him.

"You were very good, *nicht wahr?*"

"No, Captain Langbach. My mother was very good. I was too young. I simply loved it."

He looked at her another long moment. "Curious," he said. "I find it curious. You interest me. People who interest me are not too lucky sometimes. Perhaps I shall make you one of my responsibilities. Perhaps," he said, his mouth flickering, "I shall look for ways to test your devotion to the Reich."

She bent her head in spite of herself. She could not understand why he seemed bent on persecuting her, unless it was some queer savage mood, but instinctively she felt it was more than a matter of mood. He was like someone trying to find an outlet for hate.

"There never was a time," said Ilse Margraven, "when I wasn't ready."

"Very good," said Captain Langbach. He raised his glass toward her and tossed it off. "You quiet ones often deserve extra attention," he said. "To an empty castle and its quiet hostess." He laughed. "I am responsible for both." His eyes still on her, he buttoned his military overcoat and took out a pair of black leather gloves. "Remember that, Fräulein Countess," he said, and elaborately touched his gloves to the visor of his cap. Then he was gone with his aggressive cadenced stride.

For a few moments she sat, as he had left her, staring down at her clasped hands. Why did he bother with such a small fish as herself? She had always despised him too much to be afraid of him and maybe he realized that and the awareness of the Americans was churning him into that unreasoning fury. For everyone was becoming aware that the Americans were threatening the Westwall; those legendary Americans might materialize into human beings behind bayonets and machine guns and tanks. Perhaps the fearsome Langbach could not stand the thought that the people were beginning to fear something else more than him. Or, perhaps, he was simply breaking, as he accused the weak, whom he despised, of doing.

She rose from the chair and walked to one of the windows, dragging her right foot slightly in her habitual limp. Standing at a tall leaded window, she hugged her arms tightly about her for warmth and stared down at the river. The mists had dispersed and the bridge was clearly discernible with its four stone towers and its three steel spans and the railroad tunnel on the east bank.

Suddenly she shuddered violently, her whole body shaking, and she whirled herself around, her back to the river and the bridge.

There was less than fifty miles of front where the First United States Army struck. Fifty miles from a point northwest of Cologne to the link-up area with Patton above Coblenz. This was the stretch of Rhineland that had been allotted to the Americans and they prepared to go after it in one fast gulp.

Across fifty miles of Germany the upper jaw widened for the bite. First Army men moved in obedience to something called Letter of Instructions 16, and fourteen division headquarters worked feverishly on movement patterns on the roads in their zones and devised their fire plans and drew up the attack orders for the regiments, the Army front with its whiplash planning dwindling to circles on maps as the orders came filtering down closer and closer to the smallest common denominator where the man in steel helmet and field jacket and trousers stuffed into combat boots, his home letters and pictures in the breast pocket of his shirt or the wallet on his hip, took as his piece of the front whatever he could see with the naked eye. And orders spread and divided and subdivided to the engineers and the truck drivers and the medical corpsmen and the communication troops and the supply depots. And the orders went by explosive little jeeps into towns and villages and down side roads into fields and climbed bumpy tracks to the crests of ridges.

Against all this Major Clay Stanton realized the futility of any personal mission. There was no time for him to sit down and talk to anyone. There was no way he could tell it right. There was no room for him to maneuver. Not at division headquarters. But he tried.

He waylaid Captain Jeffrey Cummings Baker, as the recon commander was leaving a G-3 briefing to return to his CP. The Book, Doke Stanton had called him.

He was wearing horn-rimmed glasses which made him look owlish under the brim of his helmet. He wore a trench coat buttoned up to his chin and he was carrying a map case, and he listened to Clay Stanton say bluntly that his brother was not fit for combat and should be sent immediately to a field hospital for observation.

Captain Baker replied in a soft voice, but there was a taut little muscle in his angular jaw that moved like a pulse. Major Stanton's brother had been returned as fit for duty. Furthermore a battalion aid station had rejected him for treatment as recently as early this morning. The Book spoke in his soft precise way, but again that taut little muscle jumped in his face.

"He needs a thorough examination," said Clay Stanton. He found himself getting angry. The Book had that effect on people. "That aid station isn't qualified for anything but a snap judgment, Captain. It's a place for quick dressings, splints, and bandages, not mental disorders. My brother is a bad case of combat fatigue."

"Most of us are," said The Book sententiously. "Your brother has a difficult attitude at present, I agree. I was obliged to take away his stripes. That may very well act as a shock treatment to steady him down. At least, to regain the stripes should be an incentive." He nodded politely. "Excuse me, Major. I must return to my command post."

Clay Stanton, speechless, saw him go. That pompous ass, he thought, with his shock treatment. As if Doke cared a whit for a whole sleeve of stripes. He moved restlessly to the Operations Section. The G-3 officer was conferring with the division commander, but he located an assistant G-3 supervising two enlisted men preparing the duplicator for turning out the overlays to accompany the field order. He broke off somewhat impatently while Clay Stanton identified himself and asked about the mission for the reconnaissance troop.

"Recon? Hell, I don't know. The Old Man gave a mission —oh, yeah, the Old Man thinks the Jerries have moved some stuff into Tettledorf and he wants to probe it." He nodded shortly. "Got to get this stuff out. Excuse me, Major."

Clay Stanton went over to the Operations map tacked against a wall of the G-3 section and studied it for Tettledorf. The division commander wanted some information in a hurry before he set his attack order and was not using an ordinary patrol. That indicated a fast, deep reconnaissance with the possibility of a fire fight and he needed the mechanized cavalry. The hell with Tettledorf. What difference did it make where it was?

He swung away from the map and left the headquarters. Picking up his driver, he climbed into his jeep.

"Head for Zulpich, Florian," he told his driver. "Getting late. We'll spend the night at Corps."

They had not gone very far when the swelling pressure of the imminent attack again engulfed him. On a narrow lateral road his jeep was forced to one side by a procession of tanks moving fast, their raucous motors gunned into a hideous sustained roaring cascade. They were heavily loaded with sandbags and spare parts, splashed with mud, the helmeted tankers standing in the open turrets. One after the other, lumbering along in thundering steel parade, a darting little one-star jeep rocketing in and out among them, heading for the front of the column. Clay Stanton saw the red board on the bumper with one star and recognized the officer bending forward beside the driver. That was Noon, who had built highways before the war, and the reckless speed with which he came threading in and out among his tanks gave an emphatic keynote of drive and speed to the inexorable armored column. They must be tanks of the 9th Armored Division shifting position for their attack. Noon's Combat Command B. Somewhere they would rendezvous with the infantry that would accompany them.

They finally cleared in a wake of halftracks and jeeps. Clay Stanton stirred restlessly in the uncomfortable seat as the jeep bolted on again toward III Corps headquarters. It was getting late, the wintry twilight hurried along by the dun-colored sky. A few miles out of Zulpich he nearly lost his life.

A convoy of trucks was hurtling toward the front, bypassing a command car that had broken down in the middle of a muddy road and was wedged, half-slewed around, in the ruts. The trucks simply roared around it into the edge of a field and came crashing and swaying back onto the road, bouncing and skidding hideously as their drivers yanked furiously at the wheels and gunned their motors for the traction to keep them plowing back into the ruts. Clay Stanton's driver had barely time to swerve off the road and up on the side of an embankment, where they hung like a fly on a wall, as truck after truck went careening by, showering them with sprays of flung mud that rattled like hail against the windshield. The truckers paid no attention to them. They slammed their big clumsy vehicles through that muddy slot of a road as though nothing would stop them, God, man, or devil.

When finally they got back off the embankment, the jeep was encrusted with mud. Clay Stanton passed a hand across his dirt-streaked face. The world behind the front was a nightmare of raw roaring power. The sense of urgent drive was like some tensed steel spring.

"Close, huh, Major?" said his driver, clearing a patch of the windshield. "Those truckers could have knocked us into a pile o' junk. We better get goin' fast. It's dark now and I sure don't want to meet any of them trucks drivin' with cat's-eye lights. They'd make applesauce out of us."

It was pitch black when they arrived at Corps headquarters. "Get some rest, Florian," Stanton said wearily. "Tomorrow we'll get back to Army."

Although, as he went into the headquarters, he felt as though that was turning his back on Doke pretty fast. He reported into the Operations section. Here he knew the Assistant Corps G-3. They had been at the Point together.

"Look, Mike," he said, "I'm down here on my own time. Get me off the hook, will you? Can you use me around here a day or two?"

"Well, I guess so, Clay," said the G-3 officer. "But I don't know how, except for some liaison job."

Major Stanton was too tired to care. "Call Army, then," he said. "Tell them I'm here and ask for me on TDY with your liaison group. Try to swing it, Mike. They're probably ready to chew me out but good."

"Okay," said the other. "You can bunk down with me tonight anyway, just off the War Room. I'll see what we can do."

Stanton washed the grime from his hands and face. He

ate a hasty meal and then returned to the billet off the War Room. Sitting down on a canvas cot, he rested his head in his hands. What did Doke expect? A miracle? What he needed was time to check on the miscarriage in those transfer orders. That was the only sensible way to go about this. What else could he do with the whole damned Army front ready to blow like a volcano? And anyhow it might do Doke good to get through that recon mission. Settle his silly idea about luck.

A fast deep reconnaissance into the German positions. Clay Stanton drew a breath tight and hard into his chest. Sure, that was a rough break, but the Army deal came up like that sometimes.

He had an odd memory of his brother, as he sat there numbed with fatigue, the smoke curling from a cigarette burning down unnoticed between his fingers. He had been just a youngster and he had fainted at a movie that had a climax of a blood transfusion scene. He just could not take things like that. It had been a Shirley Temple movie and the family had kidded Doke about it for years. Clay Stanton dropped his cigarette on the floor and stamped on it. He could hear the War Room duty officer giving some coordinates over the phone and the screech of tires as some jeep braked hard in the road outside. He stretched himself out on the cot and flung an arm over his eyes.

The only way to have done it, Doke, was simply to have taken off, as you wanted to do. But I have a career in this army, you know that. This war is my big chance. You know that. If you wanted to go AWOL, you had to do it by yourself. And why didn't you? But, hell, Clay thought moodily, Doke just did not have enough nerve left to take even that much of a chance. He was like someone completely transfixed on the middle of a tightrope.

He must have slept, for he was suddenly shocked wide awake by the blast of artillery fire. He came half-lunging to his feet, not knowing where he was for the moment. Then, as he remembered, he sank back on the edge of the cot, his ears ringing with the sharp ripping crescendo of the guns firing along the Corps front.

He sat there, feeling the floor reverberate under his feet and listening to the windows rattling behind the blackout curtains, as the big 105s fired with the speed and continuity of a message flashed by the shutters of a blinker light. They were really pouring it on—guns of Corps Artillery firing at something out there in the night between them and the Rhine.

5.

THE Division Commander was fighting a tough war. He was always willing to fight and with a little luck he might get a Corps. He was a grizzled man with steel-rimmed glasses, who smoked a pipe and looked philosophical, yet had a gleam in those professorial eyes and liked to take a chance.

The reason he had ordered out the recon troop was an enemy strongpoint centering around a crossroads town called Tettledorf that formed a bold salient from the German main line of resistance. This had really challenged the division commander, this Tettledorf, which had never enjoyed the slightest claim to distinction before, but because it was an enemy position that might defilade the railroad track that was the axis of advance, the division commander puffed on his pipe and studied the map as though he were considering a chess problem.

Intelligence reports indicated that the enemy had withdrawn from that exposed position and then suddenly occupied it again. The division commander was not particularly bothered, but he did not like loose ends and he preferred to know whether he had a salient on his front or not. Salients could be stubborn. Of course, he could bypass it and belt an artillery preparation. But he had to know and so he ordered the reconnaissance troop to get the answer and fast. Was the enemy holding Tettledorf, and in approximately what strength? That meant the recon troop had to draw fire.

The recon troop was startled at this sudden mission. It had been preparing for its part in the division attack, which was to spearhead a mobile task force on the right flank of the division, in company with a platoon of tanks, a platoon of tank destroyers, a platoon of combat engineers, and a company of infantry. Now it had to gear itself for a fast reconnaissance with the possibility of a sharp fire fight.

The division commander regretted the necessity of the reconnaissance, of course. But he did not intend that anything should bog down his attack right at the start and, if there was a salient at Tettledorf, he had to shape his attack accordingly, because this was to be no static front, like before the Roer, and the Corps commander was a cavalryman who wanted speed, the way all these people did who had ever fought under Patton. That was the division commander's own Little Picture and he would have been quite willing to sympathize with the recon troop's Little Picture as an occupational hazard of the trade.

They had moved out while it was still dark, that heavy drape of darkness before the dawn hours, the lead jeep of each platoon driving with cat's-eye headlights, the narrow slits in headlamps painted black that gave only a semblance of light on the road ahead. At the beginning, in those first stages of the dark advance into enemy ground, men swept for mines, because the Germans often mined the approaches to their outposts.

Then the darkness had filtered into a somber dusky gray, with ground mist rising like chill fingers dripping with foggy tendrils, and shapes became distinguishable in vague outline and somehow the motors of the jeeps seemed louder, as though the early morning had pulled away a cottony undercoating of darkness.

It was like a sliver of steel, the reconnaissance troop, with the ghosts of old cavalry patrols jingling along with it; the column of jeeps, interspersed here and there with armored cars, pushing out into the dead territory between the lines, the point jeeps reconnoitering ahead and then the whole column hitching itself along, leaving their division outposts behind and probing toward that suspected salient.

It was fired on suddenly in the first grayness, the spiteful chatter of a machine gun. Part of the point platoon covered the German outpost with fire, while the rest of the recon troop sideslipped on past and accelerated its pace along the winding road, and suddenly the German countryside was around them, still veiled here and there in a slight ground fog so that it was like looking at a panorama through gauze. It was barren in the grip of winter, yet with its clusters of deserted farmhouses it gave the impression of grazing country. The long regular ridges ran generally north and south, undulating gently, with smooth hillsides, dun brown with scattered patches of snow and girdled by small black patches of forest.

Doke Stanton, riding in a three-man jeep crew in the middle of the column, hunched down beside the machine gun mount, his hands clamped tightly between his knees. With luck there would be nothing at Tettledorf. With luck they would get there without drawing artillery fire. With luck they could hightail it back to their lines and maybe Clay would be there. With luck—only where was the luck? The sharp *pi-toon* of a sniper's rifle could find the guy in the middle of a whole column whose luck had run out.

There were marks of savage flaying by artillery here and recently. Trees stood at grotesque jagged angles and shot-up vehicles and litters of equipment lay in great gouges across the road and into the fields, the flung earth of the craters a dull sandy color, and there were lanes off to the sides of dugout firing positions with heaped bundles of brush against shellbursts. Doke began to hope. This must have been part of the enemy salient and nothing was here. Maybe they could cut around and go speeding back. The Germans had pulled out. They must have pulled out. There was nothing here.

But a few minutes later the point jeeps abruptly signaled the column to a halt. The Book's armored car moved up to the head of the column. Immediately the point platoon dismounted and deployed into the fields on either side of the road and the rest of the troop was signaled to advance.

Paul Kelso, Doke's jeep sergeant, grunted as though he had been hit in the stomach. "Here we go," he muttered. "Have your tickets ready."

The Book was out of his armored car waiting to talk to Doke's platoon commander. The lanky Milroy dismounted from his car and together with the captain reconnoitered a short distance up the road. A hundred yards to the front their road crossed another.

"What do you think, Lieutenant?" asked the captain. "Do you think it is Tettledorf?"

"It should be," said the platoon commander. "But probably it's just the nose of the position." He squinted toward the crossroads. There was a farmhouse, solidly built of stone, with red-tiled roof and damp stains on its walls. A cobbled courtyard adjoined the house and near the side of the road was a haystack with a hooded truck parked beside it. Across the road was a patch of pine woods. There was nothing else. The grayness of early light hung murkily over the quiet crossroads.

The Book arched his heavy dark brows in a frown. "If it's the Tettledorf crossroads, the Jerries certainly must have pulled out. Don't you think so, Lieutenant?"

Lanky young Milroy glanced at him briefly and then again at the crossroads ahead through the trees. "Maybe," he said. "And then again you've got to remember the Tettledorf position would be held in depth. The real strength would be beyond those crossroads." He nodded negligently toward the smooth slopes that broke the wooded ridges. "Fields of fire for defense positions. Could be."

"But chances are we'd have drawn fire by now," said The Book.

Milroy shrugged. "Jerries aren't wasting artillery these days. Could be they'll let us make our move."

The captain spoke and there was a queer taut note in his voice. "We've got to hurry. Send a dismounted patrol in to point those damned crossroads."

"Okay," said Milroy. He turned and called softly. "Kelso. Paul, get your bunch."

The three-man crews of two jeeps dismounted and gathered around the platoon commander. He was saying something. Doke Stanton did not hear him. He slipped a clip into his carbine with hands that shook perceptibly. "Get going," said Milroy. "We'll be covering you close."

He found himself walking through the patch of leafless trees toward the crossroads ahead, his legs moving as though of their own volition. His knees felt as though they were wobbling on bearings. His heart and mind and everything worth a damn were way back there behind him, way back beyond the American lines, and what he was pushing through this scrofulous growth of winter-lashed trees was just something to drape a steel helmet and a muddy brown uniform on. But it was all he had and he had been pushed, pushed, pushed—the Army, the whole huge selfish impersonal mass, The Book, the pipe-smoking general at comfortable division headquarters—pushed until he was here, a sensible intelligent man actually walking through some trees with a gun toward some crossroads and just one little hunk of lead could end the whole damned foolish business, but it only mattered to him, and was there any luck left, any luck at all, just enough to get him through this day, this morning, maybe even the next hour, just the next hour?

They paused and crouched, strung out on the edge of the lateral road, a little bit above the house, and they could hear Milroy's M-8 moving up slowly back there on the east road. Doke glanced about him quickly. There was that beat-up truck parked next to the haystack. Nothing else. Nothing else? Wait a minute!

"Wait a minute, Kelso," he said fiercely and grabbed the sergeant's arm.

"Now what the hell?" growled Kelso.

Doke pointed to the patch of firs across the road from the house. "On that southeast corner of the crossroads—that black cloth."

His eye had caught it and he pointed again, his voice urgent. "It's covering a cut of fresh meat—pork ribs or something—"

As he spoke, the breeze caught the cloth and, as it blew lazily back, they could see the newly butchered sheaf of ribs hanging there.

"So?" said Kelso.

"That's the way a soldier lives, Kelso, on the land. They're in there. That's a position—the Germans are holding Tettledorf—"

Kelso shook off his arm. "Maybe. Come on," he said, yanking Doke to his feet. "Let's get going."

"Fire a burst in there, Kelso," said Doke Stanton tensely. "Get the jump on them, for God's sake. They've got the road in their sights, you know damn well—"

Kelso looked irresolute a moment, then reverted to his orders. "Come on!" he barked. "It's getting lighter by the minute." He made a sweeping gesture with his arm. "Break!" he ordered, and pushed Doke headlong. "Move!"

Doke Stanton found himself breaking from the cover of the trees and racing across the road, a tightness in his throat and his knees buckling loosely as though they were double-jointed. Any good recon man could sniff out this deal. The Jerries were back in the salient and they commanded the crossroads and the railroad track, and, if there had to be a fire fight to prove it, you didn't have to set up a whole patrol like ducks in a shooting gallery.

"Ellison!" he muttered. "Ellison—"

The patrol reached the other side of the road just above the house. "Spread out," said Kelso. "You're bunched like beets—"

His words were snapped off by the sudden ripping burst of machine-gun fire from the direction of the fir trees. It tore into the grayness of the morning, the real grayness of a new and imminent day, not the murky grayness of thinning darkness. The patrol threw themselves flat. Doke Stanton did not look for cover. He just hurled himself at the ground and sprawled there tight. Immediately the recon troop covering them opened fire. Milroy blasted from his M-8, the trigger pedal mashed to the floor, his .37mm gun firing through its slit. The dismounted platoon opened up on the crossroads from the fields on either side of Milroy's armored car.

Glass shattered in crashing blasts as the American fire swept across the farmhouse, splintered ricocheting chunks of stone, kicked among the cobblestones of the farmyard, slashed at the pine woods like scythes. Suddenly the German truck parked near the haystack exploded in one huge yellow acrid cloud. The blast turned Doke Stanton over as though he had been flipped by a spatula. Instantly a geyser of smoky tendrils shot up from the exploding truck and little streaks of fire burst out in a fan. Then the smoke billowed with traces of flame.

Kelson groped to his knees. "Christ!" he choked. "That must have been an ammo truck." He choked again as the acrid smoke spread its blackish-yellow veil over the crossroads. "Back across the road!" he yelled then. "Jump for it! There's Jerries all over the place—"

Doke Stanton came to hands and knees. He did not have his carbine or helmet, but he was not aware of it. He groped to his feet, spun dizzily, staggered to one side, his mouth open in a soundless scream. There had to be a hole. There had to be a hole. The whole world seemed exploding around him. Someone grabbed at him in the veil of smoke and he tore himself away with a frantic lunge. A piece of flying tile from the roof caught him a glancing blow in the forehead and he went to his knees momentarily. He could see the outlines of the farmhouse through the drifting smoke and it appeared as though men were running through the veil across the farmyard. He came to his feet and plunged toward the house and reached a door, hanging half on its hinges. Instantly he flung himself through it and found himself in a big kitchen.

He half crouched, looking for the cellar. There had to be a hole. There was a door at one side of the room and he leaped for it, pulled it open and plunged through. The next moment he bounced back from a stunning collision with shelves of crockery and went down in a crash of cascading china. This time he simply lay there in the litter, panting, clutching at the floor. The solid farmhouse seemed to shake around him. Plaster fell in powdery lumps and pieces, bullets splintered the wainscoting of windows, from a long distance away someone screamed outside somewhere, and he lay there among broken crockery and nearly strangled with the bile in his throat.

Something prodded him hard and he groaned with the sudden pain of it and stirred. A hand yanked him by the shoulder and he struggled up on one knee. A shabby German soldier was holding a machine pistol on him, a little unshaven man with an overcoat so big for him that it hung around his ankles and the sleeves draped his knuckles. But there was nothing ludicrous about the weapon in his hands, nor about the officer who stood beside him, young, blue-eyed, clean-shaven, with a tightness about his mouth that gave a nasty impact to the Luger in his hand. He rapped out something in crisp staccato German.

Doke could not seem to hear. He shook his head dizzily. He could not see very well, either, squinting against the blood and plaster dust that streaked his face. But as the German officer spoke again and he was struck across the shoulder with the barrel of the Schmeisser he realized that he was a prisoner and instinctively raised both hands quickly. Strangely, he had never considered that possibility. He could imagine himself being cut in half by machine-gun fire, but he had not been able to imagine himself a prisoner. He came to his feet, and with the undersized private at his back and the officer in front, made his way unsteadily up a long narrow hall that ended in a side door. He shrank from leaving the protective shell of the farmhouse and then got a merciless prod of the Schmeisser in the small of the back that made him wince with pain and stumble out through the door.

Following the officer who ran, bending in a slight crouch, he ducked through a wide low vineyard of dormant gray grapevines, his hands still at the level of his shoulders, advancing deeper into Germany in a numbed unsteady run.

The village was east of the crossroads, a small village with the quaint old worldliness of a curved meerschaum pipe or a figurine of Dresden china. But it was a victim ready for sacrifice because it was the hub of a network of inter-locking defense positions that formed the salient and the Americans were sure to hit it hard when they knew about this.

A German major, his overcoat draped across his shoulders like a cape, stood at the sandbagged entrance to a cellar of the village schoolhouse and talked in swift expletives over a field telephone.

"There is an attack, Herr Oberst," he said. "It penetrated the crossroads, but now has moved south of the village." He listened a moment. "I will have it located for the flak battery," he said hurriedly. "It does not seem to be an attack in depth. There is no great force, I believe. *Jawohl,* Herr Oberst."

He slapped the telephone into its leather case hanging on a post. Then he looked at the prisoner. The American was leaning back against the sandbags, his face a streaked mask of dried blood and grime and plaster dust. The imperturbable stocky lieutenant stood nearby. His Luger was back in its black leather holster. Even the undersized private had lowered his machine pistol. The prisoner was like someone dead on his feet.

The major made a restless movement. "I have no use of English," he said crisply. "Nor do I have the time."

The lieutenant smiled thinly. "You do not wish prisoners, Major? There is no problem to that."

"Look at this one," said the major, jabbing with his thumb. "Either he is stupid or he is in shock. Take him to Division. They can question him there better than we can here."

"I made a reconnaissance of the crossroads for you, Major," said the blond lieutenant smoothly. "But I am not at your orders. I came here on orders to take an officer to the rear for court-marital. You will pardon me, Major?"

The major scowled impatiently. These paratrooper cubs had the arrogance of emperors. But they could fight and they would die for the Führer where they stood and there really should be more of them right now.

"Can you not drop him off at Division on your way?" he asked.

The lieutenant shrugged. "If you wish, Major."

The major nodded shortly and bent toward the cellar entrance. He called curtly and a tall officer stepped out and stood, waiting. He wore a cloth forage cap instead of a helmet and carried no side arms. "If you are ready, Colonel," said the major.

The tall officer listened a moment to the spat of small-arms fire south of the village and nodded absently. "Surely a feeler," he commented. "They are trying to break off, I think. I suggest you show as little of your strength as possible. Yes, I am ready." His glance moved to the American prisoner. "I am to have company, I see," he said.

The lieutenant gave a brief perfunctory salute. "After you, Colonel," he said. "The truck is just ahead."

Doke Stanton was prodded into movement. He found himself walking behind a tall German officer toward a hooded truck with three soldiers lounging around it. He still could not hear very well and it seemed to affect his balance. He weaved in his walk, those treacherous knees buckling on him.

The tall officer stepped into the rear of the drab little truck with its battered, sagging canvas hood and Doke was pushed in after him. He sat down and rubbed his knees. Two soldiers with rifles climbed in and the door was shut. Then the truck began to move.

The officer crossed one leg over a knee and folded his arms across his chest. "So you are an American," he said to Doke. His tone was wondering, softly introspective against the noisy little truck and Doke did not even hear him.

Doke Stanton was trying to think again. He sat there, bemused, staring at his knees, groping mentally out of a cottony cocoon of semideafness and the ringing clangor in his head. The big fact was that he had been taken prisoner. He tried to build around that. If he could get safely stowed away in a Stalag, he had a good chance to survive this war. He figured the odds the way a gambler might scan a poker hand. To get into a Stalag was the goal. But maybe just repeating name, rank, and serial number would not be enough. The Geneva Convention did not matter a damn when information was really wanted. Doke Stanton knew that. He was alone and that meant they really might not want to bother with him, if they did not get anything out of him. He might have to barter for survival. They knew when they could crack a prisoner and a man was a fool to throw away his chance of survival by clinging to name, rank, and serial number. The hell with what they told you about the Geneva Convention. He stared fixedly at his hands, as though hypnotized. No, you had to know how to barter. He would have to learn that fast.

The truck bumped and swayed over a rough road and then jolted to a halt. Doke's head came up swiftly. Already? The stocky boyish lieutenant slid out of the front seat and disappeared. They waited in the hooded gloom of the truck, the two guards and the tall quiet officer and the American. It was very quiet here. They must have come several miles from Tettledorf. Then suddenly the paratrooper lieutenant was back. He gave a curt command to the driver and the truck jolted into motion again.

Doke found the German officer's glance resting on him. "Division headquarters has displaced," the German commented, nodding. "Our young officer in charge will not bother to find it, I believe. That is not so good for you, hein? Now you are getting deeper into Germany. Now you are perhaps a burden to him." He nodded briefly toward the dangerous young officer riding in front.

It was as though he was helping Doke figure the odds. Doke recalculated the chances for getting into a Stalag. In a way, missing Division was a break. He was afraid of Division. The farther to the rear he went the less likely that he might be shot out of hand. But that paratrooper in the front was to be watched. They were fanatics and killers, the paratroopers, and Doke knew that he was excess baggage to this one.

Suddenly the truck began to sway crazily as the driver put on speed and the racking motor coughed raucously under the pressure. Above the wheezing motor there emerged another sound, a steadily increasing drone. There was a screech of tires as the truck skidded under the whiplash of the brakes. Doke pitched heavily against the other side with one of the guards, the truck spun in a half circle, then righted itself and braked to an abrupt halt.

They were stopped in the shadow of something that smelled of creosote. The pursuing droning sound suddenly flashed above them and was gone.

"American planes," said the German colonel reflectively. "We found the shelter of a culvert."

Doke picked himself up off the floor of the truck. He was not fast enough to suit one of the guards, and received a nudge with the butt of a rifle. He sank back, rubbing his shoulder. The German officer folded his arms again.

"It has been like this since Normandy," he said in that same reflective way. "We could supply or relieve units only by night." His eyes rested on Doke Stanton again. "Your planes and your artillery," he said. He scanned the American a moment longer. "But not, I think, your men. That has not been proved."

The truck waited a while longer; then, at the lieutenant's impatient command, the driver gunned it back into motion and they went careening out of their shelter. Once again they sat in the bumping hooded little prison, sealed off in semi-gloom from the road, the sky, and the German countryside. The two soldiers braced themselves with their rifles and tried to stay awake.

The German colonel spoke after a lengthy pause. "Strange," he said, "here we are in my country and yet I am more likely to be shot than you are. You may be shot, of course, even sooner than I, but it is more likely not."

Doke could hear him a bit better now, as his hearing gradually returned. For the first time he really looked at the colonel. The officer seemed a youngish man, with a lean handsome face, absently fingering at his throat as if there had once been a decoration at the collar of his blouse. Doke looked away again. This calm talk of shooting started that maddening buzz in his head again. He had a chance for a Stalag; he held on to that thought, going over it again and again in his mind.

There seemed no end to the ride. It was like an endless string to nowhere. It was as though the banging little truck might have been churning motionless in a quagmire. It was a ride to the rear, right enough, but it did not matter, it did not matter, as long as there was a Stalag at the end of it.

And then the colonel spoke for the first time in all that while, as though he, too, had been thinking and his thoughts had finally built up and spilled over with the sum of them.

"I would do it again, I think," he said, speaking to no one in particular and yet, strangely, as if to someone somewhere. "A useless and exposed position. My men could be slaughtered or cut off and starved into surrender." Again he fingered absently at his throat. "I could get no permission, of course. Withdrawals are not permitted. One must go all the way to the Führer for permission to withdraw a regiment."

Doke Stanton looked at him impatiently, his eyes rimmed with fatigue in the caked dust of the long ride and the dried blood from the cut on his forehead. He had been thinking of life in the Stalag, a bit rugged perhaps, but merely a matter of counting days, and life was merely a matter of following rules, simple, rudimentary, with combat a distant thing beyond barbed wire and blessed survival an eventual reality. It was a numbing, lulling vista, like a self-administered hypodermic, and the German officer broke into it with his abrupt soliloquy.

"But I withdrew them anyway," the officer was saying. "Not too much. Eight hundred meters. I thought if I called it a consolidation, you understand, it might pass." He shook his head. "But no. It was eight hundred meters of the Reich. *Ach,* such orders! Give not an inch! How many times can a soldier be shot than once? You cannot lose your men in the wrong place and the right place. One or the other. Not both."

The lieutenant, in the front of the truck, turned and looked at him through a ragged rent in the canvas. The cold blue eyes in that expressionless boyish face had the impact of a fist. The colonel smiled slightly and said nothing more. Doke

Stanton was glad that the colonel had become silent. He reminded Doke of the war and that was something which should be finished for both of them, each in his fashion. Besides, it was unnerving to be riding with a man who expected to be shot. It was a realistic thought that disturbed his dream of a Stalag.

The lieutenant suddenly swung out on the running board, held on there staring at the sky for a long moment, then pulled himself back inside the cab. Instantly that racking cough of the motor became evident again as the laboring little truck began to shudder with increased speed. They were swaying all over the road. Now what? Doke heard it, then, and froze in his seat, gripping at the board bench with tightly tensed fingers. That droning sound was coming up on them, trailing the bouncing, scurrying, fleeing little vehicle, the droning deepening, deepening, deepening into a deep-throated swooping roar—oh, God, those American planes—those P-47s that raided and hunted and strafed deep behind the German lines. There was no hiding, there was no hole—damn it, *here it was*—the roar was upon them and a sudden sound like a stick rapidly raking against a picket fence. The truck spun, careened on two wheels, skidded to a violent stop, nearly turned over in a sickening heave, then flopped back on its wheels. Doke had clung fiercely to one of the ribs of the hood. He found himself stuck half through the tattered canvas. There was a smell of petrol and he could see a licking flame coming out of the engine. Feverishly he fought clear of the truck, tearing at the canvas and twisting his body to get clear. He fell out in a tangle of bushes and struggled to his feet.

The truck had skidded off the road into the edge of some woods and was partly nosed over in a growth of saplings. One of the German guards was crawling out through the back and a plume of black smoke was thickening from the engine bonnet. Doke rubbed a sleeve swiftly over his eyes and then looked around him irresolutely. The whole front of the truck suddenly became transformed into a sheet of flame with a soft slurring sound. He started to plow through the bushes to get around the truck and back on the road and collided headlong with a figure. He found himself looking into the pale blue eyes of the stocky boyish lieutenant, a jagged cut along his cheek. The lieutenant gripped him by the shoulder and with his other hand tugged at the revolver in that black holster. Doke frantically flailed at that restraining arm and wrenched away from the death in that boyish face beneath the snub helmet.

A searing gust of flame shot out of the canvas hood, practically into their faces, and as the fiery red lash darted at them the German recoiled. Doke flailed again, knocked aside that revolver arm, and lunged free of the grip on his combat jacket. He was clear, fighting blindly to get away, forging into the woods, fending off pine branches with outflung hands, tripping and stumbling but lunging on in sheer driving panic. There was the sound of a shot behind him and another and another and he sobbed with uncontrollable spasms wrenching at him as he wrestled and clawed through the undergrowth, tearing at it with both hands.

He broke into a clearing, ran through it in a staggering zigzag, flailed his way up a bank, got back among trees again, tripped over a root and fell to his knees, crawled on all fours a few feet and then sprawled flat in a tangled fernbrake. He lay there trying to get his breath, a taste of copper in his throat and his face hot against the cold hard earth.

Even after he caught his breath, he lay motionless a long time. Once he thought he heard the thrashing sounds of pursuit and he could only hope that they would give him the chance to come to his feet with his hands raised. But he doubted it. That crazy killer of a paratrooper lieutenant would be more likely to shoot him in the stomach and watch him bend over gasping in agony and clutching at himself and sinking down to smear his face in dead leaves at the toes of those polished black boots.

Why did those American planes have to shoot up a drab little truck? Wasting ammunition on targets like that. Those crazy pilots would be shooting rabbits next. Doke Stanton cursed that P-47 pilot. Between him and that paratrooper, he had been dumped into a stretch of woods far behind the German lines.

Finally the cold galvanized him into movement. He came cautiously to his feet and looked around him, rubbing his hands nervously against his thighs. He had to find someone to surrender to safely. He did not care who it was, just so he could get back on the track to a Stalag. That bastard lieutenant. Doke Stanton cursed him, too, briefly, savagely.

He could hear the vague sound of planes high overhead and also the subdued muttering of what might have been trucks off to the left somewhere. He stamped his feet on the ground, blew on his fists, and then pushed on slowly through the woods, more to keep moving than with any definite idea in mind.

A patch of light ahead in the shaded gloom of the pines caught his eye and he pushed toward it, feeling the beginning of hunger and the bite of fatigue, and finally stumbled into a clearing. He stood there vaguely and all he could think of were the roads around his home in Connecticut—the one that he used to take to the village and the road to the beach and the road to his mother's house with the big sugar maples interspersed with dogwood and spruce.

"Mother," he said softly. "Mother, mother—" He spoke the word, as though he were trying it out.

He dashed a hand across his eyes and then noticed what appeared to be some kind of a child's playhouse built in the spreading branches of a tree on the edge of the clearing. That could mean a house somewhere near and he was again wary, tensed, as he moved over to investigate. It was a well-built little house in the branches, reached by a wooden ladder up the trunk, and he seriously considered hoisting himself up there. But, as he noticed a path leading off through the woods, he decided to try this instead and he moved along it at a steady plodding walk, following the dim little path matted with dead leaves and hoping that it would lead him back to a POW.

He pushed through a screen of evergreens and found himself suddenly on a paved way. The shock sent him back instinctively into the shelter of the evergreens. But all was quiet and he ventured out again on the road. To his left it curved on through the woods, but to the right he spied two gateposts of yellow brick surmounted by an arch of iron grillwork. Again he was irresolute. The winter twilight was setting in and he could remember now, as though it were in a dim previous age, that he had not been able to eat anything before the recon troop had moved out on its mission, and he was hungry now and all he asked was to be fed and told what to do, and any chance was worth getting him out of this cold and isolated void where he hung like something on a meat hook.

Skirting the edge of the road, he made his way to the gateposts and found they were the driveway entrance through a stone wall into a courtyard paved with brick. He hovered there, studying it closely. Across the courtyard stood a large yellow brick house with twin turrets that made it look something like a castle. Many of the windows were shuttered, giving it a deserted appearance, and at one side of the courtyard a small military car stood on blocks, its wheels gone, surrounded by a large heap of empty boxes, old tires, and discarded petrol tins.

While he was scanning the place, a sudden noise on the road behind him caused him to whirl, shivering with cold and uncertainty. It sounded like a motorcycle and it was coming fast. All he could think of was the baby-faced paratrooper lieutenant and he spun again and dashed into the courtyard, running through the gray mesh of wintry twilight toward the pile of litter. He ducked around behind it, saw a small potting shed and crouched down among broken flower pots and empty boxes, just as a motorcycle and sidecar roared in through the gates.

A German soldier was astride the cycle, with an officer riding in the sidecar. It swept up before the door of the big brick house and the officer dismounted and went in, while the soldier stood astride the cycle, flopping his arms about him against the deepening chill in the air. A few minutes later the officer came out, settled himself again in the sidecar, and they sped back out through the gates and were gone.

Doke leaned against a post of the shed, his arms clasped about his knees, and looked at the big quiet house. It might be some kind of headquarters, although it appeared withdrawn and deserted. He did not know. He was just too tired. He lowered his head on his arms. He would have to do something. But not now. Now he was just too tired and even this little shed gave some slight feeling of protection to which he clung.

He did not sleep, but he was jarred into attentiveness as though he had been asleep. Crouched there, with his head in his arms, he heard footsteps coming across the courtyard. More than one person, because there was a clumping tread accompanied by gentler undertones, as if they were walking with different strides, and it sounded as though they were coming straight toward him.

He kept his head ducked in his arms, as if he could avoid the reality of the situation bearing down on him. He was too tired to run and he could not seem to summon the decision for anything else. All he could do was keep from seeing them and they might not see him. It was the only shred of protection he knew and he tried to cloak himself with it.

He knew that the footsteps had stopped very near him and there was a long silence. Someone cleared his throat with a guttural sound and muttered something in German. But the voice, when it came, was lighter, different.

"Amerikaner? American? Are you an American?" It was a girl's voice, the question in it compounded of wonder and incredulity.

6.

THE DATE of March 3 would have meant no difference between March 2 or March 4, except it was the day that the Americans went headlong after the Rhineland.

March 3 was simply the date on which a general named Bradley threw a switch and the big attack crackled all down the line.

At Corps headquarters there was no way of knowing that an attack was underway. Corps was a big quiet headquarters with the solid steady imperturbability of a frigate under full sail. There were places of tension, to be sure—in the Commanding General's trailer, in the War Room where duty officers waited for reports from the fighting divisions, and the quarters of the Corps Surgeon, among others. But mainly Corps' composure was outwardly unbroken, a big tactical headquarters that you could hang divisions on like a hatrack, close enough to the fighting to feel kinship with its divisions, far enough back to carry on its functions in the rarefied serenity of the Big Picture.

Berkham knew that Corps was busy, all the same, and he stayed out of the way. There were some billets in a nearby gasthaus and he waited over there after first letting it be known casually here and there that he had brought a bottle of Scotch down from Army in his bedding roll. It was late in the morning when Lieutenant Colonel Mike Morrow, an Assistant Corps G-3, dropped in at the gasthaus where the correspondent was lounging at a blue-tiled stove, more ornamental than effective.

"Thirty-six hours getting things to suit the Old Man," the officer said. "But before I knock it off for a while, what about that bedding roll, Berk?"

"Patented for sleeping or drinking," acknowledged Berkham, and tossed him a mess cup.

He poured out a drink and the officer sat back in a wooden chair before the stove and half-closed his eyes. Berkham said nothing, tamping tobacco into his pipe.

"Here's to your next dispatch," said the officer.

"I've been trying to guess this attack," said Berkham. "I'd like to get closer."

"We can't send you down to any of the divisions yet, Berk. They're swinging from the heels, all of them."

"Okay," said Berkham. "But how are you doping this Corps attack?"

"Well, the 9th Armored makes the link with Patton," said Morrow. "If Leonard breaks that armor of his through, it could be damned interesting. Anyhow, we're watching it close. We even have an extra liaison officer with the 9th Armored—a friend of mine we borrowed from Army." He finished his drink and set down the mess cup. "If that armor can break up the front, we're going to catch Jerry but good. We're piling a lot of stuff right down the Ahr valley." He drove a fist into his palm. "Bang! Like that! And brother, would we love to grab ourselves a Rhine bridge."

Berkham looked at him attentively. That thought of the Rhine bridges had attracted him to this Corps in the first place.

"You're playing yourself a long shot there, aren't you, Mike?"

Morrow laughed. "Right out of this world. There isn't a chance in a million—we know that—but we're not forgetting about a bridge. The artillery boys are sore as pups. No arty fire on the bridges when we get them in range and how they hate that. All they're permitted is time and posit fire above the bridges."

"According to the book," said Berkham.

"You're damn right, Berk. We're not doing anything to make our chances worse." He grinned and came to his feet, stretching. "We'll settle for reaching the Rhine, but as long as there's a bridge on that river we're not going to forget it." He sighed. "Unfortunately neither will Jerry. Thanks for the drink. I'll keep you in touch."

He waved and departed and Berkham sat there, going over it in his mind. This Rhineland attack had interested him deeply. He was not sure why, himself, except that Bradley had wanted this chance so badly and Ike had given it to him, in spite of the grousing of the SHAEF planners, and somehow the thought of the Rhine out there ahead stirred his jaded energies. The Rhine barrier before the heartland of the Reich and the Nibelung would get a look at some men who had come a long way from Normandy.

He took out a pencil, feeling that restless itch to get something in his mind down on paper where he could really look at it. He wanted to be on top of this attack. Maybe he would have done better over at VII Corps. Joe Collins always put on a rousing show and there were hell-for-leather combat commanders like Terry Allen with his 104th and Maurice Rose with that tough 3rd Armored.

But this Corps might really open up, too. He reviewed the divisions—Clift Andrus and the 1st, the Big Red One; the 9th with L. A. Craig, the 78th with Edwin Parker, and the 9th Armored of John Leonard. Watch the Ahr valley, Morrow had said. If armor punched through that German crust, things might become interesting.

Berkham twisted his big shoulders. Watch one of those lozenges on the acetate map. At a time like this, he felt how inadequate that was. Those lozenges had jumped off against the German 15th Army this morning, this very morning. They were cracking into the Westwall defenses and with the tick of his wrist watch someone was a casualty. He had been over here too long, but a correspondent should get away from a big rear-area headquarters and purge himself once in a while by getting down with the combat men.

He began to write, a pad propped against his knee.

"There are no guns to be heard at the moment here in Corps headquarters. But Americans have been attacking since dawn and there are voices here. What are the voices of an attack? Here are some of them. *'Red Three calling Red Six. They're firing* 150s *at us direct. Over.' 'Keep on going boy, keep on going.'*

"Other voices?" wrote Berkham. " *'All right, here's the way we jump off. Able Company to lead attack with platoons in line. Left platoon to be echeloned to left rear. Mortar platoon to follow left platoon—'*

"And still they come. *'Look, Tony, here's what you do. Take your platoon straight down the main drag. A section of heavies will follow and set up a base of fire to help cover you. Then Ed will bring up the second platoon and a section of mortars in case you run into anything.'*

"Voices of the attack. *'Baker Two to Baker One. We've reached the railroad tracks and we don't see anyth—'*

"Yes, sometimes a voice will stop like that. Because through all and over all is the shout of *'Medic!'* That call has begun since shortly after the jump-off. It has been called in the first gray hours of morning, at the very beginning of the day, with the earliest waking hours, with breakfasts barely finished.

"Voices of the attack. *'What the hell's the matter with our artillery? Haven't they any observation? Haven't we got any*

Cubs in the air? Can't someone find out where those goddam shells are coming from and blast the hell out of Jerry? Thirty-six rounds of heavy in ninety seconds and it's too damned much.'

"Voices of the attack. *'We're three hundred yards out. We've got the first pillbox, but we can't find the second. We don't think it's there where you said it was. Who plotted these damfool maps, anyway?'*

"Voices of the attack. *'Captain says can you get us some litter bearers. We gotta get these wounded outta there.'*

"Voices of the attack. *'The tank commander says he has a ditchful of Krauts in front of him and he wants the infantry to move up quick—'*

"There are so many voices, each an infinitesimal private world of its own, but together they swell into a thundering crescendo that the German 15th Army can hear plainly enough and, soon, also the American people—"

Berkham stopped abruptly, frowned moodily, and tossed his pencil and pad over on his cot. That kind of thing would never make a dispatch. But he knew what he wanted. He wanted someday to write a dispatch with the lead, "Here in this one place, at this one time, the whole war can be told." What a lead that would be! But he had about as much of a chance of finding something like that as the army had of grabbing a Rhine bridge.

He lighted his pipe, folded his arms, and leaned back with his feet propped on the tiled stove.

"Berkham of Arc,"" he muttered. "With his voices."

It was like coming up through the water from the deeps where it was cold and black and heavy. It was like straining toward light and air, flailing toward the surface, reaching for it just as suffocation closed around like a stifling blanket.

Doke Stanton stirred in his sleep, suddenly fought into wakefulness with a wild yell, and came to his feet, swaying blindly. For a long moment of complete stupefaction he stood there trembling, trying to understand this strange, this completely mysterious place where he found himself.

It was a darkened room with pale ghostly silhouettes around him, like a prison cell with silent watching figures, as though he were entombed, and again he yelled out of sheer numbed terror. He thought he saw a door and he lurched toward it and yanked at a knob. The door was locked and this seemed to snap the last vestige of control. He hammered on the door with his fists, shouting incoherently. Finally, breathlessly, he stopped and leaned heavily against the door. "God!" he muttered huskily.

The sound of a key turning in the lock made him recoil. He moved back a few steps, rubbing his hands tightly against his thighs in his nervous way. The door opened and a flash of daylight knifed into the darkened room. Doke Stanton moved back yet another step. Then he stared. A girl was standing on the threshold.

She was a slight person in dark skirt and gray sweater and her blond hair braided around her head.

"What is happening?" she asked. Her English was easy and sure, somewhat accented. She came a step farther into the room.

"What is this?" said Doke. He sounded feverish, hurried. "Who are you, for God's sake?"

She studied him gravely for such a long moment that he became resentful and uncomfortable. "You are an American?" she asked, and from some distant memory he seemed to recall a question like that being asked him in a tone of both wonder and incredulity.

"Yes," he said, "I'm an American. I'm a prisoner of war. I want to surrender. I want to surrender right away."

She nodded. "I think perhaps you are not well."

She took a few limping steps toward him and put her hand on his hot forehead. He felt the brief light cool touch of her hand. It was the first touch of spontaneously kind interest he had known since one time when Ellison had gripped him by the hand after his first Normandy reconnaissance. It was as simple as that. It was as important as that.

"We have something for you to eat," she said, and returned to the door. A shapeless elderly woman, bundled in a voluminous woolen scarf, was waiting there with a tray. She took a fearful sidelong glance into the room, but the girl said something to her in soft German, gave her a swift smile, and took the tray from her. She turned and placed the tray on one of the sheeted objects and then, with that odd hesitation in her walk, went to a window and pulled back the heavy black curtain. Murky gray light flooded in and he saw that he was in a small paneled room and that the ghostly shapes that had so startled him were pieces of furniture under protective sheeting.

She nodded toward the tray. "Eat, Herr American. It will be good for you, I think."

"What is this place?" he demanded.

"The Castle Rimburg-Clewes."

"How did I get here?"

"You do not remember? Ach, so. You—you"—she made a motion with her hands—"collapsed."

He did vaguely remember then. Yesterday evening it must have been. He remembered now walking between two people, feeling as though he were walking on stilts, and suddenly he did not recall anything. So he had collapsed.

"Passed out," he muttered, rubbing his unshaven chin. Yes, now he seemed to remember. He had hidden in some shed or other. That horrible day. He had started it on reconnaissance and ended it by collapsing in complete and utter exhaustion. She gently reminded him about the tray of food and he discovered that, even though he felt hot and feverish, he was hungry. He sat down on the edge of the sheeted couch where he had slept and took the tray on his lap.

There was a bowl of thick broth, two meat sandwiches, and a pewter cup of milk. He ate hungrily, famished, in that same feverish jumbled way as his thoughts. The girl sat on a window seat, crossed her knees, and watched him, chin on fist. It was only as he found that cool curious glance on him as he finished that he realized how he had wolfed down his food and again he became resentful.

"Thanks," he muttered, and put the tray aside.

"You are the first American I have ever seen," declared the girl. "I have been so curious."

He did not answer. All he wanted from her now was the quickest way to get back on the track to a Stalag. He was a prisoner of war, couldn't she understand that?

"Last evening Martha told me someone had crossed the courtyard and was hiding in the old carriage house. We thought it was some deserter from the Volksturm. Or perhaps he was drunk and wanted to sleep. There are often such nowadays. Then after the Provost officer notified us that an American prisoner had escaped, I became wondering and I made William go out with me—I was so curious," she said in her soft even voice.

"But I didn't escape," he said quickly. "I mean I didn't intend to. It was after our truck was shot up by a plane—the officer was going to shoot me. That's the only reason I got away into those woods." He wanted to be sure she understood that. "That paratrooper lieutenant," he tried to explain. "He didn't want to be bothered with me. He was bringing back an officer for court-martial—"

Yes, of course, that youngish colonel who had withdrawn eight hundred meters without permission. And that damned P-47 out strafing everything in sight. The pieces of the whirligig resumed recognizable form. Sure, that was how it had been. And now they were hunting for him. He ran a hand quickly over his forehead.

"There must be so many of you," the girl said. "They must be close, is it not so? They must be just behind you?"

He looked at her warily then. Oh, no, none of that stuff. He wasn't giving any information free for nothing to a Nazi bitch. What he had to barter he would barter where it counted—with someone who could make a POW out of him.

"Look," he said, "you know I'm a prisoner of war."

"Yes," she said, "I know that."

"Then how about notifying the military that I am ready to surrender?"

"That must be done," she acknowledged. Again she studied him with that deep curious attention. "It is too bad," she said finally. "The SS have charge of security here. Langbach will skin you like a rabbit. He would love this chance." She gave a little sigh. "He always knows what he can break. He will be brutal, I'm afraid."

Doke Stanton did not like the sound of the SS. "Why should he be?" he asked uneasily. "I'm just a GI who got taken prisoner. What has he against me?"

"It is hard to explain. He is afraid of the Americans and what he fears he hates." She shook her head. "And, of course," she added meditatively, "when he knows someone is afraid—when he feels the fear—"

"But isn't there any military installation?" he burst out. "Can't I surrender to someone else?"

"I have always wondered about the Americans," said the girl. "I have never met one. Even when I was in England. I remember an old vicar saying once at the end of the season that the Americans had gone home, because their voices were no longer heard. I was so interested to know what was so unusual about an American voice."

She considered Doke with her grave eyes and he abruptly was aware that he was unshaven and disheveled and probably his face was still streaked with grime and dust.

"Not the SS," he said tersely. "Will you help me?" Can you help me?"

"I do not know," she said slowly.

"I'm not well," he said. "I couldn't take it."

"No," she agreed.

Again she was silent a moment. "You know how close your troops are," she said then. "You know when they should be here."

"How can I know?" he said desperately. "I don't even know where I am."

"Look out the window," said the girl. "And you will know."

He stared at her uncomprehending. She sat quietly on the window seat and waited. He stood up and made his way to the window. He stood there and looked out anxiously.

There was a gray river below, a wide river flowing beneath a steep blunt cliff, a river with a long slender steel bridge. Doke Stanton stiffened. That river—my God, he had ridden a long time in the truck—but that couldn't be—

He wet his lips. "That's the Rhine?" he managed.

"Yes," said the girl.

The Rhine! He looked down at it incredulously. The Rhine! Why, you talked of the Rhine as though it were something in another world. He had been trucked all the way back to the Rhine. The American attack must be forty or fifty miles behind him at least. It might take them two weeks, three weeks, a month—hell, they might bog down entirely trying to get through the Westwall.

He looked down at the wide gray river and felt the shakes bitting him again at the very sight of it.

"The Rhine," he repeated numbly. "It really is—"

"The Rhine," said the girl, "and the Ludendorff Bridge."

It was framed in the window—the roofs of the town below, chimney pots smoking lazily, and the wide gray river flowing beneath the heavy overcast. A train was moving slowly along the other bank, close to the steep blunt cliff, and several trucks were rolling across the bridge. Men were working from small boats at the piers of the bridge with something that looked like a wooden barrier or screen. And distantly, incongrously, a bell was ringing leisurely in the town below, like a school bell.

Doke looked at it spellbound—that frontier river—and it did not seem possible that he could stand here looking down at it from a window, when he remembered that Americans were attacking behind everything they could throw into planes and tanks and guns to reach this spot and they would die all along the way.

"We have been bombed many times," he heard the girl say meditatively. "We are so tired of it."

He turned to look at her. She was moving toward the door, her right foot dragging a bit as though it were weighted. At the door she paused.

"I do not believe there is any harm in you," she said, "but I shall have to lock the door."

Doke suddenly hated to see this steady, soft-spoken girl leave him. He walked toward her quickly and she watched him calmly.

"Look," he said, "I have been taken prisoner. I'm through with fighting. I'm tired. I'm very tired and my head is bothering me, and—" He paused, realizing he was speaking in that jumbled way again and perhaps she could not follow him. "All I want is the treatment of a prisoner of war. That's all. Can't you help me get that?"

"I can see that you are not well," said the girl.

"My name is Stanton. Douglas Stanton. Private Douglas Stanton—"

She said nothing and he looked at her closely to see what hope there might be for him. Her eyes were a deep blue, long and clear, and the lashes were dark brown and thickly curling. Her eyes were like a cool deep frontier in themselves.

"I am Ilse Margraven," she said. "I am employed by the owner of this castle. There is only so much I can do. The Wehrkreis has the administration of security here and the Wehrkreis is the SS, you must understand. I must go now."

He felt that he could talk to her, if she would only give him the chance.

"Will you come back?" he asked restively. "Soon, I mean."

"Yes," she said. She swept him with those remarkably lashed blue eyes. "For years I have wondered about the Americans. I though they would be big men, chewing gum, and very practical and confident. They would need no help. They would be terrible in battle, but then they would give help. Friendly, masterly men."

She nodded. "Please be quiet," she requested. "Do not scream or shout." She went out of the room and closed the door behind her. He heard the key turn in the lock.

Doke passed a hand over his cropped hair. Of the millions of Americans in Europe, he had been spewed up here on the Rhine. And he tried to think who would have fitted her idea of an American—Paul Kelso, Nick Halsema, Joe Bosky, The Book, Major Clay Stanton? Ellison, probably. But Ellison was dead.

He looked around him slowly at the little shrouded room and felt the nearness of the great river down there below the window and fought down the hammering thought that he might be long dead before any other Americans saw it.

7.

THE DAY of March 4 was no different from March 3 or March 5 to the slave laborers who worked at the Ludendorff Bridge. Their days ran together in an endless repetitive round, like the monotonous lap of water against rock. They lived on the west bank, in a labor camp, and worked all day down at the bridge, dragging, carrying, piling, digging, wherever the rifles of their guards pointed, sometimes on the west bank, sometimes on the bridge, sometimes on the east bank, a huddled mass of men who had been born in Poland but had not seen their country for over five years.

To one of them, March 4 was a bit different although he knew it only as an overcast day, with a chill in the railroad tunnel where he happened to be working. But somehow, somewhere, he gleaned an inkling that the Germans were having trouble holding the Westwall defenses against the Americans. The Germans were having trouble. To Paul Karski this was the time to strike a blow—when the beast was in a death grip with the Americans—when the Nazi beast was in trouble—strike a blow. And to Karski this meant the bridge.

It had to mean the bridge. The bridge was his whole waking life. It had been for eight months, since he had been assigned to the Construction Platoon after the terrible illness that had decimated the labor camp near Arnhem. Karski had survived that. He had survived everything so far. He was a big man, badly stooped now, with eyes sunk deep in the creased folds of his face. He had only a few teeth left and there was a nagging pain in his chest and he could no longer close his gnarled and swollen hands. But he had survived.

Once he had thought constantly of his village, as he had known it, the good farm and the feast days and the power in his arms behind the plow with the clumping fat horses of his father. Karski had not thought of those things recently. He now thought of the bridge.

Karski had loved the bridge ever since he knew the Germans were planning to destroy it. If the Germans wanted to destroy it, then he wanted it to survive. If it would help the Germans to destroy it, then it would help the Americans if it was not destroyed. That was like a plow furrow in soft spring earth—there was no trouble following a thought like that. The doomed bridge became his friend. It had become identified with a shadowy whisper of freedom that recurred once and again every so often.

He spoke about this guardedly with Jan Lewandowski, the onetime medical student at the University of Kraków, for whom he had a great and abiding respect.

"It can be done somehow," he murmured, as they crouched over their battered mess cups inside the railroad tunnel during the half-hour pause at noon. "You hear me, Jan. When I think, I, too, have brains. Listen, then. The ignition switch is at the mouth of the tunnel. But the generator is inside the tunnel. What easier to cut the wire from the generator to the ignition switch."

"They check the connection regularly," said little Lewandowski, holding his mess cup in both hands and whispering between sips of the watery stew.

"Listen," said Karski. "I tell you—"

"Be quiet, Karski. Do not be so excited."

"Excited!" Karski lowered his voice. "The Americans are breaking through the Westwall. This bridge could carry us to freedom. Lewandowski, I can do this. I can have all ready to stop the demolition. Listen, listen." He tugged eagerly at the small man's arm. "With the edge of the old shovel I have saved, the wire can be cut. It is in the darkness of the tunnel. Then to tie the ends together so that the wire will look taut. Then at the moment they make ready to explode the bridge, I jerk the wires apart."

"No," said little Lewandowski fiercely. "It has not been planned well and it is not the time. The demolitions are not yet set. There is too much time for them to discover the loose splice—"

"It is in darkness," insisted Karski. "They care only that the ignition switch works."

"They check too carefully." Lewandowski laid a hand on his arm, trying to steady him down.

"When we go out of the tunnel," whispered Karski, "I will fall behind. The group will hide me from the guards, and after the platoon has left the tunnel they will not miss me so soon. I need only a minute, perhaps two—"

"Raus!" suddenly shouted a sergeant at the tunnel entrance.

The labor platoon came slowly to their feet. Lewandowski tied his mess cup to his belt. "It will not do, Paul," he began helplessly. Karski nudged him forward. "There may not be another chance. I will do this thing."

The labor platoon shuffled out into the daylight. Lewandowski could imagine the big bent man sidling off across the tracks to the generator, stooping and feeling for the broken piece of shovel blade from inside his ragged jacket, feeling for the wire that ran to the ignition switch, grasping it. . . .

Suddenly a shot rang out. The whole platoon stopped, frozen. There was another shot, a loud sharp explosion with a fuzzy ricocheting echo from inside the tunnel. Lewandowski swallowed hard and stared down at the ground. There had been some merit to the idea, but the timing was all wrong. Karski had been like some feverish child held in the grip of an alluring prank. But the Germans were allowing no pranks. They were serious and thorough and they did not intend to lose a Rhine bridge.

All that was left of the big stooped man was a piece of shovel blade and an idea. Lewandowski murmured a few words of the Polonaise, as though draping him with a flag.

Occasional shots near the bridge and along the river meant nothing in the town or to anyone at the Castle Rimburg-Clewes. The security troops at the bridge occasionally fired at floating objects in the river and the 20 mm flak batteries atop the Erpeler Ley would blast into the sky from time to time. The big 88s were usually silent however. There had been no American planes swooping in low and fast during the last few days.

Doke Stanton did not hear the shots down at the bridge shortly after noon. He was sunk in sleep in the little secluded study, sprawled on a sheeted divan, sleeping the drugged exhausted slumber that was only oblivion and not rest.

He came out of it gradually and grudgingly and woke with a sense that someone had just left the room. Then he sat up quickly. A small table had been cleared of its sheeting and on it was a basin of water, a piece of soap, a towel, and a safety razor. He contemplated the articles sullenly for a moment, then shrugged and walked over to the table. The water was still hot. Evidently she had just left the room. Funny, he thought, how that would have awakened him. Like a touch of breeze waking someone in a stupor. She wanted him to shave. Okay, okay. Be all cleaned up for the SS.

He washed and shaved and was just toweling himself when the key turned in the lock and she re-entered, carrying a tray.

"You would like something to eat, Private Stanton?"
He was struck by her use of his name. He had told her,

of course, but he was surprised that she had remembered it and still more that she had used it. This time when he ate, he took it more slowly, and she waited, sitting on the edge of a chair, chin on fist in that pensive posture of hers, but saying nothing while he finished his meal.

"Thanks," said Doke. What was her name, he tried to remember. "Thanks, Fräulein," he said.

The girl inclined her head, apparently preoccupied with something. He walked restlessly back to the settee, sat down, and clasped his fingers.

"Well," he said, "what's going to happen?"

"I'm sorry," she said. "There is no way to avoid the SS. I had thought that a unit headquarters would move into the castle. You could have surrendered to them. But now," she said slowly, in that introspective way, "I do not think they will come." She paused. "Perhaps they would have turned you over to the Wehrkreis just the same."

"So that's the answer," said Doke Stanton. "The damned Nazi bully boys."

"I know," she said in a low voice. "But, Private Stanton, there is nothing I can do. If the Wehrkreis should learn I have not reported a prisoner— And there is danger of that. William is frightened. I have told him that it will be good for the castle when the Americans come, if we have helped an American. He and Martha are anxious about the castle," she explained. "They have been in the Rimburg service for a long time. I think perhaps William may say nothing as long as he is more frightened of the Americans than of the Wehrkreis."

She lifted a slim shoulder in a brief shrug. "And I, Private Stanton, can risk so much and no more. I do not like to turn over a weak man to Captain Langbach."

He stared at her. "Weak?" he said. "You're calling me weak?"

"I am sorry," she said. "I should have used a different word, possibly. I have insulted you."

"I'll call myself a coward," said Doke Stanton, "but all my life I've tried to stop anyone else from calling me that. Weak? I'm afraid of pain. I can't help it. I wish I wasn't. But I am. I'm ready to surrender, if they'll put me in a Stalag. I don't want to be worked over by the SS, that's all. You can call that weak. Okay, I'm not a superman."

He bent toward her tensely. "Maybe I can hide out. I noticed an old tree house in the woods near here."

"I know," she acknowledged. "I used to go there often with the Rimburg children. I was their governess."

"If I had enough food, I could hide out there."

"In a tree?" she said, genuinely astonished.

"Why not." He became restive again under her direct glance. "I'll live in a cave, or in a tree, or under a rock, until my chances are better."

"Better for what?" she questioned, interested.

"To survive," Doke Stanton said succinctly. "To live through this war. That's all I want. I've been in the Army for over three years. I've been in Italy and Normandy. I've been wounded. I'm tired. I'm sick of it. I've had enough."

"I have heard," she said, hesitatingly, "some of our men talk that way recently. And we here feel the same way about the bombings. But you are winning—" Her voice trailed away, perplexed.

"Look, Fräulein," he said, "I know we're winning. But you can still want to live. You can still be scared. You Germans have caused a hell of a lot of trouble in this world and you're still doing it. I know what your 88s are like and your flak guns and your machine-gun nests and your lousy pot-helmeted Krauts planting mines and booby traps and lobbing grenades. We're winning, but a lot of Americans are going to be killed before it's over. But not me. Not if I can help it. Not me."

She listened to him, her lips parted slightly, her hands clasped about one knee, that indefinable air of natural grace about the way she held herself, and, always, that compelling attentive look in her long blue eyes.

"I suppose the Americans are very—very angry—at us?"

"You can bet on it. Mad clean through."

"Mad?—you mean angry?" She was silent, considering. "They will be very hard on us—the German people?"

"They could be. Have a white sheet ready to hang out the window. They'll come up to this river plenty trigger-happy."

"I don't mean that. I mean—" She paused, her lashes lowered as she studied her clasped hands. "Not the army. Any army will have its savagery. Many of the American troops may be terrible and we must expect it and live with it. But the American people, Private Stanton, do they despise the German people?"

"Why not?" said Doke.

She glanced up at him. "You speak like the blow of a fist, Private Stanton."

"The Americans aren't quite the fools you might think. Not after getting into two of these European things."

"They blame the German people, then?"

"Look, Fräulein, don't talk to me or any other American soldier about the German people. If your troops were going the other way instead of this backwards goosestep, there'd be all the cheers in the world out of the German people."

She spread the fingers of one hand and surveyed them thoughtfully, her blond head bent. "That is probably true," she acknowledged. "A sign that all the suffering has been worth it. *Gott mit uns*. But there are some who would not cheer, who never have cheered."

"The closer the fighting comes, the more people you find who never liked the Nazis," said Doke Stanton tersely. "All of a sudden they're just poor misguided, misled people, who never heard of the concentration camps—"

"Like Augswien, you mean?" she asked in a low voice.

He shrugged impatiently. "Somebody else always seems to have been the Nazi."

She was silent and he stood up from the little divan and stretched himself tensely. He was bored with this stuff, this bootless philosophical twaddle. If she was going to turn him over to the SS, let her be about it, or help him figure how to find that hole, like the old song, no hiding place down there, I went to the rocks to hide my face, the rocks cried up no hiding place, no hiding place down there, but there had to be some way to outguess this; this damn castle must have all kinds of places, cellars and things, and what would he need to do to get her to hide him?

She was saying something and he looked down at her, with the feverish restlessness in him making him jumpy and taut and bitter. But he would have to listen. Another newly shriven Nazi, probably, and she had something in mind and so did he and the trick was to use her some way so that he could feel safe. So he would have to play along with this stuff awhile. She certainly had taken everything he had thrown so far and that meant she was playing along, too. There was something she wanted. There must be.

"The American people," Ilse Margraven was saying in her intense low voice, "they can be angry, but they surely do not wish us destroyed."

"You mean massacred?" he said. "Oh, hell, no, of course, not."

"No, I mean they will raise us up someday? They will be our friends? They will help us?"

Doke Stanton stared at her speechless. Of all the damned nerve. Help, she wanted, and hell blazing all along the Westwall this minute and the Rhine to crack, and the Ruhr to crack, and the Hitler gang still calling the signals.

"I have studied a great deal about you Americans," she said, that same intense note in her voice. "You are always a mysterious people. A lengendary people. Everywhere people would like to see America. It must be, I think, because America is a world culture. Is it not so, Private Stanton?"

He frowned. "I don't know," he said.

"But it is so simple," she pursued eagerly. "The Americans have always drawn the best from the rest of the world. Their people have come from many countries. And even today they draw to them great minds and intellects. They welcome everyone's ideas and arts, I think. The American mental climate must be healthy and secure for creative minds, is it not?"

"I suppose so," said Doke.

"There was this book by the English author, Hilton. About the hidden valley in Tibet where the best of human culture was to be preserved. You have read it?"

"Yes," said Doke.

"But America must be like that today," she pronounced. She shook her head. "I can remember when America entered the war against us. To me it was as though Germany had tilted and we were all sliding headlong into confusion and disorder and defeat. And the Reich was everywhere powerful then. That was the seeming."

She was silent a moment and he watched her curiously. Soon he should know. She was working something out—there was a reason to all this, he was sure of it.

"They say that America is a great soulless machine for the making of profits. That the financial barons pull the strings of American thinking. But how could that really be?" She sounded as though she were working out a geometrical theorem. "They are too young, the Americans, to have lost the feel of liberty. What could they want from Europe? Even our leaders have said this is not America's war."

He waited, still listening warily, but somewhat uncertain about her now, because she gave a strange impression of voicing something for herself alone, musing with words, and he knew what that was like.

"So it is possible of the truth that America is a big, friendly, creative nation with feeling and heart. If it is not there, where is it? Where would one find it in the world? In Tibet, like in the English novel? Where is it in the world, Private Stanton? Are the Americans a nation of mechanical toys, who are generous because they can afford it? Are they disinterested in *Lebensraum* because they have plenty of land of their own? Do they not care about world power, because they have two big oceans? Or is it the thinking? I am so curious," she said apologetically. "It does not seem to me that America can be so great as I have imagined it to be."

"You would like your country to lose this war?" Doke said.

"What I want," said the girl, "is to see a victory—of thinking."

He whistled noiselessly, a deep long exhalation. That was as neat a bit of sidestepping as he could imagine.

"You don't think artillery might have something to do with it?" he said curiously. "And enough men to mount a counterattack at the right time and plenty of bomber fleets with fighter escorts?"

"We have had all that," said Ilse Margraven. "And we are in trouble. Now you have all that." She shrugged slender shoulders. "It remains to be seen about the—thinking."

It irritated him, this preoccupation of hers, and mainly because it was something withheld, a mental approach that he could not grasp and yet, perhaps by reason of her even, balanced manner, had some peculiar basis for validity.

"If you mean," Doke Stanton said between his teeth, "we haven't won the war yet, I grant you that, Fräulein."

She did not pursue the point. "Private Stanton, you were perhaps a schoolteacher before the war?"

He had to adjust himself to the sudden change in her interest, from the intensity of her introspection, that had been almost like a private world, to this direct question.

"No," he said, "I was trying to be a writer."

"Ah, yes," she said, nodding. "Something like that. I used the wrong word before. It is not weakness, but sensitivity."

"Use any word you want, Fräulein. But I still want a place to hide. If I can't be a POW, then show me a hole."

She winced slightly. Well, what did she expect? Did she think he was forgetting for one minute his problem of survival?

"The situation still exists," she admitted. "My curiosity has not been practical for either you or me."

She rose from the chair and made her way over to the window. For some moments she stood there pensively looking out, one hand idly twisting a fold in the rough blackout drape.

"Private Stanton," he heard her say softly, "look here a moment."

He joined her at the window. There were the roofs and winding cobbled streets of the town below the castle window, the wide river and the long steel bridge.

"Do you see what is happening at the bridge?" she asked.

He could see a long train of cars crossing to the east bank behind a puffing locomotive.

"They have cleared a track," the girl remarked, studying the scene. "Hospital trains and empty goods wagons. Rolling stock that must be saved. Next it will be guns. And lastly men. There must be real pressure from the Americans."

He found himself suddenly hoping. Perhaps the GIs would make it here sooner than he had thought.

"The pressure will really tell," he said, "when the Germans have to blow that bridge."

"Yes," said the girl. "The bridge will have to be destroyed. That will have to happen."

There was a silence. He studied the long bridge with its single track of rail traffic and then, as the girl remained curiously silent, he looked at her.

To his surprise, she had turned her back to the window and was holding her face in her hands. He stared, astounded. Her shoulders quivered perceptibly as she stood there, her head bowed in her hands, and he suddenly had the amazing impulse to put his arms around her. It was crazy, but the completely feminine loneliness of that slender figure drew the fleeting impulse like the strike of a match. But, even more, she suddenly was three-dimensional, not a shadowy person talking on an obscure mental plane, but a person, who, for whatever reason, had been kind to him, and somehow it gave depth and impact to everything she had been saying and maybe her curiosity about the Americans had real and vital roots.

"Fräulein?" he said uncertainly.

She took her hands from her face and walked, limping, toward the door. She paused to pick up the tray and then moved again toward the door and he thought she was going to leave without a further glance or word. But then she turned. Her face was expressionless.

"Herr American," she said, "be sure that you will sleep undisturbed tonight and be satisfied with that much. Let tomorrow come. Who knows what it will bring? We Germans are living that way. You, too, will have to be content with that."

She turned and left the room and the door closed behind her. A moment later there was the click of the key in the lock.

Doke Stanton sat down slowly on the window seat and rubbed a hand across his forehead tightly. Something certainly seemed to have struck her all of a sudden. She had been companionable in an intense eager way, he could realize that now, and then abruptly she had become impersonal, almost stern. He could account for it only in some connection with the bridge down there on the Rhine.

Involuntarily, he turned in his seat and glanced down at it again. A long slender bridge on four stone piers across the river, with a freight train jerking its way to the east bank; if the Americans kept coming, the Germans would blow it sure, why did that break her up?

It could not be that she thought the destruction of the bridge meant that the Germans had lost the war. Not by a damned sight. The Americans who came through to the west bank would eventually have to cross that river first to the German heartland and the river down there was the Rhine front.

No, he thought, it must be something else, and he pondered about it a long time.

8.

THE DATE, March 5, was no different from March 4 or March 6 to Anatole Heudlak, requisition clerk at the big supply depot at Dedenbach.

Dedenbach was a few miles from the Ludendorff Bridge, closer to Bonn, a depot of gasoline, tires, and bridge-repair material. In the office of the long narrow brick warehouse Anatole Heudlak worked with the requisition slips that had been certified by the administrative officer and made out order forms in quadruplicate for the supply officer. After that Heudlak had no further interest in the matter, although he was well aware that once the supply officer's signature was on the forms, the pink copy went to the transportation officer, the yellow copy was sent to Army, the green copy to the administrative officer, and the white original was retained by the supply officer. This was the routine at Dedenbach and in this routine Anatole Heudlak played an inconspicuous role, with just one vestige of power—he had custody of the certification stamp that the administrative officer used. The administrative officer of the supply depot at Dedenbach had become content to initial batches of stamped requisition slips with only cursory examination and sometimes none at all. Anatole Heudlak had worked at Dedenbach for nearly two years.

He was a small graying man with horn-rimmed glasses and a grayish complexion and a gray uniform. He was neat, precise, and quiet. Nobody gave any thought to the fact that he had been born in Czechoslovakia.

As a matter of fact, studious little Feldwebel Heudlak had not given too much thought to the fact either. Not for a long time. In the beginning he had been glad to serve under the conquerors of his native Sudetenland. It had not seemed like treachery in the beginning. His mother was Sudeten German and his Czech father had died long before the crisis. Heudlak worked as a clerk for a German merchant and when the Germans had moved in, their troops garlanded with flowers and greeted by flags and kisses, he had at first been bewildered and then swept along on the tide of enthusiasm. After all this was the New Order and he had German blood and he did not wish to lose his job or his life, and it was easier to forget that many Czech families in the Sudetenland wept behind closed doors when the conquerors thundered across the frontier. No, it had not seemed like treachery then. Nor even when he had felt it advisable to join one of the "Ost" Battalions as a company supply sergeant. His German employer helped to arrange that.

He was not sure when he began to feel that he had betrayed his country. He simply and gradually found that he was living with that awareness. He was, he discovered, a Czech. It had never occurred to him in his unobtrusive, compliant nature that he could be anything so marked as a traitor. But during all the time he worked effectively and quietly at Dedenback, Anatole Heudlak thought of the country of the Moldava and Prague and the great range of the Carpathians and the fine little army that had not been allowed to fire a shot in defense of the homeland. Then he let himself remember the Czech families in the Sudetenland who had wept behind their closed doors.

It was on March 5, as he busied himself with requisition slips at the depot, that the idea came to him and he at first simply sat there, blinking behind his glasses, little beads of perspiration breaking out on his forehead. On his desk was a requistition slip calling for six hundred kilos of military powder for the engineering officer at the Ludendorff Bridge. They were getting that bridge ready for demolition, then?

Things were that bad? The Americans were threatening that much? There were no sounds of guns yet, although American planes were strafing the roads, and trucks went out from Dedenbach only at night. But there were no signs of any planned withdrawals and no orders had been received to evacuate Dedenbach.

However, as Feldwebel Heudlak thought about it, there were certain signs all the same that the Americans were making gains. There was more drunkenness around the depot, for one thing, and some of the officers were often absent from their desks, and there was a much reduced guard at the depot—some of the Volksturm had been brought in to replace army personnel. The Germans were in trouble west of the Rhine. That was an awesome thought.

He looked down at the requisition slip in his fingers. Six hundred kilos. More than enough to blast the Ludendorff Bridge into a sunken steel hulk. Feldwebel Heudlak knew that bridge well. It was an obscure bridge and maybe that was why he liked it, but it had been his custom to spend a few hours' leave drinking beer in Remagen and visiting the bridge, watching the swift Rhine water swirling around the stone piers.

The idea came in swiftly, unsought. He would alter the requisition slip, make out the supply forms for, say, three hundred kilos and, instead of military powder, industrial powder of the most inferior grade. That supply officer, Colonel Ramfit, would never notice. Not with the liquor he kept constantly in his desk now. The idea came like that. It came as simple and complete and thought out as that.

The requisition slip quivered as his fingers trembled. He laid it down and then sat back from the desk, gripping the arms of his chair. He wet his lips. It was a wild chance, this. In the first place, that engineering officer at the bridge would come storming into Dedenbach when he found his requisition had been mishandled. And, in the second, he was smart and cool, that officer, and it might be that this explosive was spare stuff that he wanted on hand. And, lastly, all these officers, of course, asked for more than they needed. Cutting down the requisition might merely be a nuisance.

But the idea would not die. He did not know where it had been born. Perhaps back in the Sudetenland when he had seen miserable sniveling informers moving among lines of loyal Czech policement and setting up victims for the Nazi firing squads with accusations of persecution, whenever it suited them. Or perhaps when he had stood in the window of his German employer's office and seen the Czech citizens being trucked off from the town square to forced labor and the muted sobbing of their families had filtered past the guard of Nazi bayonets like hot tears between the tight fingers of a blinding hand. Or perhaps the idea had grown from the number of times German officers had cursed dud shells and defective fuses that had been manufactured at the great Skoda works, where this one or that one of the Czech labor force had risked his life to contribute his mite for the country he remembered and had lost.

It did not matter. Feldwebel Heudlak wet his lips again and reached a shaky hand for the supply forms. His hands still shook as he slid the sheaf into his typewriter. This was the first time he had ever broken a regulation or made a mistake or exerted his own judgment. He worked quickly, the perspiration glistening on his forehead and his heart drumming against his ribs.

Jerking the forms from the typewriter, he swiveled back

to his desk and reached for the certification stamp. His glasses seemed to have become filmy with his perspiration and he removed them and polished the lenses feverishly. He wiped his eyes and the palms of his hands and put on his glasses again. Then he sat transfixed in his chair.

Through his office window he looked out at the wired compound of the depot and saw a powerful figure standing there in helmet, combat dress, and a machine pistol cradled under one arm. There was something oddly and forcefully familiar about the thrust of that powerful fleshy figure, the helmet strap under the broad jaw, the blunt shoulders. Suddenly Anatole Heudlak recognized him. It was Captain Langbach, the SS security officer. Usually he wore the black garrison uniform, high peaked cap, black boots, black belt and revolver holster, but there was no mistaking him now even in that battle dress, and instantly the little Feldwebel was alert. He was standing out there in the compound near his staff car, the Schmeisser under one arm, glancing casually around him, and Feldwebel Heudlak watched him, thinking not as a national who had thrown his lot in with the New Order, but as a Czech national in an alien uniform.

He did not like this. If the American threat was really developing, this would cease to be a rear area and become a combat zone and, with that, all security responsibilities of Himmler's Wehkreis would be taken over by Army headquarters. Langbach, out there in battle dress like some posturing statue representing the last-ditch defense of the Reich, could well be staging one of this periodic roundups for "security investigation." It would be like the sadistic bully to stage one last flare-up of terror before he and his outfit were moved east of the Rhine.

Feldwebel Heudlak saw him make a negligent motion of his machine pistol toward the administrative building and two helmeted troopers stepped out of the staff car. Heudlak licked his lips. Perhaps it was one of those roundups, but it could not have anything to do with him. Still, his throat was dry suddenly and his fingers were trembling against the desk in a nervous tattoo. Thinking as a Czech national, he remembered the security interview he'd had with Langbach several months before and, though it had seemed routine, there was a belief that Langbach never forgot anyone he interviewed. It might be that Langbach had marked him privately in that evil little mental book of his. It might be that he would be marked for the net of little fishes that

Langbach would pull in during these last days of his power here.

The two security troopers, battle-dressed, with revolvers at their belts, were coming toward the administration building. Anatole Heudlak saw that before his glasses filmed over again with perspiration. This time he did not bother to clean them. It could not be that they wanted anything with him, but when you thought as a Czech national you felt sure they did. The graying little man felt his whole being contract, like something trying to get within a shell. At a time like this, God, right at this time! How close it had been!

Although how ridiculous to think his forgiveness could be tied in with the survival of that bridge. At a late, late moment he'd had nothing to offer his country but a wild idea, and it was doomed like the bridge itself.

Early that morning Doke Stanton had awakened. He had slept undisturbed, as she had promised he would, but this, he had an uneasy feeling, was to be a day of decision. Waiting in the chill little room, he had sat on the window seat, his hands jammed in the slit pockets of his combat jacket for warmth, and looked down through the morning grayness at the river. They had evidently finished running rail traffic to the east bank and replaced the planking, because now there was a trickle of vehicles.

It did not seem possible that the Americans could be anywhere near, or there certainly would be a much bigger flow of traffic down there. Maybe the attack had hit a snag. There were a lot of Jerries west of the Rhine, that was certain. Well, damn it, if that First Army attack was doing anything, why weren't the Jerries showing more signs of pulling out? He became uneasy again. It would be tough to try to hang on here from day to day.

The girl was the key, of course. She was sticking her neck out, maybe, but he had to be sure she would continue to do so and he speculated on the best approach. He was the first American she had ever seen and she seemed to have a consuming interest in America. But it was an abstract interest; strangely enough, it seemed involved in values and attitudes, an intense preoccupation with a people's thinking, and he did not know how he could keep her going on that. He did not know what it was himself.

Suppose he took himself as a representative American. Well, he was moral, of course. That is, he figured he was honest—he would not steal or forge checks or cheat at games. He respected other people's opinions. He figured he was tolerant. He liked to be friendly. He hated injustice. It did not sound like much. Anyone in the world could be like that and probably was.

Well, where the hell did anything unique about an American arise? Americans had a high standard of living and were generous and believed in democracy. But he sat here on a chilly March morning, trying to think of something that might intrigue a German governess who limped, and realized instinctively that her mind sought for something that he could not identify or explain and, for all he knew, did not exist. It would be a rough deal, if his life came to depend on his translating a girl's ethereal and idealistic concept of the American people into realistic terms. His best chance was to try to arouse her interest in him as a person.

She had nearly given way at some thought connected with that bridge. He kept remembering that. He could remember her with her face in her hands and her slim shoulders bent. Amazing. A grave, steady, soft-spoken girl, who could hide an American prisoner and yet apparently be overpowered by something connected with a bridge. It was down there in the gray morning, spanning a gray river, like a slender steel link between two cliffs, and that seemed all there was to it and yet there was something about it that could break her down so completely. If he could only dope that, Doke Stanton reflected restlessly, he might find the approach he needed.

He found himself awaiting her impatiently and she seemed delayed this morning, so that he gave himself over to anxiety that something had gone wrong in this quiet cold stone heap of a castle and he had to restrain himself from flailing at the door with his fists, as he had done that first morning he had awakened here in this little sheeted room. Only the memory of her warning had stopped him.

When the key turned in the lock he was pacing up and down, his hands jammed in the pockets of his combat jacket, and he stopped short and whirled, as the door swung open. She was standing there with his tray and he could not tell from her face just what he might expect today.

She wished him good morning in her grave courteous way and said that she was sorry she was late with his breakfast. Then she set down the tray and started to leave.

"You're not going!" said Doke, alarmed. She had always stayed before.

She looked at him in some surprise. "Why, yes," she said. "Why not?"

"But I want to talk to you, Fräulein," he heard himself say.

"Later, Private Stanton," she said. " I must do things."

"I want to talk to you," he repeated. "You won't go making any decisions until I have a chance to talk to you? You'll come back soon?"

She inclined her blond head. "Yes. I shall come back soon."

She closed and locked the door behind her and he flung himself down on the settee and stared at his breakfast. He felt like some child who was afraid to be left alone. Some feverish child who wanted a person to sit beside him and run a hand over his forehead. Yeah, he muttered, yeah. A sunny afternoon, say, in the Pomfret hills of Vermont, one of those grassy slopes warmed with the sun, he lying there with his head in the lap of a girl and looking through half-shut eyes across the valley where growths of pine girded the bright green mowings and gray rock outcroppings jutted out of snug upland pastures dotted with grazing Jerseys and the sky hung over it all like a bright blue inverted bowl and occasionally a girl's cool hand brushed across his forehead like the skimming touch of a breeze and spoke volumes in the afternoon silence— "I am your healing touch of companionship and understanding. I understand you and I am here and you know it."

God, thought Doke Stanton, and pressed a hand tightly across his eyes; he must be going crazy. His thoughts seemed to be all mixed up, so that he could slip into fantasy like a person taking a cat nap. It was like the time in Normandy when he had seen a farmer wring the neck of a pigeon and toss the bird on the ground to thresh out its life in the dust, until it fell over on one side and one wing was extended, in all its delicate symmetry and miracle of creative design and trim feather beauty, wasted, done, finished in the dust, and that was the way of a man's life, too, in this damned war.

It was hours, it seemed, before the girl returned. She came in and sat down on the edge of a chair, holding herself in that effortless straight way, her hands clasped in her lap. Doke Stanton looked at her. "Well?" he said. "What's the verdict, Fräulein?"

"Verdict?" she repeated. "I do not understand your use of the word."

"Any news that has to do with me," said Doke, "is a verdict."

Ilse Margraven regarded him thoughtfully a moment. "Oh," she said, "I see. There has been some news—a rumor that this area will become a combat zone. The Wehrkreis would have no further authority. But," she went on slowly, "Captain Langbach is simply away on one of his security inspection trips. I do not know when the Army will take over here. Soon, I should think, but I do not know how soon."

"And then?" said Doke. "What happens to me then?"

"You would be handed over to the nearest Army unit," she said simply. "What else is there?"

The simple logic made it such a flat statement that he was jarred. Then he stood up and looked down at her, hands on hips.

"Do you think some Army unit is going to bother with one prisoner, Fräulein?"

"They would be fair to you."

"I was a POW once before," he reminded her. "And I was going to be shot, because I was a nuisance. And do you think some Army unit with its back to the river and the Americans moving in are going to feel any differently?"

"I think," she said, "you would have a better chance than if you were fighting at the front."

"You don't seem friendly any more," said Doke.

"What do you expect?" she asked, perplexed. "You are an enemy soldier. Would you expect me to do nothing? If you shot just one German soldier, it would be my responsibility, Private Stanton. Do you think by any chance that I am not loyal to Germany?"

"It's not a question of loyalty. It's a question of humanity. You did not turn me over to the SS."

"The SS are beasts," said the girl with finality. "And you —you seemed so helpless. Never would you have stood up against Langbach."

"Was it that?" said Doke Stanton. "Or because you were curious about Americans?"

She hesitated and bent her head slightly. "It seemed that one gave me the chance for the other," she said, somewhat indistinctly.

"If your curiosity could have lasted until the Americans came," said Doke, "it would have been more fair. But instead you finish with your curiosity before the Americans arrive and I risk a revolver bullet in the back of the neck."

Her head came up and she looked at him startled, as though she had never seen him before. "You truly think that?" she questioned.

He did not, exactly, but now was the time to pile it on. He sat down on the settee again, bending toward her, and she sat there very straight, watching him with those blue eyes and listening, her lips slightly parted. "When the Americans get through to the west bank," he said, "fighting will stop for a while, probably for a good while, because a river crossing takes plenty of planning. That will give me a chance to arrange for a transfer to Paris and I'll spend the rest of the war drawing maps. The only German soldiers I'll see will be prisoners of war." He took a breath. "All I need is some time to arrange that. I'm finished with fighting." His voice rose slightly with his intensity. "Kill anybody! Hell, I never wanted to kill anything in my life."

She was silent a moment, then again studied her clasped fingers. "You want me to continue to hide you here?"

"Yes," said Doke Stanton. "Finish what you started, Fräulein. You said yourself there was no harm in me."

"I know," said the girl. Again she was silent and he carefully said nothing, because he had a feeling it was going his way. "I do not believe," she said finally, "that you have thought of everything. But perhaps you have. Yes, perhaps, you have." She gave a little sigh and arose. "I must go now."

Again he had that queer reluctance to see her go. There was a sense of response and perception about her that made her an interesting person to talk to and when she became interested or curious her ideas had a free flow that certainly passed the time. Now that he was sure the matter had been settled, he wished she would stay and talk.

She looked at him thoughtfully, twisting her slender fingers together. "I think," she said quietly, "that you always will pay heavily for what you want and sometimes you may find it is not worth what has been given for it." She nodded to him, a polite little inclination of her braided blond head, and left the room, and for some reason there was something a bit pathetic about the limp in her walk. Her country was in a fair way to be beaten and she had just been beaten herself. And also possible was the likelihood that she had lost interest in him as either an American or as an individual.

He shrugged impatiently. Maybe he had whipsawed a kind heart or a sensitive conscience and maybe he would not like to think of it later. But it would be much later, it would be after the war, and a lot of things would not matter after the war, like whether you were a coward or a hero or a combat infantryman or a PX clerk or went AWOL or always looked for the deepest hole you could find. People did not think about those things very long. A German governess might not think very highly of the first American she had ever seen, but, if that was what she called a stiff price to pay for survival, she did not put much value on life.

She did not return until late in the afternoon. He had spent most of the time in a restless pacing, or lounging in the window seat watching the river and the bridge. A slow steady rain was meshing out the whole steep bank across the Rhine. There was traffic going east across the bridge, in spurts, then in only occasional trickles, vehicular traffic and some towed batteries, with a few straggling formations of troops. There was a lack of haste about it that infuriated him. There should be a pell-mell rushing retreat. He knew this was a fantastic expectation, that he was trying to telescope weeks and weeks of bitter Westwall fighting into days or hours. But instead of adjusting himself to the probable realities, he clung to the fantasy, like a person trying to shape an iron horseshoe into the form of a rose with his bare hands.

She came in with his tray, set it down, and drew the blackout curtain. The rain and the late afternoon had already pulled down a curtain of darkness. She switched on the one bulb in the room and it glowed a pallid yellow. She made only a little gesture toward the tray, then again turned to leave, and suddenly checked herself.

"William is gone," she said. "I find that disturbing."

"William?" he repeated.

"The old manservant here," she said. "He has been gone since early this morning. It may be that the Volksturm has impressed him into some defense work, but I do not think so. The Volksturm is losing all organization."

He felt uneasy. "But why is it disturbing?" he asked.

"Because he was always so nervous about your being here. Martha is nervous, too, but Martha trusts me. I—I think William's fear may have finally overcome his trust in me. You must realize, Private Stanton, that the SS has not yet left town. They have been in authority so long—people are so disciplined about such things—"

"You think William has told them?" He spoke the words and the shakes came into his stomach as he spoke them.

"I do not know," she said. "I don't really think so. I just feel disturbed."

The shakes rippled up from deep in his stomach, into the middle of his chest, pulsed against his throat. The fantasy to which he had clung during the long lonely afternoon began to disappear into thin air and he groped for it. "Damn it!" he burst out. "If they would only blow that bridge!"

She stared at him. "What?" she said, astounded.

"That bridge out there!" He nearly yelled it. "All day long I've been hoping they would blow it. Because, until they blow it, I know the Americans aren't close enough to threaten, and until they get here I've got to live on in this nightmare—"

She cut him short. "You want to see that bridge destroyed?" There was a tautness in her voice that brought him up short.

He looked at her blankly. "Why, of course—"

Ilse Margraven drew a long quivering breath. Then she reached into the pocket of her sweater and brought out the key to the room. She laid it on the table beside his tray. "I cannot guarantee you an undisturbed night," she said, her soft voice still taut. "I will not lock you up. Besides, Herr American, I think you are your own jailer. And you probably always have been."

She left the room, closing the door behind her, and this time there was no punctuating click of the key. Doke Stanton looked after her stunned, and the fantasy and irrationality were vanished, like some sort of a jag, and in their place were left the realities and a key.

9.

THE NIGHT of March 5 was no different to the young American lieutenant than March 4 or March 6. Except he was especially tired that night, more tired than he thought he had ever been and that included the days and nights of the Bulge. This was a particular type of fatigue, the kind that ached all through his bones from the soles of his feet to the throb in his temples. This was the fatigue that brought a hot pain behind the eyeballs and hung an invisible weight around the neck and dulled perception and reaction with a terrible anesthesia and forced the mind to concentrate on actions like lifting the feet. It was a fatigue born out of an incessant, unremitting attack, where motion and impetus were to be sustained and the needling spur of speed and drive pricked relentlessly at the men moving through the spitting, splitting defenses of the Westwall. It was a fatigue of mind and body and soul and there would be precious little time to recoup before the same hard driving orders would spark another same hard driving day.

His name was Birmingham, the young lieutenant, and he had just been made company commander at the meeting at Task Force command post. His company had lost two commanders in the past ten days and now he had it, a second lieutenant who had been churned up out of the welter of fighting through ambushes and pillboxes and stabbing emplacements of automatic weapons and flak guns to the command of the company.

It was pitch black when he came back from the meeting with the Task Force commander, stumbling wearily down into the cellar of the shot-up, raddled house that was his company command post. The breathing of the exhausted men asleep in the cellar was like a heavy slow wash against his clouded senses. He yawned prodigiously, felt about the floor for a place, and spread his bedroll. He took off his helmet, sank to his knees, and then simply fell over on his side. Tired, God, he was tired, but he had made it through the day and as of now he commanded a company of infantry accompanying an armored task force.

Lieutenant Birmingham turned over on his back and clasped his hands across his stomach. His whole body seemed to throb against his bedroll and he knew he needed desperately to sleep these few hours he had, but he could not sleep. He lay wakeful in the darkness and thought of this Germany, the part of this Germany in which he lay wakeful in a cellar, this rugged hilly terrain of wet bare forests interspersed with towns and narrow black-top roads and broken by stretches of farmland. He could hear the anti-tank guns dug in along the defense perimeter and firing like artillery, while the big 105s were being towed up through the night to catch up with the advance, to be somewhere in supporting range when the leading elements jumped off tomorrow.

The division had taken a town called Euskirchen today—or was it yesterday?—and now they were changing direction and instead of attacking toward Bonn they were to attack southeast through Rheinbach and Stadt-Meckenheim, driving through a valley called the Ahr, pushing as fast as they could, riding halftracks if necessary with the tanks on a slanting approach to the Rhine somewhere off there in the darkness. That was what the orders said and that was what the maps said, but it did not make any difference which direction you attacked, nor did the names on the maps mean anything. The only thing that meant something was the Rhine, and to Lieutenant Kurt Birmingham that meant a great deal. In particular, the black line on the Rhine near the confluence of the Ahr. That was the Ludendorff Bridge.

He thought about it with a growing wonder that he would be heading in its direction. To think of it! For the bridge had affected his entire life. In a way it had, because his father had crossed that bridge with the Army of Occupation in the last war. December, 1918. The bridge had been recently built then.

Lieutenant Kurt Birmingham pillowed an arm behind his head, an island of perverse wakefulness in a sea of snores and sighs and long deep breaths pulled up out of the chest and exhaled in slow tides of exhaustion. Yes, sure, December, 1918, and his father crossing the bridge and then deserting soon afterward and marrying a German girl, having a son, naming that son Kurt.

Kurt Birmingham living in Germany until he was seven and maybe he would have always lived there. Maybe he would be fighting in the Westwall tonight, if it had not been for one of those American charitable organizations that managed to arrange for the return of his father and his family.

Of course, America had not been at war when his father deserted, but still it had hung over his life always and the somber shade of it had enveloped his family. Kurt Birmingham could remember life in that little railroad town in Pennsylvania, the house across the tracks with an ineffectual father whose record always seemed to be with him, like some taint in his blood that marked him just a bit apart, that kept him just a bit off balance, that hurt his confidence and ambition just enough to make his life a complete failure.

It was funny, thought Kurt Birmingham, remembering, how he had always felt so keenly about something he never fully understood, that he learned only in bits and pieces. The bitter, bitter years of poverty, of odd jobs, of obscurity in high school, a slender youth who spoke German as fluently as he did English, who was an American citizen yet could not feel absorbed into America. Pride, when you couldn't afford it, he thought, remembering, could strangle you.

He reviewed those years and reflected that he had never thought of that far-off bridge in Germany. It had nothing to do with things. He had not thought of it when he joined the Army, or during OCS at Fort Benning, or coming over on the *Queen Elizabeth,* or fighting in the Ardennes. He had not thought of it until he saw it on the map in the Task Force command post. Now he could think of nothing else. Now he could only realize that the bridge actually should be on the sector map of his division.

He was a second lieutenant and a company commander. He had been a good platoon leader. He would be able to handle this company. And in all of this he had felt the sense of belonging and at once realized that a Rhine bridge was tied up with his allegiance and his sense of gratitude that he was on this side of the Westwall tonight. His father was dead and his mother, back in that little Pennsylvania town, probably would not understand, but Lieutenant Kurt Birmingham would have asked nothing greater in life than to cross that bridge as an American fighting man.

Pride in reverse, he thought somberly in the darkness of the cellar. But maybe something more. Maybe, he thought. Maybe a balancing of accounts with his country. Maybe this was what they called *noblesse oblige.* Maybe this was just a little offering of gratitude that would be utterly unimportant to anyone else but himself. Yet Kurt Birmingham thought that such little things did gradually enter the fiber of a country. Like bringing a brick to a construction job on a skyscraper.

He grinned wearily to himself. Okay, okay. He probably would never see the bridge and, if he did, it would have been most efficiently destroyed by the Jerries who were masters of military science. But, while he was putting his life on the line, he could offer this private little idea of his own to his country at the same time.

He closed his eyes and it seemed he had hardly done so, when a hand shook his shoulder and a voice was saying in the murky cellar light, "Lieutenant, the Old Man has sent for you to come to the CP."

Lieutenant Birmingham put on his helmet and came up out of the cellar. It was just beginning to get light, and, as he heard the rattle of mess kits, he smiled. The kitchen crew had come up. Good boys.

There was a light rain falling as he made his way toward the rendezvous, mushing through the mud, and he could just imagine what he would hear. "Everbody to push hard today. When you meet fire, try to overrun it. Don't get bottled up in towns. If there's any stopping, I'll be on your necks, because the Old Man will be on mine, and somebody will be on his."

All right, thought Lieutenant Kurt Birmingham, more of the same as yesterday and more of the same tomorrow and more of the same again, until finally they reached the Rhine. And let it be somewhere near that bridge.

Locomotive headlights on the east bank of the Rhine were misty in the rain that was filtering through the darkness. There was a strange tensity to the night. The flak batteries on the Erpeler Ley opened up once, savagely stabbing at the night sky, and then were silent. There was a sound of cars careening about in the town below the castle, klaxons screeching violently, and what looked like a flare of torches down along the west bank of the river.

They were fitful things. In the darkness they were like the tossings and moanings of a person heaving against uneasy sleep. Doke Stanton huddled in the window seat, his arms clasped around his knees, looked out through the gleaming black panes and felt the same fitful uneasingness. Endless, endless, endless, like the waiting for a firing squad or a guillotine or a noose. Something was going to happen, but there was no knowing when or what it would be like. It was simply abroad, a tension and a dread and a high keening note of fear like a desperate dissonant note of a violin. He sat there and realized that what he imparted to the night was also his.

He sat there because he did not know what else to do. She had turned the tables on him with a clicking decisive move that left him bemused. One moment he thought he had her cornered. Keep him hidden, keep him fed, keep him secure, until the Americans overran this place, no matter what that might mean to her personally. The next moment she had cooly put him on his own. Escape if you want. Stay if you want. Was that what she meant? She thought something might happen tonight. You're on your own, Herr American. Was that it? Whatever she meant, it had been a skillful riposte. Because he was lost right at this moment.

He did not know what he wanted to do. A Stalag, which had seemed the answer at one time, the perfect answer, was no longer attractive, if the Americans were actually shaping a break-through. But if she was taking no further interest in him, what was his next move? He was sitting here behind an unlocked door. "You are your own jailer," that amazing girl had told him. My God, and why? Something he had said about wishing that bridge would be blown in a hurry? He could not believe that had anything to do with it, but he kept coming back to that remark. It had appeared to spark that gesture of hers.

But he could not continue sitting here as though the door really was locked. What would someone like Ellison have done? George Ellison, who had urged him to take a battle-field commission. "You'd be a hell of a good recon officer, boy." George, if you hadn't been killed trying to outpost that sketchy line, held by recon men and those resistance guerrillas of the Armée Blanche, what would you have done?

Look, George, I never wanted to be an officer. Your odds shorten when you're one of those brand-new second lieu-tenants. Anyhow, that's over and done with. What would a really brave Joe do in this situation? All right, Ellison, you'd try to duck a Stalag, wouldn't you? You'd want to lie low, wouldn't you, as long as there was a chance the GIs would break through to the river? Well, what's the difference be-tween a great guy like you and a psychoneurotic like me? What do we do differently? Escape? Escape where? Just slip out into the night and start working back toward our lines? The Germans are between us, the whole damn Westwall. That's brave? How many times can a brave guy get killed?

You were brave at Aachen. What would you do, Ellison, here, on the Rhine now? Wouldn't you figure the odds? The odds certainly weren't on escaping in the night to nowhere.

The key was that slim German girl, that thoughtful girl, that governess with the limp, who had left him calling his signals to empty air. How would Ellison have handled her? Wouldn't Ellison have wanted to see that bridge blown? Good Lord, it's sure to be destroyed, so what difference does it make if the GIs come through here and hurry it up? Yet, somehow, Ilse Margraven seemed to react strangely to that bridge. It didn't make any sense, but there it was.

Let that go. The door is unlocked. Well, you just can't sit here. She left it unlocked. At least, see what kind of escape route you might have. The door is unlocked and she warned you something might happen tonight. Something might happen tonight.

Slipping off the window seat, he felt his way across the dark room to the door and cautiously tried the knob, as though it might have been affixed to a booby trap. He pushed it open slowly and peered through the opening. A faint aura of light ahead encouraged him. He could see that he was at the end of a short narrow passage. He worked his way along the little hall, feeling the dank chill of the place, the dimly diffused light, the remorseless silence. It was like venturing into a mausoleum, and his own little prison of a room that he had just left seemed a friendly familiar place by contrast.

Okay, Ellison, stick around. You tell me what to do and I'll do it. There were some men who seemed to have a built-in sense of feel about these things. Remember the road from Sittard to Gangelt, Ellison? It was the most advanced lateral road the Americans used, and when you got on it, you bucked along as fast as you could, because the Jerries were watching your every movement from the ridge to the south and maybe they would shoot and maybe they wouldn't and you took a breath and held it the whole way until you ducked through that old Roman arch in Gangelt and got around behind some woods. Ellison always seemed to know when to run that gantlet. He always could get the recon troop through. Ellison was like the old frontier fighters and cavalry leaders. Big, friendly, fearless guy. *Beau sabreur*. Born able to read the signs and reach for the answer.

He stepped out of the little passage into a broad, high-ceilinged hall with a ponderous chandelier. A massive staircase of carved dark wood rose to the second floor and it was from up there that the light seemed to originate. Doke Stanton rubbed his hands tightly against his thighs and looked nervously around him. Across the hall was the entrance to what seemed a huge cavernous room. At his left was evidently the front door, wide, of the same massive dark wood as the staircase, studded and banded with bolts and strips of brass. What was out there? Oh, yes, he could remember a paved courtyard and a gateway to a drive through some woods. And then, of course, the town was out there somewhere, the town and the river and the bridge. This was the way he must have been brought into this place, collapsed from tension and exhaustion.

He looked away from the door and up the staircase in the direction of the light. It was like the diffused light from inside a room near the head of the stairs. It was the only light in this whole place, like the dawn of creation in the dark of the deeps, the one sign that anyone might be drawing a breath in this chill brick pile besides himself.

The scream hit him like a cold flat hand across the face. It pierced through the shadows and silence like a knife suddenly slashing through the wall of a tent. It was a sudden scream, somewhat muffled, but a scream of unutterable pain, and it had been the scream of a girl.

He stood at the foot of the staircase shocked into sheer rigid immobility, that terrible war drum of fear pounding in his chest. He wet his lips and stared up the staircase. All was quiet again. But it had been a scream. He could not expunge those few seconds of voiced agony. She must have screamed. It must have been she.

He took a brief sideways glance at the short passage to his room, as if to make sure he had somewhere to run, then grasped the banister.

"Fräulein?" he called tentatively in a low choked voice. Then he started up the stairs, pulling himself along the banister by main force. Hell, what could have made her scream? The memory of it came back and nearly halted him dead in his tracks, but he grabbed the banister again and pulled himself on until he reached the top and then once more he stopped and listened hard.

There was a small lamp burning on a table near the head of the stairs and, just beyond, a door slightly ajar emitted a narrow oblong of yellow light. He stepped cautiously to the door.

"Fräulein?" he said in a low voice, and gave the door a

push. It swung open and he saw her, then. She was in a heap on the floor, supporting herself with one arm, and her head was flung back. She seemed to have hurt herself, he thought, and he started to move into the room.

Then, indefinably, he hesitated barely over the threshold. It had seemed to him he heard heavy slow breathing somewhere very close. He hesitated, and even in that moment he knew this was all wrong; there was something dangerous here and he was hung in space for that irresolute moment, watching the fallen girl, her body rigid with pain, and yet sensing the threat somewhere near, close at hand. And, even as he sensed that another step was a great risk, he suddenly found he had already taken one step too many, for there was a panting grunt just to the left of him inside the door. Something struck him across the side of the face with stunning steel impact and he staggered sideways, the salt taste of blood in his mouth and his jaw paralyzed with the sharp pain of that short heavy blow. He felt himself seized by the jacket and swung around and he had only a blurred impression of a face under a helmet before he was struck again, this time not as hard, but it split his lip and he reeled backward and came to a stop, buckling at the knees, his whole face shot and streaked and raddled with pain. Numbly he raised a hand to his mouth and felt the blood there. He stared at the man standing in the room, looking at him, stared as though it were impossible that this could be true.

He was a big man in German battle dress, with a machine pistol cradled in one arm. It was the steel barrel of the Schmeisser that he had used in those two sharp paralyzing blows. Even now, as he took a step, that menacing steel barrel jutting from the cradle of his arm, the memory of those two blows sent Doke Stanton backward in a couple of reeling steps until he brought up hard against a piece of furniture. The German stopped moving and studied him deliberately.

Doke looked over at the girl. She was still on the floor, over near the side of a narrow bed, but she was looking at him now, her expression horrified. She put an arm on the bed and tried to pull herself up. Doke could not understand what had happened to her, but she seemed shattered.

"Why," she gasped, "did you—come—?"

"You screamed," he said numbly. "You screamed."

"He stamped on my foot," she said painfully. "He brought his heel down on my bad foot. I could not help the scream.

Be careful of him." She was breathing hard as she tried to lift herself from the floor. "He's—Langbach—SS—"

The German said something in sharp command and Doke's eyes swung back to him again. He tried to blink away the hot tears that clouded his vision, tears of the shocking throbbing barrel-whiping. The German's face seemed like a pudgy blob between the brim of his helmet and the strap under his powerful jaw. He was talking German to the girl, his head turned slightly toward her, but his sharp blue eyes under the heavy black brows were scanning the American.

Doke wiped the blood from his chin with the back of his hand. It was a mechanical gesture, the way he would brush at a fiy. The German had stamped on her foot, on that foot she dragged around like a bird with a trailing wing, and the pain of it had made her scream. He focused on that thought. But, my God, why had he done a brutal thing like that? He was a German and she was a German. Or was it somehow because of him?

He dashed a hand across his mouth again. The SS. This was the way it went, you twisted and turned in your burrow and you always met the ferret eventually, grinning and waiting for you. The fear and the punishment and the pain and the helplessness—always there, and never more so than in this little bedroom near the head of some stairs where a shattered girl was struggling to get off the floor and a tough SS man was speaking his hoarse guttural German.

The girl had managed to get up on the edge of the bed. She braced herself with both hands and looked steadily at Langbach. Her lips moved in undistinguishable reply, as though she were speaking through set teeth. Langbach moved the barrel of the Schmeisser in a slight gesture toward Doke Stanton.

"He wants me to tell you, Private Stanton," the girl said slowly, "that he has been all day rounding up those who would be traitors to the Reich. Now, when the Reich is passing a critical hour, the rats raise their heads." Her voice trembled and she paused. Langbach's eyes flickered to her immediately. "He is stamping on them one by one," she said, then. "This is what he says, Private Stanton."

Langbach spoke again. His words sounded as though they came through phlegm and for the first time Doke realized that this dangerous brutal executioner might be drunk as well.

"He says," repeated the girl tonelessly, "that tonight he has caught another rat. He always thought my heart was not with the Reich. He has always promised to give me his attention. He is going to be sure everyone knows what happens to those who enter into a conspiracy against the Reich."

Langbach cut her off impatiently and started talking again. He was beginning to shout now and the heady lust of his temper was making him excited. His lips were wet.

"Conspiracy?" said Ilse Margraven. "God in heaven! He is claiming that you are a part of an American force dropped behind the German lines to attack us from the rear. He means to uncover the whole conspiracy. Oh, God in heaven, he is crazy—"

"Tell him," said Doke, "I am a prisoner of war—" He stopped. It sounded so foolish to him.

Her long blue eyes rested on him imploringly. " I have told him. I have told him. But he will believe only what he wants—"

Doke braced himself against the piece of furniture at his back. There was law somewhere and reason and protection. Somewhere. Not here. Not in this modest little bedroom. Not here. There was torture here and there was savagery and screams and death and silence. This was the world and the universe. This little bedroom. This was all.

"I am sorry," said the girl in a low voice. "He came here to my room—"

"Sprech deutsch," Langbach suddenly flung at her.

She paid no attention to him. "I don't know," she went on in English. "Perhaps William showed him the side entrance. I do not like to think so, but William must have been a badly frightened man—"

"Sprech deutsch," Langbach said fiercely. *"Deutsch! Deutsch!"* Doke Stanton wanted to beg her to do as he said. Langbach was being ignored and it was infuriating him. What was the matter with her anyhow? How could she sit there and ignore the temper that was beginning to crest like a wave.

"I am afraid William may have told him you were here," she said. "Or perhaps this brute guessed it from something about William. He's a brute. Private Stanton, a beast. But he is clever—"

"Sprech deutsch!" shouted Langbach. The rest of his words boiled up in a guttural stew and he took a step toward the girl, the barrel of the machine pistol moving back in an arc, and Doke Stanton could remember the pain of that metallic crash against flesh and bone and it was as if he were to be

whipped again himself. He launched himself off the bureau behind him and made a desperate grab for the end of that sweeping steel barrel. It was not something he had planned for or watched for or waited for. It was the blood in his throat and dripping from his chin and the bruising ache in his face and the memory of a scream—and he moved in an instinctive lunge as Langbach pivoted toward the girl, he lunged with both hands outstretched the way he would have tried to stop a car bearing down on a child in a street.

His lunge carried him on top of the German and he had his hands on the threatening swinging barrel. With a frantic yank he twisted it away and in just a few seconds he had it, the machine pistol, as simply as that, with no premeditation, no planning, just a jet speed at the right time.

But, as he tore the weapon free, he was so astounded at his own action that for a moment he could not get his mind regeared to take advantage of an unthinking impulse. He had not planned this and, in the moment he took to realize his luck, the big figure in battle dress was on top of him. He had barely time to club awkwardly with the Schmeisser before he was enveloped in a pair of powerful arms, lifted from his feet, and borne backward over a small chair that splintered beneath him. A stale smell of brandy and tobacco blasted against his face as he was slammed to the floor, still holding desperately to the barrel of the weapon, and it was only as the tough stubby fingers dug at his windpipe that he let go and fought to pry loose that tightening grip on his throat.

The specter of suffocation was in those fingers shifting, feeling for the grip that he would never dislodge, that would destroy him in one minute, two minutes, and his whole body arched in a desperate muscular contortion. Lambach held on to his throat but shifted his body to get more leverage on that contorting, struggling khaki body. Doke Stanton jerked up his knee savagely into the groin and Langbach's stale breath suddenly exhaled in a gust as he came lurching down on top of him with a gasp of pain. Doke tried to claw those fingers loose again, then instead jabbed his fingers into Langbach's eyes. The German yelled something and, as the pressure on Doke's throat slackened momentarily, he heaved the heavy form off him with a sobbing desperate surge of strength and rolled free. He came up on his feet, choking, looking frantically for the Schmeisser. But already Langbach was coming up off the floor and Stanton snarled and launched a kick aimed right for that fleshy face beneath the tightly strapped steel helmet. And Langbach, a touch of froth at the corners of his mouth, caught the kick in his hands, twisted and shoved, and Doke Stanton went careening against the wall with an impact that jarred him nearly senseless.

But he was conscious of one thing. Langbach still had hold of his foot and was coming up on his knees and in another second that heavy body would be pinning him down and those fingers would be at his throat again. He lashed out with his free foot and this time he got Langbach in the face and he kicked out again, threshing to twist himself away from the wall, and again he was free and rolled over to get to his feet, nothing in his consciousness but a blurr of light and Langbach and that machine pistol.

He nearly tripped over it, as he came surging back to his feet. God, where was it? He could not seem to focus. There was nothing but this terrible blur and the knowledge that Langbach was near, close, coming for him, a form, a something, a terrible presence, and there was no time— even as he grabbed down at something near his feet, the time was running out. That panting gasp was in his ears as his fingers found the Schmeisser. In the next second Langbach had it, too, and was twisting it away savagely. Doke was forced back through the door and out into the hall, the Schmeisser bending, twisting in his hands like something alive. Suddenly the German crowded close on him, lifted his boot and drove it down hard on Doke's instep.

His own heavy combat boot saved him somewhat, but a flash of pain shot up his whole leg and he found himself shouting gibberish, recoiling, then lowering his head and butting into that face and feeling the crash of bone against the top of his head and suddenly seeing a spurting smear of crimson across the features under the helmet. The reaction was terrible. Langbach nearly flung him off his feet with the fury of his struggle for the weapon. Doke felt his strength ebbing from his fingertips, deserting him, flowing away, leaving him even while his mind tried to keep up the grasp on that slippery writhing barrel. He lost his grasp, lurched, made a last dive for that battle-dressed figure and desperately threw his arms around it to pin that weapon. And then suddenly he and Langbach went pitching headlong, as if the floor had collapsed under them. They had gone over the edge of the stairs and they went down with a crash, Doke on top, dazedly clinging to the figure beneath him, for protection now, as they turned as though flipped by some giant hand and went sprawling on down the stairs in a bruising, cascading tangle of arms and legs, like bundles carelessly flung down a chute. A report went off almost in Doke's face. His foot caught in the balustrade and there was a splitting crackle as a couple of the uprights were snapped off. He lay on the stairs, head down, stunned, pinned by his foot, while the thick battle-dressed figure turned over in a slow ponderous somersault and then slid face down to the foot of the staircase.

Doke braced himself with one arm against a step, his chest churning that familiar taste of copper into his throat and his breath coming in quick congested gasps. He saw Langbach groping heavily to his feet and clutching his stomach, staggering a few steps toward the great brass studded front door, reeling in the semidarkness of the hall below like some vague shapeless shadow. He staggered headlong against the door, spun, dropped to his knees, then still clutching at his stomach, like a person clasping a lot of loose apples, he fell forward on his face and lay still.

Doke Stanton pulled his foot out of the balustrade. He could see the Schmeisser lying a few steps farther down and he reached for it with a great, painful effort. Then he turned and dragged himself up the stairs on his knees.

The girl was clinging to the banisters at the head of the stairs. She sank down slowly as he dragged himself to her and he suddenly pitched forward with his head in her lap and his whole body contorted again, this time from the inside, in a searing retch, and he was shaking with great shuddering involuntary sobs that would not stop, that he could not control, that simply welled up from his chest and seemed to pull him inside out.

All of it seemed trying to escape, the pain and terror, the tension and pressure and the strain, the bitterness and the fantasies and the close face of death behind the writhing, wrenching, twisting steel barrel of a weapon; like the body trying to throw off an illness, he crouched on the stairs, his face in her lap, shaking in the grip of a reaction that seemed bent on turning him inside out like a glove to preserve his sanity.

Then slowly he realized that she was trying to get him to listen to her. She was raising his head, holding her hands tightly over his temples, and her soft urgent voice came again and again.

"Listen—please—listen—he did not come here alone—"

His self-control slipped back to him from its truancy. He became aware of things, that he ached all through his body and his whole face was stiff, and the tight clasp of her hands at his temples. His shoulders shuddered, but he was still. He could hear her now.

"There is someone—coming—downstairs—"

"Yes," said Doke Stanton huskily. His throat hurt him, too. "We have that Schmeisser."

"No, listen. There is only one chance for us. Please let me do this my way. *Ach, lieber Gott,* please listen—"

"I'm listening," he said.

Her voice was urgent, low, but he could hear her. "Get out of sight—*please!* Hurry—hurry—*now*—"

He pulled himself up over the top step and crept to the door of her room. He lay flat on the floor, holding the weapon. He could see part of the front door. The girl caught the banister and raised herself to her feet. She stood there, holding to the banister with both hands.

A voice came from downstairs, a man's voice high-pitched with excitement. The girl spoke in German. She paused, then spoke again. There was a silence. Suddenly there was the sound of the front door closing with a slam.

For a long moment the girl continued to stand with her hands gripping the banister. Then, abruptly, she crumpled to the floor. She seemed to melt into a heap beside the balustrade.

10.

THE GERMAN Field Marshal, Walther von Model, commanding Army Group B for the Reich, had many things to think of in that early dawn of March 6. Not that Model was worried. The Field Marshal was not one to worry. His glacial reserve and tough professional competence were his insulation, along with what was expected of him by direct orders.

But he could be concerned, a more localized condition of mind than worry, and the Feldmarschall felt some concern about his front west of the Rhine as March 6 began to develop into a new day.

He had been awakened by a call from Keitel at OKW headquarters in Berlin. Evidently the Führer had been holding one of those late staff conferences. Keitel sounded irascible as he asked for the situation on Model's front.

"It is fluid," said Model.

That was quite a word and both he and Keitel knew it. What it conveyed was that the situation was unfavorable and OKW had better be prepared for big American gains. But it was a safe word to transmit to the Führer.

"The Führer has directed me to tell you that there is to be no withdrawal. He had Westphal here tonight."

Model heard that with interest. Westphal was Von Rundstedt's Chief of Staff and it was no secret that old Von Rundstedt did not think much of the Westwall defenses nor did he think they could be successfully held.

"The Führer told Westphal that there was to be no withdrawal," Keitel went on in his drillmaster's voice. "The Führer says the Americans are quaking before the Westwall. All German troops to hold their ground. That is the order from the Führer."

"Heil Hitler," said Model, as the call from Berlin was terminated.

Before he went back to bed he spent a few minutes reviewing the latest report from his Operations officer. The commander of the 53rd Corps had been captured by the Americans. He would have to get someone down there right away. It had better be Botsch. True, he had only recently assigned to Botsch the responsibility for those two bridgeheads, the important Hohenzollern Bridge at Bonn, and that other one, the railroad bridge, the Ludendorff, at Remagen. But Botsch was a good combat commander, and if the Führer insisted on holding the present front, the situation near Coblenz had to be patched in a hurry. Von Bothmar could take over the defense of Bonn, and as for Remagen, that was not important in the present situation.

Model made a note of that decision and then glanced at the situation in the center of the front. Americans were threatening Cologne and also the town of Euskirchen had been captured. Euskirchen—there was that drive on Bonn he had predicted. There was the place he had to watch, that Cologne-Bonn area. The American main effort would be clearly discernible now.

He bent musing over his maps. Out of those stand or die orders some holes were likely to develop in Von Zangen's line. His problem was to see that those holes were plugged by bits and pieces. But he did not question the Führer's orders. Those orders had been established and reaffirmed. The Führer told Keitel and Keitel told him and he told Von Zangen and Von Zangen told his Corps commanders. The army and the people had to become used to those orders. War was a matter of complete discipline. It was a blind and complex machine and all that mattered was that each of the parts performed as directed. Parts could be replaced or patched up or thrown away, but they never had any choice as to their function. Von Zangen was to hold west of the Rhine. That was the final, irrevocable yardstick of responsibility.

At the same time, Model, reviewing the situation map with his steady professional's eyes, knew that the Westwall was becoming dead bark. It would be necessary to cut away that crumbling layer to see down to the green and alive—the battle for the Rhine. That was the real front. As long as there was a Rhine front, there was a chance to stabilize; there was a chance to get the new jets into the air; there was a chance for Herr Goebbels to work his way with the people; there was a chance to keep the iron collar of discipline and unquestioning obedience yoked about the army and the nation; there was a chance that the Anglo-Americans would negotiate.

Model surveyed the river line on his big operational map. All bridges had been readied for demolition and might have to be blown soon, if the situation remained fluid. No problem there. But the Westwall needed stiffening, and when he went to bed that night he was concerned about Coblenz where armored troops of that reckless devil, Patton, were chewing up the 53rd Corps, and Cologne and Bonn where the Americans would be hammering hard. Von Zangen would have to counterattack to wipe out those penetrations. He would issue immediate orders to that effect.

Yes, the Field Marshal was concerned, but he was not worried. Because he would, of course, pass along the Führer's orders, which was what was expected of him, but the real front was the Rhine and he knew it and no threat existed there on any map in his headquarters.

The Americans still had their Armageddon ahead of them. They had the Rhine ahead of them.

At first Doke Stanton thought she had been shot, even though he was sure that sound had been the front door closing. She had gone down all of a heap like a plant struck down by a scythe. Swiftly he gathered her up and carried her into the plain little bedroom at the head of the stairs. She was absurdly light in his arms, not the lightness of a wisp, but a gossamer quality of lithe balance.

As he laid her down on the bed, he caught a glimpse of her foot and drew his breath sharply. It was swollen and seemed turned sideways slightly as if unhinged. There was something about that foot that bespoke complete and utter agony, as of something delicate that had been shattered. How she could ever have stood on it, let alone to have made her way out of the room as far as the stairs, he could not comprehend, but suddenly he remembered the single scream she had given, and that agonized cry could have been as much from her realization that she would never walk again with that foot, as from the pain of it. Good Lord, thought Doke Stanton. What a thing to happen to her. Before, that limp had been something that had clipped, but could not destroy, a poised and natural grace in the way she carried herself. There had been, he could realize now, a sense of living with her disability, of even somehow a quiet dignity because of it. But now the chances were she was really crippled.

He rubbed one of her hands gently as she lay back on her pillow breathing slowly, her lashes like shadowy crescents. Again he glanced back at her foot. Something had to be done for her. There had to be some way of getting help. That elderly woman servant, that Martha—where was she?

"Please," he heard the girl's low voice, "do not look at it. Please."

Her eyes were open and resting on him. "Does it pain you very much?" he asked.

Her head moved slightly on the pillow. "I can bear it," she said simply. "There are other things. Just do not look at it. Just do not think of it."

"But a doctor—" he said. "Can you not call a doctor? Is there a phone?"

"No," said the girl. "It has been some time."

"Martha—?"

"I think," the girl said somberly, "Martha has probably fled. This will have been too much for her. But she has always lived here. She will come back. If she doesn't—what difference will it make? The SS make it all very unimportant."

"The SS," muttered Doke. "Yeah." He felt sick enough as it was.

She looked at him through half-lowered lashes. "They will be back, I'm afraid, Private Stanton. Never will they suffer a thing like this. Captain Langbach is quite dead." She shifted her body slightly and in the process gently freed her hand. "I thought that he might have come here with his squad. But we were lucky. He came here with his driver only."

She clasped her fingers together and there was a sudden flitting expression of pain in her face. Then she relaxed again, but her breath came quickly for a few moments. "I do not believe he really thought an American soldier was hidden here," she resumed. "Perhaps William may have talked—but William is an old man and a bit cloudy in his mind and everyone knows how afraid he has been of the Americans. No," she said reflectively, "I think Langbach would have come here anyhow, Private Stanton. I was on his list and his days were ending. I was among his—his unfinished business. But the rumor of an American here gave him his chance to bully me. To have his sport."

She flushed slightly, then, and wrinkled her forehead in distaste. "You see," she said, trying to explain, "he has contempt for the weak, quiet ones, as he calls me, and so when he finds he is at a disadvantage, he loses control of himself. So when his bullying failed—he stomped on my foot—and I screamed, because I could not truly help it, Private Stanton. I could think of nothing else than the pain and how much I had lost in my life. But he must have heard someone coming—and to his amazement it was—an American—"

"I heard your scream," said Doke Stanton. "And—" Then he fell silent. It was hard enough to talk, even when he knew what he wanted to say.

"Thank you for coming," said the girl gravely. "But we both might have ended up at SS headquarters. What a grand climax for Captain Langbach. But I do thank you, Private Stanton."

She contemplated him at length. "You have been badly hurt," she said. She reached up a tentative hand and again he felt that cool healing touch of her fingers.

He tried to grin with his swollen lip. "It's not much—" He was going to say it was not much compared with what had happened to her, but he left it unsaid.

"That driver of his," said the girl suddenly. "I told him that I had shot Captain Langbach while resisting him. And when he stood there thinking it over, I told him he had better look quickly to Captain Langbach. Even though—Langbach was dead—but he did not think of that. He carried him out on his shoulder. But the SS will not leave it so easily—Colonel Blum will not permit such a thing—"

Doke nodded numbly. Her quick thinking had gained some time. But the reckoning must come. An SS officer had been killed.

"Listen to me, please, Private Stanton," she said. "I do not know what Blum will do when he comes. But if you are found here, there will be a terrible vengeance for Langbach. You know that, Private Stanton."

"What will happen to you?" he asked.

She tried to smile. "If I was unfinished business for Captain Langbach," she said, her voice trembling a little, "I will be unfinished business for the SS."

She came up on an elbow and again her voice was quick, low, and urgent, as it had been when he first heard it through his hysteria. "I do not care about myself, Private Stanton. I am a finished thing. Look, how I talk to you now as an ally. But we are not allies. I am a German. I am a loyal German."

She fell back against her pillow, breathing as though she had been running hard and had dropped down to catch her breath. This time he tried to get through to her.

"Ilse," he said, and even at that moment was conscious that he had used her name, even though he had not realized he knew what her name was. "You never felt the SS was Germany."

"It is too easy," the girl said. "You know that. All of us will be held responsible for the SS. All of us Germans. Can we say we never felt that the SS was Germany and would that be accepted? You would not accept it. Too easy," she repeated. "Too easy. I hate this feeling of disloyalty."

"You proved that you did not think the SS was Germany," he tried to tell her. "You proved it."

"Please," she said again. "I feel far away from everything. Let me think, Private Stanton. I do not know how much time I have and I must think it out. Once," she whispered, "it was never to dance again. Now it is never to walk again. A cripple and a traitor. Am I that? Please—let me think, Private Stanton."

He stood at the foot of the bed, the machine pistol in one hand, and carefully did not look at that twisted swollen foot. A sensitive, finely tuned consciousness was hideous with dissonance and some protective barrier that had guarded her inward peace was smashed. It was strange how clearly he could sense that. There was not a thing he could do for her.

"I will be near," he said, and left the room. He made his way slowly downstairs, still carrying the machine pistol that had killed Langbach. He was nearly dizzy with the pain in his jaw and inside his mouth, but his knees were steady. He could be scared now without the terrible bodily weakness that used to overcome him as though some diabolic chemistry began to brew in his vitals. He could think. He felt like someone who had emerged from a long drunk.

In the little room off the hall where he had been locked up, he took a look at himself in the small shaving mirror she had provided him. The visage horrified him. There was a spreading blue-black bruise on one side of his face and his lower lip was swollen and there were bruises at his throat. His mouth and chin were caked with blood. He washed himself at the basin of water, rinsed out his mouth, bathed his bruised lip. Then he picked up the Schmeisser and returned to the hall. He stood there in the pallid glow of light from the upstairs lamp, listening in the deep quiet of the dank stone confines all about him.

Although he could not explain it, there was a quality to the silence that made him think of the river out there below the town, black water swirling thickly past a long steel bridge. He glanced toward the head of the stairs, again listening. All of a sudden it would come, he thought; the screech of tires outside, the heavy click of boot heels, and the crashing summons at the door. Night things. Like Langbach. Night things in battle dress. His hand tightened around the weapon. Then he looked around for a place to keep his watch.

He found it in an alcove under the stairs where there was a small room that still smelled of coats and rubbers. He sat down against the wall, the machine pistol between his knees. How many would come? A whole damned squad, probably.

As time passed, he found himself becoming gradually drowsy from sheer fatigue and jerked himself awake to listen hard in the quiet of the castle. But finally he awoke to find it was daylight and he realized that he must have slept for hours. He pulled himself to his feet and hurried upstairs, all drowsiness gone instantly. The night prowlers could not have come without awakening him, he was sure, but there was no telling what had become of that girl.

On the threshold of her room he stopped, startled. She was up, sitting in a chair, and hovering over her was the elderly Martha. The old servant shrank away as she saw him. The girl spoke to her quietly and finally the old woman plucked up the courage to sidle toward the door. He stood back to let her pass and she still shrank from him until finally she had worked past him and scurried out to the stairs. She was the first person to be afraid of him that Doke Stanton remembered.

He went into the room and stood beside the girl's chair. Her foot had been bound closely with strips of fresh white cloth and looked far less horrifying, but he knew that she must have had it bound tightly against the pain.

"Ilse," he said, again trying out the name, "they didn't come."

"No," she agreed. "Not yet."

He was struck by the way she looked this morning. Her hair, which she had always worn tightly braided around her head, had been brushed clear and fell free past her shoulders in a thick ash-blond mane that curled slightly at the ends with an appealing sense of resilient life. Her cheeks were wet and so were her lashes. As she sat back in her chair, propped by pillows, a light shawl across her knees, he had again that odd and compelling instinct to put an arm around her. She made him think of some priceless little domestic interlude, as if he had found the faceless, nameless girl he had always thought to marry looking like this, and he wanted to move close to her to comfort her against something, anything.

"Martha returned," she said. "William is staying away. But Martha is lost away from here. She has helped me so much—no matter what she may feel." She sighed. "I am sure she does not feel the same toward me."

"I can see," he said, still studying her, "that it has been—difficult." He had to ask it. "Did you think it out, Ilse?"

She tightened her fingers together. "People have a right to resist brutality."

He put the weapon carefully on the floor and sat down on the edge of the narrow little bed. "We can be allies?" he asked.

"No, we cannot be allies, Private Stanton. When they come for me, you are not to try to prevent it. I will not have you shooting Germans because of me. You have a right to protect yourself, but not me."

"But," he said helplessly, "doesn't it go together?"

"You must stay out of sight. If they should search for you, then you have a right to protect yourself. But I think they will be interested only in me. I doubt if they really believe an American is hiding here. Langbach did not really believe it, except that he could convince himself of anything that would serve his purpose. No," she said, looking at him seriously, "you must promise you will not try to interfere."

"You said we had a right to resist brutality."

"Yes," she said. "But now an SS officer has been killed. These people have a right to investigate that and I will not see Germans shot," she repeated, "because of me."

"You forget one thing," said Doke Stanton. "I've captured this place and, if I want to hold it, I can damn well try."

She stared at him. "You've what, Private Stanton?"

"I've captured it," said Doke. He knew it sounded foolish, but he had to try to change her perspective.

She contemplated him speechlessly another long moment, then leaned her head back against the pillow and smiled faintly. "I think," she said, "that is really an amazing viewpoint."

It certainly was. It was like a child trying on his father's trousers. It was foolish, pathetic, and ridiculous. Sure, say anything. Whistle for a wind.

"Let's just wait," he said tensely. "Maybe they won't come."

"Yes, of course," she assented readily. "Let us do that."

They were interrupted by Martha returning with a tray of food. She set it down on the girl's knees and then waddled hastily from the room. Doke slowly sipped at a cup of hot bitter brew that might have been coffee and that stung his mouth. The girl did not touch the food. She simply sat quietly in her chair, her hands clasped on the shawl over her lap, and looked out the window pensively.

"But really you are right," she said then. "The only way we can sit here like this is to expect they will not come, Private Stanton."

"Why don't you call me Doke?" he heard himself say suddenly.

Her glance moved to him. "Doke?" she said questioningly. "Why should I call you Doke? What is that?"

"Well," he said, somewhat embarrassed at his impulse, "It's my nickname."

"Your childhood name? Doke?"

"My mother used to call me that when I was little," he explained. "And then everybody started to call me that. I never liked it," he said, "except when my mother used it. But I'd like you to use it, too."

"Doke," she repeated.

"It's a silly name. My real name is Douglas Kendall, but my mother rigged Doke out of it. When I was very little," he finished aimlessly.

"I can see your mother calling a little boy Doke," she said. "I can see it very clearly." Her discerning glance swept him thoughtfully. "You had lovely times in childhood?"

"No, not very. I spent most of my childhood at Army posts. My father and mother did not get along. I don't think those times were lovely exactly."

"But you had a happy life in America?"

"It could have been better, but I was happy enough. I sure wish I had it now."

"Many people must be thinking of you."

He shook his head. "I don't have much family. And I'm not married. I know a lot of people, but they don't do any extra special thinking of me."

"You are a writer, Doke? I think you said."

"I was trying to be a writer. But I don't think I would ever have been a really good writer. I always lost too much of what I was trying to say."

"When you know what you want to say, that will not happen."

He was struck by that thought because of its very simplification. It made him think that perhaps he still had a chance, that he might yet be able to write the kind of thing he liked, that it was a matter of growing up to it and that he would find, miraculously, the missing ingredient he needed.

"If I live long enough," he muttered, and felt again the short odds of it all. He had been wandering in his mind.

She started to say something and then changed her mind and they were both silent. There was a faraway drone of planes, American bombers, most likely, winging deep into the Reich, and from below the castle, somewhere in the town, there was the sound of steady hammering that for some reason made him think of the building of a scaffold. He became uneasy again, as though a brief hypodermic had worn off. Her quiet poise had made this seem like the stage of a picnic when you just sat back and chatted and relaxed. Only there was no threat of an SS squad around a picnic. He stood up near the window. She seemed preoccupied with something out there. By God, that bridge down there, probably. It reminded him.

"Why did you unlock the door, Ilse? Why did you say I was my own jailer?"

"Please, does it make some difference now?"

"Yes," said Doke. "It makes some difference."

"It is not easy. Perhaps it was that you seemed so blind, so selfish, so thoughtless."

"But why?" he insisted. "It was something I said about that bridge out there, wasn't it? I wished they would go ahead and blow it up? If the Americans are ever to get here, they'll have to blow it up. Why shouldn't I wish that?"

"Please," said the girl again. She almost whispered it. "I cannot talk about it, I cannot."

He stared down at her, baffled. There was something from which she barred him. Her mind ran deep and somewhere in its depths was an answer that intrigued him, but it was not for him. Maybe neither of them were in their right minds, but it looked as if that long slender railroad bridge over the Rhine was some kind of key to this suffering girl.

"Please call Martha," she said in a low voice. "I must have help now in loosening this bandage. My foot is numbed. I must not have it too tight for too long. There is a push bell in the wall—near the stairs—"

He moved instantly to comply. He found the bell, set in the wall near the head of the stairs, gave it a long push, and returned to the room.

"Ilse," he said, "can't you send for a doctor?"

"Not now," she said. "Later, perhaps."

"Am I the reason?"

"Please do not think of it that way. There are many difficulties about obtaining a doctor at a time like this. And Martha will talk, if she leaves here. She could be arrested herself. Believe me, it is better to wait. And also," she said in her soft, thoughtful way, "it is not important to the SS that I can walk. There remains that."

Yes, there remained that. He left her as Martha came ponderously up the stairs. There was something unnerving in the fright of the elderly woman when she saw him. With the machine pistol under his arm, he made a restless prowling scout through the little castle with its chill stone walls and somber dark woodwork, its rooms of sheeted furniture behind drawn blinds, its empty dim halls.

He located a place that had a good field of fire on the head of the stairs, the door of a turret room at one end of the upstairs hall. There was a heavy oaken door, and if he kept it ajar for a firing niche, he could cover the head of the stairs, while presenting an almost impossible angle for return fire. It was a good position and he thought that a tough Joe with ice water in his veins could really keep anyone clear of the girl's room for as long as he could see to shoot and had enough clips. His hands began to tremble at the prospect of his trying it. He had only one clip and Ilse did not want anything like this, but he had to set it up; he had to have a plan. It would do no good; eventually he would be squashed like a bug and everything would be all the worse for her. You could not be a realist, though. No, you could not. You had to resist. As inexorable as a compass bearing; you had to resist. Maybe Ellison could have figured it some other way. Men like Ellison acted with instinct. Other men were psychos and nothing was sure or instinctive to them. Men like Ellison should live forever; blot up some of the excess fear that other men could not handle.

Finally he stopped at one of the leaded windows in the main hall and drew aside the blackout curtain. For a long time he studied the bridge. There was slow steady traffic moving across it now, he could discern. Looked like some guns being pulled by horses and some motor vehicles that might have been ambulances and staff cars. But still no sign of long lines of snub-helmeted Krauts in their drab battle gray retreating across the Rhine. Still no sign that the GIs were anywhere near. There was only this steady ooze of traffic to the east to testify that the GIs might be making some headway.

He rubbed a hand absently along the barrel of the German weapon under his arm. Strange to think of the girl upstairs being keyed in somehow with that bridge over the Rhine. It was strange, too, to stand here thinking about it when a squad of SS troops could arrive any time and make the whole question unimportant.

And yet, as he looked down at the slender bridge below the town, with its towers and piers and graceful spans, he felt that, whether he ever knew or not, it was important.

11.

A TRUCK came roaring into the courtyard of the castle and braked to a screeching halt that nearly spun it around. It was a drab truck, its camouflage color of olive with wavy black streaks weathered and faded. Three helmeted soldiers leaped down to the courtyard, rifles slung across their backs, and ran to investigate the heap of petrol tins by the shed at the side of the courtyard. They kicked the pile apart, picked up one here and there, shook them, threw them aside with a clatter, kicked among them again with their heavy boots, and then ran back to the truck and leaped aboard. The truck swung around with another screeching of tires and sped on out through the gate posts.

Doke Stanton saw it go, standing at a window of the turret room. He saw it go, incredulously, and leaned heavily on the sill, his head bent, and his knees weak with the flood of relief that swept over him. Sixty seconds—in and out—and in sixty seconds it had been doom and salvation so close that his nervous system was left jangling like a stuck motor horn. It could have been the SS. He had felt sure it was the SS. But it had been an army truck apparently scouring the town for petrol. Sixty seconds in which his body had been frozen, then released in prickles of sweat. He swept the back of his hand across his forehead and took a long breath. Then he left the turret window and made his way down the hall to the girl's room.

When he had looked in on her before, she had been asleep and he had known that was the greatest mercy she could receive. But now she was awake, propped up in the chair, her injured foot, again tightly bandaged, resting on a small wooden box that Martha had evidently found for her.

He told her about the truck. Ilse Margraven nodded. "I know how hard that must have been for you," she said. "Please relax. Put down that weapon, Doke. You carry it as though it were part of you."

"They could come any minute," he said vaguely.

"Doke, we are hoping they will not come. Don't you remember?"

"But that's foolish," he said restlessly.

"They haven't come. It isn't foolish so far."

"But why wouldn't they come?" he insisted. "They're bound to come."

"You make so many rules, Doke. The SS is bound to come. The bridge is bound to be destroyed—" She stopped suddenly then, as though some thought had broken away from her involuntarily. She leaned her head back against her pillow and closed her eyes.

He regarded her attentively and rested the machine pistol carefully against the wall. Then he sat down on the edge of the bed and rested his hands on his knees.

"You don't think the bridge is bound to be destroyed?" he asked.

"Not bound to be," she said. "No."

"Well, of course," Doke assented, "if the Americans don't get through. But I think they will."

"Oh, I think so too, Doke."

"Then—" Doke began. He felt as though he were trying to discuss something with a child, but he realized it was not as with a child, but with something childlike in her thinking, something that was none of his business and perhaps of no other person alive. He sat there and said nothing.

"Doke," he heard her say, "if I thought it would help you, I would tell you what I mean." She hesitated, not looking at him, but at the window that overhung the roofs of the town.

"Anything would help me," said Doke. He laughed shortly. "Anything would help a psychoneurotic who's reached the end of his rope."

"A what?" she questioned. "That I do not understand."

"Psychoneurotic. It's hard to explain. It's just somebody not geared mentally for what other guys have to face." His mouth twisted. "It's like an alcoholic. Only with fear instead of liquor." Then he fell silent. It was perfectly true, but he had gone too far. The emptiness within him could at least have held a little pride. Like the pride at that U.K. hospital. Yes, like that.

The girl seemed to be considering both him and his words. "Why," she said finally, "do you think no one else must overcome something? All of us have to face down some kind of lie about our true being." She looked out toward the window again. "I lived in a dream world, Doke, and only gradually did it seem to become the reality. Now I think it is the reality."

She hesitated again and he thought of some swift wild bird skimming down over a lake, unwilling to trust completely to the strange waters, delaying, ready to wing up and fast.

"You see," she went on then, "I was trying to be a dancer. I had been studying for years. My mother was teaching me and she was really lovely, Doke. And I do not know whether I would ever have been as fine as she, but I was content with the poetry of it, the feeling of it, the expression. Then I had such a foolish accident. Oh, such a foolish accident. And gradually I came to realize I would have a limp instead of a dream."

He could understand her better now, swiftly, in that one revealing moment, the compelling grace and effortless control that shone through the badgering limp, the flashes of spontaneous feeling and decisive expression, the quick veil of reserve that hid her away quickly and completely.

"I spent some bitter days, because the accident was so foolish, you see," she explained. "My mother sent me to England to stay with my grandmother quite often during the next few years, because I always was so content there. But nothing ever happened for me. I mean," she said, feeling her way. "I could find nothing to do in life. And then finally I had to return to Germany. There was something I must find to do."

She made a brief indefinite gesture of her hand. "Here there was Strength through Joy and martial Mädchen organizations and I shrank from these. Finally I became a governess to the children of the Count von Rimburg." She smiled. "Wolfgang, Theodore, and Sophia," she said, reminiscently. "I had to work hard, you understand, because it is difficult for a person with a disability to take part in games with three lively growing children. I used to cry often, at night, by myself. But drawing I could teach, and music, and I learned to row and to swim and I learned patience and it went well enough. It went well enough," she repeated, thinking about it. "And my home was close by, at Stadt-Meckenheim, so that I could often watch the pupils at my mother's dancing school and listen to my father's choral groups."

Doke Stanton thought that she spoke of her life with the same detachment as he felt about his own, a remoteness, as of something gone and finished, to be viewed the way you looked at the moon.

"The war, of course, was terrible," Ilse Margraven went on. "It was as though Germany was removing itself from the world my family and I knew and loved. But I did not know how terrible it could be until my father was summoned to Berlin. For questioning and consultation, it was called. And yet he seemed to know it was serious and so did my mother. I do not know why they should have felt he was unreliable. True, he never was a party member and his family was of the Social Democrat tradition, but he was devoted to Germany. I think," she said, considering, "that he must have refused them something. I do not know, but I believe it must have had to do with his wife's English connections. I do not know, but I think this may have been so. But he was judged politically unreliable and that meant Augswien."

"Augswien?" said Doke. The way she had said the word, it sounded like limbo.

"It is a concentration camp, Augswien," the girl said. "For those to be politically rehabilitated." Her voice shook slightly. "I used to wonder what it was like. We did not know for some time that he was there. But when we were informed, my mother left here to live as close to Augswien as she could. She followed him. She crossed that bridge to take the Frankfurt train. I went with her as far as the bridge and said good-by to her there." Again she made that indefinite movement of her hand, like brushing aside a cobweb.

"For a time I heard from her. She lived a few miles from the Augswien camp and she had not yet seen him, but she had arranged so that he knew she was there. But as time went on I heard less often. Six months ago the Count decided to remove his family to Bavaria. I could have gone with them. But I could not bring myself to cross that bridge. I could not bear to go over that river into what seemed to me would be the terrible inferno of defeat and punishment and chaos. I shrank from it, as though it were actually a fire. Instead, I offered to stay here and look after his property, with his old servants, until the Rimburg family returned. So I said good-by a second time at the bridge."

She rested her head back and he thought that she might have exhausted herself not physically, but with the sheer effort of recalling a period in her life of mental struggle with ghosts and fears.

But she apparently wanted to go on. For the space of a few seconds she made tentative futile efforts to move the position of her bandaged foot.

"Can't I help you?" he said. "Is it very bad?"

"Martha and I have arranged a time system," she returned. "It is no worse."

But the reminder of that serious hurt seemed to have broken a spell during which he had ceased to listen for sounds, when he had not imagined the coming of a car, the slam of doors, the footsteps, the crashing climax of a sharp banging on the front door. Now he was conscious of that again. Doke stood up and took a few steps toward the hall. They could come in without warning, they could appear in this room as Langbach had done, they could suddenly be here with the heart-stopping impact of their presence, their guns, their merciless faces—

"Doke," said the girl in a low voice, "live in the present minute. Believe me, it is the only way."

"I get the feeling," he said, staring out into the hall, "that time is running out for us."

"It is running out for the SS too." She gave a little sigh. "If you only knew how I have needed someone to talk to."

He turned, struck by the remark. "You, too, Ilse?" he said. He returned to her side and sat down on the floor near his weapon. "All right," he said quietly. "There's nothing more important. What is it, Ilse?"

"You must not think that I am out of my mind," she said. "Although, perhaps, that can happen without our realizing it. I built a new world around a bridge, that bridge out there, and I lived in it."

He looked up at her attentively. Was she going to tell him that? Abruptly he could remember all she had said and out of it all was forming the picture of a bridge, a long bridge across the Rhine, taking form like something coming out of a mist.

"I should have joined my mother near Augswien," Ilse Margraven said in her grave, introspective way. "But I did not dare. To me the bridge had become a connecting link with the outside world, for the world of the west ends at the Rhine, and beyond is the heart of the barbarism, the paganism, the medieval torture rack for my whole country. Whenever I thought of the coming defeat, I saw that bridge destroyed and Germany sealed off by a river into a beleaguered citadel that gradually became a funeral pyre. There was no connection with the rest of the world. There was no connection with humanity, help, friendship. There was no connection with the legendary and magical Americans. That is what the destruction of that bridge meant to me."

Doke Stanton started to speak, then checked himself, for

this was not the time to interrupt her. He had never before in his life glimpsed so clearly the attack of fear in another mind.

"Gradually," she went on, "I tried to see the bridge, as I wanted it to be. To me there is nothing greater than a bridge. It is a link. It means continuity. And therefore it is indestructible." She paused. "Have you ever thought of that?"

"Ilse," he said gently, "nothing is indestructible. Nothing is going to last forever. No bridge can do that."

"The concept can last forever, Doke. There is always a bridge. There must always be a bridge. That was my dream world. It was my refuge. I looked at that bridge out there as the concept of continuity. To me it stood for my country's imperishable link with the world of America. And so a bridge becomes a great manifestation of a spiritual fact. There is no end. There is no defeat. There is no void. There is always a bridge."

Doke swept a hand slowly over his hair. She had spoken simply and unemotionally, reviewing something aloud that she had always voiced only mentally before, talked about it as though the words might tear its fabric, testing it the way you would hold something to the light to test its texture and strength.

He was afraid that she had finished and he hoped she had not, because he had come to respect her thinking, but this was a lot for him to take all at once.

"That bridge," Ilse Margraven said, "became a great friend of mine. I used to watch it often. I have seen it at many different times of day. I do not look at it as a structure of iron and steel and stone, but the symbol of a great truth. Do you remember what an English writer says—I do not remember his name—but he says something about 'Man's puzzling station in eternity between the birthless Past and the Future that has no end.' Man's puzzling station must be at the approach to a bridge."

She turned toward him and her wide, delicately modeled mouth curved into a smile. "Perhaps you do not agree, Doke?"

"Just that I do not understand," he said.

If she was disappointed, she did not show it. "I will always be glad I spoke it aloud. It is very kind of you to listen."

"I would rather listen to you than anyone else I've ever met," said Doke Stanton, and found that he meant exactly that. It was strange how true some thoughts became when they were spoken aloud.

"Thank you," the girl said. "You are nice to talk to, Doke."

It should have been late, on a Sunday evening in his Connecticut home, after the eleven o'clock news, with a fire expiring slowly and gracefully and in showers of crackling sparks in the open fireplace, two persons alone together—it had that feeling. It would have been wonderfully right that way.

"It is difficult, though," Ilse Margraven said seriously, "to try to establish the reality of a person's world. For example, I know perfectly well that my people must destroy that bridge. I would not do anything to prevent it, even if I had the power, because I would do nothing against my country. And besides," she added, considering, "a truth or principle is not at the mercy of a human being.

"I really prefer my own dream world to the real and the actual. Yet is this the true, Doke, this cold, this darkness, this knowledge that the bridge is doomed and nothing can stop its destruction?"

"I wish, Ilse, I could say no," Doke Stanton said gently.

"Oh, that is quite all right, Doke. My beliefs would be no good if I cared whether anyone else disagreed with them. I simply say that I have come to believe that the dream world I built up around myself is truly the actual. That bridge represents an indestructible spiritual idea."

"Well," he began, then stopped.

"I believe," she repeated. "But I can't know it. That's a difference. If it is destroyed, I shall still believe in my spiritual concept of a bridge. There always is a bridge. We are never cut off. We are never ended. I will believe that. I just would wish that we could be given a renewal of faith in this world once in a while. I just wish that we could know—a little—"

She was silent, studying the window, with her hands clasped quietly in her lap. She had permitted Doke Stanton a glimpse of the thinking behind the thickly lashed cool blue eyes and it ran deep and quiet and strong, as he had expected. But the realities were that it was cold and she had been crippled and both were in a desperate situation. The realities were that the bridge out there was doomed and if the Americans kept coming nothing could prevent the Germans from efficiently and methodically blowing it sky high.

"I'm sorry," he said suddenly, "that I told you I wished the bridge would be blown up. I don't wish that at all. I wish we could capture it. But that isn't the same, is it?"

"Doke, if that bridge were not destroyed, your people

would certainly seem to have an excellent chance of capturing it."

"But you don't want that."

"It would be best for Germany, but my people must do what they have to do."

"Then I can't figure it, Ilse." He felt confronted with an abstruse mathematical problem.

"We're human beings. We get ourselves in the way. We outline what we want or what we expect. A truth exists independent of us or what we like or don't like. I would believe in my concept of a bridge whether this was a time of war or peace, whether the Americans were six thousand miles away or as close as Stadt-Meckenheim, whether every one, every last bridge on the Rhine, were destroyed tonight. You could not destroy the truth of mathematics by throwing every textbook into a furnace. You could not destroy the truth of man's continuity and progress by destroying every structure you could find on every river in the world."

"Yes," admitted Doke, "I see that. The material symbol does not limit the truth it represents."

"It goes beyond symbols," she corrected him. "It's a spiritual truth made manifest in human terms. Nearly always we have to take it on faith, but every once in a while it happens —every once in a while—"

He looked at her carefully, because there was a note in her voice that hinted she might be at the end of her endurance. But after a moment she spoke again.

"I've stayed on in this dismal place, because I've lacked courage. The final reckoning for a country is going to take place over there beyond that river. My place is with my mother and my country. I have thought that if I only could go over there with some real hope . . . but my dream world had not become real enough to me. Now I could not go, if I wanted to do so. I shall always be sorry."

She stirred restively against the pillow that propped her in the chair. "I shall always love that bridge down there. It's like so many of the people in the world, obscure, unimportant, overlooked, yet doing its work, ready to serve, filling a function. If I should look out the window and see it destroyed, I will feel as though I had lost a—beloved—friend. But"—she seemed to be breathing with some difficulty—"I shall—know—there is always—a—bridge. Please—call—Martha—"

He immediately pressed the bell for Martha, then hastened back to her. Ilse Margraven had fainted. Doke swiftly began to get the tight wrapping off her foot. His fingers fumbled in his haste and he cursed wildly as he searched for the intricate fold of the bandaging. Finally he had the cloth strips loosened and practically tore them away. Martha hurried into the room and elbowed him aside, kneeling and holding the girl's foot to her capacious bosom, working with quickly kneading fingers. Doke Stanton watched a moment, the perspiration breaking out on his forehead. Then he turned away and walked blindly from the room. That fainting had been a merciful thing.

At his lookout position in the tower window he crouched close to the sill and rested his chin on his folded arms. He could see the courtyard and the gate to the drive and the blurry greenish-brown tops of the nearby woods. It was raining again, lightly, enough so that the paving of the courtyard took on a wet gray sheen. He could not see the bridge, but he had it so clearly in mind that it was there before him. It meant everything to her and there was a strong pull to her simple straightforward belief in the ranging scope of meaning in a bridge. A person could believe what she chose and what she had evolved in her thinking undoubtedly sprang from the kind of life she had led, but there was a pull. He mused over it, looking down at the wet pavement of the courtyard. There is always a bridge. He moved the simple statement around in his mind, as if turning a gem to the light. There were facets he tried to catch. There was something about this he would like to understand.

It had been a long time since he had believed in anything very much. This war? He believed in victory so he could go home. God? Well, he would like to believe in a deity and he certainly called on Him enough, but that was because everyone needed to believe in a protecting strength beyond himself. You needed something for your morale but you actually didn't have a reason, he supposed. On the other hand, it was so easy to believe in pain, and the blow of a fist, and the comfort of a bed, and the feel of thirst and hunger, and the response of a thoroughly aroused girl. You did not need to take those things on faith. They were damn well there and yet a girl, whose life had been marred by what she called a foolish accident and now probably ruined by the brutal stomp of an SS officer, built a whole world around herself based on that unimportant and obscure and doomed bridge out there on the Rhine.

He found himself trying to remember how long he had

known her. He had been captured, he thought, on March 2. He had first seen her the following day. This must be March 6. Around three days, was it? He had known her three days? It did not seem possible that he could have come to know her so well in three days and yet, even as he mused on that, he felt that there was something about her that would keep one on a questing study for a lifetime.

Suddenly he was shocked into immediate alarmed alertness. A car had driven into the courtyard. He came slowly to his feet, his eyes riveted on it, and that familiar racing of his pulse in his throat and his eardrums. It looked like one of those Opel staff cars, with its usual dun and black camouflage paint. This was it, then. The bastards had come at last. They had come when he had become almost lulled by the long day and he might have known they would not forget. They were here.

But only one man stepped out of the car, the driver, a soldier in helmet and overcoat and black belt, but apparently unarmed. He walked quickly to the side entrance of the castle where Langbach had entered last night. A moment later Doke heard the faint jangle of an old-fashioned bell pull. Then, and only then, did he realize he had left the machine pistol in Ilse's room. The sight of her injured foot had driven everything else out of his mind and here he had been crouching, thinking, and all the while completely defenseless.

He went quickly to her room. She had managed to move to the bed and was lying there propped up, with a blanket over her and one arm flung across her eyes. As he entered, she took her arm away quickly. There was a telltale glisten to her pale cheeks.

"Ilse," he said hoarsely, "there's a soldier downstairs." He looked around for the weapon. "Where's that Schmeisser?" he asked urgently. He could not locate it. He could not see it anywhere. "Ilse," he said in a low voice, "what happened to it? Hurry."

Her head moved against the pillow. "No," she said. "I will not have this. It has nothing to do with you."

He began to perspire again and he had to push his words out as though he were trying to talk against a wind. "I'm not going to let you be arrested." The tightness nearly choked him. "You're not going out of here unless it's to a hospital. I'll use a chair. I'll use anything I can find. So help me, I will, Ilse."

She studied him through her lashes. "I could not bear this,

Doke," she said unsteadily. "He must not be shot. He must not be harmed."

He started to speak, then whirled, listening. Someone was mounting the stairs. No, there were two. Martha must be accompanying the soldier. Quickly he turned back to the girl and looked at her for a long moment. Her grave, steady glance did not waver.

"All right," he said heavily. "As you wish."

She smiled, then, and, reaching under her blanket, drew out the Schmeisser. "You will know when to use it, Doke," she whispered, and gestured toward a door standing open at the end of the room. "Hide there. Hurry."

He took the weapon and crossed swiftly to the door that she indicated. It opened into what was a large closet-dressing room and he had barely time to slip inside and pull the door nearly shut before he heard the footsteps in the hall and, a moment later, Martha's voice. Leaning toward the crack in the door, he could see the soldier, standing in the room near the bed. He looked youthful, boyish, something like that homicidal paratroop lieutenant, but this soldier was not armed. He was speaking now and there was no way to tell from his German just what his mission was here. Ilse was replying, her soft voice barely audible. The soldier nodded and then spoke again for a few moments. To Doke Stanton's amazement, he suddenly gave a short little bow and left the room, with Martha waddling along behind. A moment later he heard the girl call softly, "Doke," and he came to her bedside, the Schmeisser still gripped tightly.

"He was Langbach's driver, Doke," she said. "He was here last night."

"Yes?" His voice sounded cracked from the strain of it.

"Please sit down," said the girl, and touched the edge of her bed. "He did not come to arrest me."

"No?" said Doke. He sat down on the edge of the bed. He felt wooden all over.

"He said that SS headquarters displaced last night east of the Rhine. An adjutant is in charge to see the files and equipment packed. Langbach's body was placed in an ambulance and sent across the river." She pushed absently at a heavy lock of ash-blond hair at her forehead. "He is about to leave with the equipment. He has made a report and he does not know what Colonel Blum will do, but he does know that the news of Langbach's death is out and there may be trouble from the Werewolves. He advises me to close all blinds, be sure all doors are locked, and be quiet. It was kind of him," said Ilse. "I think he realized Langbach would end someday as he did."

"These Werewolves," said Doke. "These—"

"They are fanatic young ruffians, most of them. Swept up into some form of auxiliary security service."

"One thing after another," muttered Doke Stanton. "More of the same."

"The SS were the real danger," she told him. "And for the present they are east of the Rhine. Something is happening—Doke, be content for the moment. If the SS displaced, this is now a combat zone. Your Americans have done something."

Martha could be heard moving around the house, shuttering the few windows that remained without drawn blinds. She came into the room and closed the blinds of the girl's window. The room was veiled in semidarkness. Doke sat down on the floor beside the bed and rested his head back. The SS had moved across the river last night and there would still be a reckoning, but they had got through the day. It was enough for the moment. His body ached from the strain.

They had been warned, but when the Werewolves came he was jarred into tension again. It was dark when their voices were heard down in the courtyard. He stole away to peer down through the louvers of the blinds in the tower room. They had brought some torches and it was like the barbaric pageantry of the Nazis to see those flickering flames spurting around running figures, making the night hideous with shuddering red streamers that gave the courtyard a look of being bathed in blood. He could not tell how many were down there, but he could hear their fierce young voices and it maddened him so that he was tempted to seize his Schmeisser and pump the whole clip down into that courtyard. He rejoined the girl, feeling sick with the sight. They could stone a person to death, or burn down houses, or rip priceless paintings. They were like a pack of fierce wild dogs.

Again he sat down on the floor beside her bed, the machine pistol across his knees. They were hurling rocks at the dark, silent castle now. The blunt sounds thudded against the walls or crashed occasionally against some blinds. Suddenly they were pounding at the great front door. It sounded as though they were hammering at it with clubs. He started violently at the sound. The girl's hand stole out to his shoulder.

"Doke," she said somberly, "it is the first sign of utter defeat. They are always the first to give way, this makeshift, without discipline. They should be manning roadblocks and guarding depots and helping transportation. They have started to run. The front is coming apart and these young jackals know it and so they scream and desert and make orgies where they can. But they are cowards. Sit quietly. I promise you."

He listened to that fierce ramming against the front door that was almost like some pagan chant, and reached up to take her hand. He held her slim cold fingers in his and felt their delicate pulsation.

"These things too shall pass," she said.

12.

THERE WAS no meaning of an actual date to Hitzfeld, commanding general of the 67th Corps of the German 15th Army. To him there was nothing of note to the fact that it was the night of March 6, but that it was the night he realized the Americans had shaped a blinding fast break-through was one of the grim and everlasting facts of life to the experienced, steady Corps Commander. He commanded troops that he could scarcely find.

He returned to the Corps CP near Falkenberg and stumbled with sheer fatigue as he stepped out of his mud-splashed car. Along the western rim of the night sky there were jagged flashes in long streaking series, and within earshot of the CP the deadly promise was being harvested in the roaring concussion of fire-hearted explosions following hard on the trail of their swift shrill warning track through the night sky. The night was a pattern of harrowing confusion, choked muddy roads, and scattered units losing all sense of contact and cohesion and the whole meshed with a light cold rain.

General Hitzfeld entered his CP and gave a flickering acknowledgment of the salute of the officers in the Operations Room. He loosened his military overcoat at the collar, laid down his cap, gloves, and stick, and sank into a large carved chair at the head of the table. An orderly set coffee and sandwiches before him and the officers waited for him to finish his light meal, but the General, after toying with a sandwich, suddenly dropped it.

His eyes, shadowed with fatigue, moved from one of his staff officers to the other.

"The Americans," he said, "were expected to attack toward Bonn after they took Euskirchen. Instead they have attacked through Rheinbach. They have knocked a hole in the line. It is the enemy 9th Armored Division. They are near Stadt-Meckenheim. We have no contact with the 74th Corps. There is a huge hole." He made a motion with his hands. "And General von Zangen wants a counterattack. He wants me to counterattack to regain lost ground. Counterattack with what?"

He made a gesture toward his Operations Officer for a map and then bent over it. "Two divisions," he said. "Two weak divisions. The 89th is trying to defend a line nine kilometers long with eight hundred men and thirty-five guns. The 277th has five hundred men and twenty guns spread across five kilometers. And I am ordered to close the hole with a counterattack. Attack across the Ahr valley toward Gelsdorf and seal off this new American drive to the southeast."

He glanced up from the map. "Always it has been Bonn, Bonn, Bonn. The Americans will attack toward Bonn. They are doing nothing of the kind. They are attacking toward Remagen."

The phone rang. The Chief of Staff took the instrument, listened briefly, and then handed it to Hitzfeld. "Army," he said. "General von Zangen."

Hitzfeld bent over the instrument. There was a thump overhead as though a heavy weight had been dropped on the ceiling and the lamp, suspended there, swayed violently. "Hitzfeld here, General," said the Corps Commander, hunching his shoulders and cupping a hand around the mouthpiece. He listened for a long moment. "It's impossible!" he broke out. "General, look at our situation. The 277th Division has just come thirty kilometers and I have not been able to locate the 272nd. I'm supposed to hold my front with one weak division, the 89th, that two divisions have not been able to—"

He paused and listened again. He started to interrupt, then contained himself with an effort. Finally he could stand it no longer. "General von Zangen," he said, speaking slowly and carefully, "there is no reason to this attack toward Gelsdorf. The enemy is attacking through Rheinbach. The fulcrum of our defense is not Gelsdorf, but Remagen. Remagen, General. Remagen."

He waited again. "Very good, General," he said grimly. "I will issue the orders. Yes." He replaced the instrument in its cradle and pushed it away. Then he sat back in his big chair. "The Corps must attack over the Ahr valley toward Gelsdorf. Continuity of the front between the Ahr valley and the right wing of the 89th Division at Münster-Eifel is not to be lost. Army insists on this."

His eyes brooded on the map in front of him. "The old orders stand. The Westwall is not to be lost at any cost. We are to attack the enemy flank with our 277th Division and with the 272nd Division from 76 Corps. The attack is to cross the line Ahrweiller-Kallenborn to Fritzdorf-Gelsdorf. A sector of our front is to be taken over by 66th Corps. The commanding general of 66th Corps is on his way here to arrange for this."

General Hitzfeld bit at his lower lip. Shocking and impossible orders. They sounded even more ludicrous when he spoke them aloud. "We will have as reinforcements a bicycle company of sixty men." His eyes rose to his staff. "Gentlemen, prepare the orders for the counterattack directed by Army. Have them ready in twenty minutes. Major Scheller, stay here, please."

The staff officers departed except for Hitzfeld's aide, the tall young major, Scheller. Major Scheller waited quietly while the General sipped moodily at his cold coffee. He had not been Hitzfeld's aide very long; in fact, he still was recuperating from the wound he had received on the Russian front and, even as he sat here, there was a nagging pain in his shoulder. But, in the time he had served with Hitzfeld, he had come to admire him greatly. Hitzfeld was a fighting general and, when he rebelled at an attack, that attack must indeed be impossible. Scheller wondered why Army did not listen to one of its experienced Corps commanders.

Although he felt that since he had come up from combat to his association with higher command he could understand the orders that had been so incomprehensible at times to the combat officers. The orders were fixed at the top and they came down that way, and, when they were handed on, someone had saved himself from court-martial and his skirts were clean with his superiors. The Westwall must be saved at all costs. What rigidity of command! There was no Westwall. The fast, flexible American attack had finished that. Those orders belonged to a past age. Why not send out men dressed in armor and equipped with crossbows? Continuity of the front, counterattack, no retreat from the Westwall—from the very highest headquarters, those orders, and it was like lighting a funeral pyre from the top. This Corps Commander, moodily drinking cold coffee, now had to issue those impossible orders or else take a court-martial. Major Scheller found one comfort in being an aide. At least, he did not bear any responsibility that might cause him to be shot by a court-martial. There, at least, he was safe.

The Corps Commander spoke suddenly. "What time is it, Scheller?"

"It is 2347 hours, Herr General."

Hitzfeld put his cup down.

"You should get some sleep, Herr General," Scheller ventured.

"Yes," said Hitzfeld. "I should. But there is no time. Scheller, take down some notes. Tomorrow I might be a prisoner of the Americans and I will not leave this unsaid."

Major Scheller flipped open a notebook and took up a pencil. The Corps Commander glanced at his wrist watch, then leaned back, looping an arm over the corner of his chair.

"March 6, 2347 hours, 67th Corps CP at Falkenberg," he dictated. "Memorandum to the Armed Forces Operational Staff. The precepts of German tactics are, of course, familiar with the conception of tenacious delaying action, if the defensive troops are in no relation to the power of the attack. Letting oneself be shot in tenacious defense in order to gain decisions in another place might be reasonable, but one can only be shot once.

"From us a relentless defense on all lines with the same troops has been demanded. Every foot of terrain had to be defended up to the last man. The result was that the forces on the fronts grew thinner and thinner and the gaps between the strongpoints greater. Penetrations into the MLR grew easier and many strongpoints, defending themselves to the utmost, were bypassed and rolled up from the rear. There has not been any defense in depth for a long time."

Hitzfeld struck the table once with his fist. "The Commanding General 67th Corps objects to tenacious resistance as the only possible way of defense. With the fall of Euskirchen the enemy shifted his direction of attack southeasterly, driving a deep hole between 67th and 74th Corps. The Westwall has been lost and cannot be held simply by orders. Now was the time for the High Command to consider possibilities."

He paused and young Major Scheller's pencil flew to catch up.

"The Rhine," Hitzfeld went on, "has acquired even greater significance as a coming defense line. If a continuation of the war, with the view of winning time for bringing it to a bearable end, should still have any meaning, all forces west of the Rhine will have to be saved up for a defense of the Rhine and transferred there in time.

"With the fall of Euskirchen, an enemy attack against Bonn was to be expected, but in attacking south to Rheinbach and Stadt-Meckenheim, it is clearly evident that the enemy is not so interested in Bonn as he is in the whole German 15th Army. He is quite likely to move from Rheinbach to Remagen. Therefore a request was made to cancel a useless counterattack and withdraw all available troops to Remagen in order to organize a new front west of there. The Ludendorff Bridge there is an integral part of the Rhine defense system and must immediately become the fulcrum of our remaining defense west of the Rhine. This request has been refused.

"We are ordered to counterattack the Americans," Hitzfeld went on, speaking very slowly. "Such orders are unrealistic. They may afford a certain measure of relief, that is to say the main point is that one has given the orders and can now expect everything. Whether the orders can be carried out or not matters not one iota. If 66th and 67th Corps are held too long in the Eifel region, we risk dangerous consequences from the new direction of the American attack."

Hitzfeld shrugged. "They surprised us, Scheller," he said in a tired, matter-of-fact way. "The Americans really surprised us. They feinted toward Bonn and then sliced across our front with a diagonal attack that has cut us in two. It is clear now."

The phone rang. Major Scheller reached for it, acknowledged, then handed it to General Hitzfeld. "The Army commander, sir."

"Please God," said Hitzfeld, "he has changed his mind about those orders." He took the instrument quickly. "Hitzfeld here, General," he said.

Major Scheller saw his expression change as he listened. The normally imperturbable Corps Commander seemed literally horrified. He rested an elbow on the table and held the transmitter to his ear as though it weighed a hundred kilos. Major Scheller looked at him anxiously as he muttered a few words into the transmitter, hung up, and leaned back heavily.

"There is bad news, Herr General?" the aide asked quickly.

"What is the time, Scheller?"

"It is 0011 hours, sir."

"At 0011 hours, March 7, I have been notified that I have responsibility for the Ludendroff Bridge at Remagen." General Hitzfeld sounded as though he could not really believe it. "I am sixty kilometers from Remagen. I am to organize a counterattack with a division that I have not yet located. And I have been given responsibility for the Ludendorff Bridge."

He squinted as though he were looking into the sun. "The Ludendorff," he repeated, dazed. "The Ludendorff Bridge. The Hohenzollern was blown at Bonn today. There are no bridges on the Rhine tonight—except the Ludendorff—and I have responsibility."

Major Scheller felt a sudden chill streak up his spine. To sit here west of the Rhine and know there was only one bridge! There were ferry points, of course—but there was just one bridge! The Ludendorff at Remagen!

Hitzfeld looked meditatively at his young aide. Major Hans Scheller. He was a capable young officer, with a fine combat record, and, to the Commanding General of 67th Corps, he was the career-type officer who could have had a brilliant future in other days.

Major Scheller heard his chief speak and the words came slowly, clearly, and incredibly. "I want you to proceed to Remagen and take command of the Ludendorff Bridge."

He had spent the winter at his home near Cologne and if he had been fit for combat he probably would have been returned to a combat command. But the inflammation in his shoulder had swung him into this assignment as aide to Hitzfeld and he had seen the gradual deterioration of the front. However, he had never felt it so graphically as when he drove away from Falkenberg through the misty rain.

The General had sketched his mission succinctly. "Use whatever forces you find at the bridge and whatever other forces you can find and establish as large a defense perimeter as possible. Prepare the bridge for blasting and give the order yourself, if necessary."

That had been the mission. The Corps Commander had added: "Take a radio operator and eight men. The Corps CP will move to Bruck in a few hours. Contact me there."

And there had been a salute and he had climbed into a little staff car with his driver and, trailed by a light truck with his detachment, they had swung off along the muddy road through the wooded Eifel.

It was a night that jabbed and poked and screamed at him, a meshed darkness broken by the rattle of small-arms fire, the glittering flash of artillery, the muffled distant thumps of explosions. There was no pattern to it, no cohension, no knowledge of where the front actually was. The whole night simply seethed brokenly and spasmodically with fragments of combat, like a ship on fire drifting in a current. There were several crackling challenges from sentries at roadblocks. And a haggard officer waved them away from a crossroads.

"You'd never get through. It's clogged with men and vehicles. They're pushing and jamming at each other. Head south, while you've got a chance. I don't care where you're going—get away from here."

They detoured there and they detoured again when they found a giant Mark VI tank slewed around in a road with a whole convoy waiting while troops in undershirts tried to dig out a road around it. The laboring little staff car picked up a side road that was scarcely more than a forest track, and the little caravan slipped along for a few miles until they ran into a village road center that was jammed with a stalled tank detachment waiting for petrol and firing their machine guns from time to time into the night. The Americans were working down through the woods, Scheller was told. He felt that it could not be true, but it tore at his nerves. There was no telling where the Americans were. He had no idea himself. The night seemed to magnify the formlessness of the front. It was breaking up in bits and pieces. It was breaking up into mobs and jammed roads and isolated detachments and clumsy abandoned vehicles standing like monsters in muddy roads or lying in ditches on their sides.

It was the driver who pointed out to him they were running low on petrol. They stopped while Scheller considered his first decision. "Can we get to Remagen?" he asked.

The driver thought they might, although with these detours it was not sure. Maybe they had better try to reach Dedenbach and fill the tank at the depot there. It was a long way around, but they ought to get there all right. Major Scheller immediately accepted the alternative. He wondered if it were because he would not arrive at Remagen quite so soon. No, of course, he had to have petrol. It would not be sane to be stranded short of Remagen.

He got out of the car and walked back to the little truck where his detachment was huddling in the misty rain. "Go on to Remagen," he directed. "Tell the bridge commander that I'm coming by way of Dedenbach to take command by order of General Hitzfeld."

Then he returned to his car and told his driver to head for Dedenbach. As they drove off, he looked back to see the headlights of the little truck looking like pale yellow circlets. Then a bend in the road hid them from view. He turned around again, fingering the map on his knees, looking ahead through the streaky windshield. He did not bother with the map; he simply let the driver work out his own way through the Eifel. They went slowly, painfully slowly, threading their way along a road that was clogged with supply and signal units pulling themselves out of depots and trundling themselves through the dripping woods in the direction of the river. Horses and oxen, commandeered to haul trucks and guns, bellied out across the road like a shapeless turgid tide and scuffed up the muddy shoulders into a morass. Occasional blasts from crews still operating their guns gave shuddering voice to the wooded slopes now emerging from the night in a cold gray canopy of morning.

Major Scheller plucked absently at his map with nervous fingers as they crawled along. There was one bridge left on the Rhine. The Ludendorff. He had never known much about the Ludendorff. The great bridge at Cologne had gone and the Hohenzollern at Bonn and the one at Engers. But the Ludendorff had been overlooked, as it had been all through the years. Why. Because the High Command thought no attack would develop there? But the High Command should know these things. So positive that the Americans would attack a certain way, with a certain objective, at a certain time. Never mind about your rearward areas, the Feldmarschall had told them. *Gott,* yes, at a meeting in that drab little castle overlooking Remagen. Never mind about your rearward areas. Keep your faces to the front. General Botsch has charge here. But where was General Botsch?—sent to command a vanishing corps in a stopgap action on the altar of the holy Westwall, and suddenly hard-fighting Hitzfeld was told to look at his rearward area. Something had been ordered. A major was on his way with responsibility for the last bridge on the Rhine. Something had been ordered.

It was nearly mid-morning when he finally reached Dedenbach and waited impatiently while his requisition for petrol was approved. It was late, terribly late, for him to be reaching the bridge. The minutes now were savagely hurrying things, nipping at him as they passed. The petrol seemed to drain into the tank as though it were dripping from a faucet. He felt as though he might be actually racing the Americans these last few miles to the bridge.

Major Scheller forced himself to calm down. The Americans would be moving fast, but they would have to fight their way into town. There was time. He concentrated on that. There was time to do all that was necessary. What he needed was the decision to blow the bridge at the exact right time. He was not coming here with orders to blow the bridge. That would have been simple. He was to blow the bridge, *if neces-*

sary. That was what he would have to decide. When was it necessary? There was a retreating army making for the Rhine. There would be guns and tanks and men making for the last bridge on the river. He had to bear that in mind. He had to be sure that the High Command would agree with his decision as to when it had been necessary.

They were able to drive more rapidly between Dedenbach and Remagen. Coming around the famous bend in the west bank, he saw the bridge ahead of him and an involuntary tremor rippled in his stomach. It was nearly eleven o'clock in the morning and the long detour had lost him hours of valuable time. That could have been a costly tank of petrol.

At the traffic control point near the railroad station in Remagen he stopped his car and asked for the commandant. A wiry little captain identified himself as Bratge, the combat commandant. Major Scheller produced his identity card and orders. Little Captain Bratge permitted himself a tense smile.

"It is good that higher headquarters has remembered us," he said tautly. "I'm glad to know what the responsible headquarters is. Since General Botsch—"

He broke off to introduce the engineering officer. He was a small quick man, too, Captain Friesenhahn. Both of them surveyed the tall young major with tense interest. Here was responsibility, at last, but the major looked tired and drawn. He was staring toward the bridge where a jumbled mass of civilians and military were streaming from the traffic control point. Some of the civilians were driving farm animals, and horses were also dragging many of the military vehicles. There was something unnerving in the desperate haste of that disordered melange of traffic to the east bank. He forced himself to concentrate on the pressing essentials of his mission.

"What is your situation, Captain Bratge?" he asked the combat commandant.

"Most of my security company is on guard near the Birresdorf road," said Bratge, pointing to the crest beyond the town. "That is the main approach. But I have only a few guards and machine gunners on the bridge itself."

Major Scheller started perceptibly. "Hein?" he said. "Nothing else?"

"Nothing else?" repeated Captain Bratge, and his voice trembled with indignation. "I have been expecting reinforcements, but they keep taking them from me, Major." He pointed to the steep blunt cliff on the east bank. "Two flak batteries were taken from there and ordered to Coblenz. I have protested and Army has said that two batteries will report there without delay. But they are not there yet. I have been promised two battalions. Two battalions have been ordered to report here. Do you know anything about them, Major?"

Scheller shook his head.

"But I have been waiting for them," said little Captain Bratge, stunned. "They were promised. They were ordered by the Field Marshal. General Botsch himself told me."

Scheller again shook his head. Something has been ordered. Something has been ordered. There seemed a whole group of people around him, all anxious for his attention. A wheezing coughing truck loaded with troops burst past the control point. Major Scheller had to raise his voice.

"My detachment," he said. "Did they arrive? A radio operator and eight men?"

It was Captain Bratge's turn to shake his head. Major Scheller drew a deep breath. His communications had not arrived. Now he could not reach Hitzfeld at Corps. He shook aside a hand that plucked at his sleeve for attention and concentrated on Friesenhahn, the engineering officer.

"Your situation, Captain?" he demanded crisply.

"I have eighty engineering troops," said Friesenhahn. "We can have the bridge ready for demolition in a few minutes. Do you give the order, Major?"

Major Scheller was shocked by the question. Blow the bridge now? And yet, why not? He was out of communications with Corps, there were insufficient troops here to protect the bridge, and he had no time now to search for forces elsewhere to build a strong defense perimeter. Blow it, if necessary. But it was necessary. Blow it now. Have done with it. Yes, blow it now, he thought.

That hand was at his sleeve again. A harried artillery captain was demanding his attention.

"Not yet, Major," he begged. "There's an artillery battalion on the way. It's very close. Let it get across first, Major."

Major Scheller hesitated. An artillery battalion means guns that would be badly needed in the defense of the Rhine front, he reflected. Yes, he had almost forgotten the combat point of view. He must think of that. And still he hesitated, trying to judge the hairline between necessary and unnecessary. The High Command would sit in judgment on this; yes, right up to the Führer.

"We may not have much time, Major," warned the engineering officer restlessly. "Our orders are not to let this bridge fall into American hands. I'm ready. Do you give the order, Major?"

The artillery captain expostulated again. He was a redfaced man with protuberant blue eyes and a voice hoarse with cold. "The battalion will be here any time, Major," he said urgently. "I beg you to hold the bridge until they can be crossed over. Those guns will be here very soon."

No, thought Major Scheller, you cannot forget that retreating army. And those guns will be useful.

"Major," began the engineering officer purposefully, "if you'll give—"

"We won't blow the bridge just yet, Captain Friesenhahn," said Hans Scheller.

His first order had been given. No, not just yet. He could never have proved that it was necessary. No, he surely must have been right to check that wild impulse. He glanced up at the town on the west bank. The Americans would have to come through the town and there had been no warning they were even close yet. He saw the Apollinaris Church and there was that yellow brick castle where Field Marshal Model had held his meeting. It looked shuttered and deserted.

"I think," he said, turning back to the officers, "I will inspect the bridge."

He walked toward it and the Ludendorff did not seem at all insignificant this close. It looked long and towering, its steel profile arched against the sky and its four stone towers standing like individual guardian forts. And every inch of it was mined, ready for the switch.

Major Hans Scheller walked steadily, his face expressionless, but the weight of responsibility began to breast at him like a strong tide, as he approached the last steel ribbon that crossed the Rhine.

13.

BERKHAM was up early on the morning of March 7. Having a nightcap the evening before with Mike Morrow of the Corps G-3 staff, he had been given to understand that the Corps attack had broken through from Euskirchen and might reach the Rhine the next day.

Strictly speaking, Berkham did not feel that was the real story. Most of the correspondents, he knew, would be heading toward Cologne, following the 104th Division into the city, because Cologne was a name that would make headlines. The Germans had blown up the Hindenburg Bridge there almost in the faces of the American spearheads.

However, he had followed up this III Corps attack on a hunch and he stayed with it. In the Corps War Room he listened to the briefing, a big quiet man sitting near the Operations Map with a pad on his knee. The Corps was closing rapidly into the angle formed by the Rhine and Ahr rivers, where the link-up with Third Army was expected. Striking successes had been achieved by the Corps' southeasterly attack from Rheinbach. Berkham listened, made no notes.

There was an air of excitement around Corps. The divisions had done it. They had grabbed those goose eggs on their maps that represented their assigned objectives. The red lozenges on the acetate war map had been moved and the scope of the whole First Army attack was clearly discernible now. They had given Omar Bradley what he wanted. They had given him relentless speed, stubborn drive, and drill-hall precision. And they had broken the Westwall wide open. Phase Three coming up—reach the Rhine, link with Patton, mop up the enemy cut off west of the river. And then they would all sit down and rest, while Montgomery pulled off the big show in the north. But all the same, thought Berkham, this was an attack to be remembered. They had made one of the most remarkable limited objective attacks that could have been imagined and it was too bad that all this generated momentum had to cool down on the banks of the Rhine. Well, that was the way of things sometimes. They were lucky to have had this much of a chance when you remembered The Plan and Montgomery's complete priority with the SHAEF planners.

But still Berkham made no notes. The story line had not emerged.

The briefing officer was continuing: "There is a strong possibility that the enemy in retiring to Bonn with his 74th Corps and trying to maintain his 66th and 67th Corps in their present position may have uncovered Remagen. At any rate, our latest Intelligence reports are that the Ludendorff Bridge at Remagen is still intact and General Millikin has notified the armor of this fact."

There it was again. The Commanding General of III Corps had never forgotten the black line on his map that represented a Rhine bridge. It was still intact and he was still thinking of it, no matter how futile the possibility.

"As of 0330 this morning," went on the briefing officer, "Combat Command B of the 9th Armored Division has orders to attack southeast taking the towns of Remagen, Kripp, and Sinzig, and securing crossings of the Ahr at Sinzig and Bodendorf. Supporting artillery will use only time or posit fire on the Ludendorff Bridge at Remagen as long as it stands. Combat Command A is to advance on Bad Newenahr—"

Berkham made a note this time. Combat Command B of 9th Armored was moving on Remagen today. CCB—that was commanded by Noon, wasn't it? Well, Corps orders couldn't be in better hands. Noon was a tough little fighter. When it came to whipcracking drive, Noon was a restless goading terror. He would boot those tanks of his along the same way in which he had built those prewar highways.

When the briefing was concluded, the correspondent stood up and made one of his thoughtful studies of the map. There was Remagen with its black line on the river denoting the Ludendorff Bridge. And there was the red lozenge with the armor symbol that marked Combat Command B. Berkham put his finger on that red lozenge. It was his way of identifying himself with the men who were embodied in that little notation on the map. The other correspondents could have Cologne. He would string along with these spearheads driving on Remagen until the Ludendorff Bridge blew up in their faces

Lieutenant Kurt Birmingham took a look at the sky the moment he awoke. It was heavily overcast again and that meant no air support. Another day when they would be going it on their own.

He did not feel so tired today. Perhaps it was because he knew he could handle the company. They had worked well together yesterday. And then, today they should get to the Rhine. If there wasn't too much stuff in front of them, they might be able to get there pretty quickly.

It was six o'clock when he reported at battalion headquarters. The battalion had been organized as a task force to spearhead Combat Command B of the division. Remsen, the tough, striding lieutenant colonel who commanded the task force, was bending over his acetate map case when Kurt Birmingham arrived in the big farmhouse kitchen that served as a CP. A kerosene lamp on a table threw a soft yellow pool in the dim grayness of the kitchen. Bert Milham, the tank company commander, was there, along with Jack Madden, who led the new Pershing tanks, and Tex Bodman, of the engineer platoon. Packey Hollis, who commanded the other infantry company in the task force grinned tightly at Birmingham.

Big Remsen looked up from his maps. "Hello, Birm," he said. "Okay, here we go. We'll move out at seven. Birm, a platoon of your company will lead. Put 'em in halftracks. We're going to push hard. Ten miles an hour is what the General wants and he'll be on my neck like yesterday. You keep that point platoon of yours moving, Birm."

Lieutenant Birmingham said "Yes, sir" and then swallowed. Speed again. More of the same. That was a tough job, keeping your men going. Ten miles an hour! That wasn't an advance; it was a blitz all by itself.

Remsen's big voice boomed out again. "Madden, your Pershings will follow Birm's point platoon. Then the rest of your company, Birm. Then Tex's engineers, then your company, Packey, and then Bert's Shermans. Got that line of march?"

Yes, they had it. "Right," said Remsen. "Look at your maps. We're going into this town, Remagen. It's on the Rhine. From Stadt-Meckenheim to Adensdorf. The division recon will screen north of the village. Arzdorf, Werthoven, south to northern edge of Birresdorf, then we recon Remagen from the Birresdorf road. Route clear?"

Well, it was clear on the maps. What they might meet along the way was not so clear.

"Good roads," said Remsen. "Second-class tarred roads." He looked at Jack Madden, commander of the Pershing tanks. "I hope those T-26s can fit on those roads. They're so big they can scare the hell out of the Germans just to look at them."

"Yeah," said Madden, with a tight grin. "They're big, sure enough."

"No air support in this lousy weather," went on Remsen.

"Arty?" inquired Packey Hollis.

"Yes," said Remsen. "Arty will have a Piper Cub hanging around. But the Old Man wants you to outrun your artillery."

Someone whistled softly. It might have been Packey Hollis.

"Now," said Remsen. "Like yesterday—no stopping. Don't get bottled up in the towns. If you meet fire, barrel on through. When we get underway, we stay underway. Keep moving. Any questions?"

Lieutenant Birmingham looked at his map and wanted to ask about that Ludendorff Bridge. It was represented by a thin black mark on the river line, as it always had been, a thin black line on a map. But it did not enter into the task force's objective and it probably could not have lasted this long anyhow. He said nothing about the bridge, merely saluted the task force commander and walked back up the road through the drizzle to his own CP.

"Keep moving," he muttered to himself. A year ago he had been attending OCS at Fort Benning. Now he had a company of his own. It was a decimated company. He had only seventy men in the three platoons. But it was spearheading the north column of the U.S. 9th Armored Division. Behind him was Remsen, and then that bundle of energy, Noon, and then the division commander, General Leonard. And beyond him was III Corps commander, General Millikin, and beyond him General Hodges of First U.S. Army, and beyond him General Bradley of 12th Army Group, and beyond him General Eisenhower, the Supreme Commander, and beyond him a little Pennsylvania town, a railroad junction town, whose snow turned dirty in winter and in summer you felt grit between your teeth from the long trains of coal cars. A man was buried there who had reached Remagen long before Task Force Remsen. The bridge had been standing then. Yes, it sure had. "Keep moving," he muttered again.

At his CP he gathered his platoon leaders. He had one officer. The other two platoons were led by sergeants, scrappy little Tony Gagliardi and big Joe Czleusniak. He briefed them quickly. The officer, Hal Grove, he assigned to the lead halftrack. "I'll be in a jeep back in the column," he said. "Any stopping, I'll be up mighty quick. Radio silence. We move out at seven."

They moved out at seven, the infantry riding the halftracks

and the huge Pershing tanks roaring cumbersomely along behind them. Almost immediately they hit a snag. The road had been so thoroughly worked over by fighter bombers of their own air force that it was impassable with craters and rubble. The engineers had to bring up a bulldozer to fill the craters with dirt and rubble and the task force waited while precious time went by. The long delay bounced back to Brigadier General Noon and ricocheted in the form of Colonel Remsen's appearance on the scene in a swearing hurry. There was nothing that could be done. They were stalled, with the vital morning slipping along.

They waited, the infantry, the tanks, the engineers, and that shout of "Keep Moving" seemed to have been washed out before they had fairly begun. Lieutenant Birmingham wiped the drizzle out of his eyes and watched the big deliberate bulldozer moving around like a circus elephant on a footstool. Let's go, let's go, let's go, he kept thinking fervently. Let's get going. Remagen. . . .

Finally the road was patched enough for them to plow on through. The spearhead reached out again into the wet gray morning. Nipping along the side of the road in a jeep, Lieutenant Birmingham anxiously watched for any new obstruction. This was bad ambush country, rolling and open for the most part, but with treacherous little patches of woods and dipping twists in the road and dangerous-looking ridges. Hal Grove rode on the hood of the lead halftrack with binoculars to his eyes, scanning the countryside for the first sign of trouble, and the gunners in the following halftrack stood behind their machine guns swiveling the barrels to and fro, their fingers on the triggers.

It was in Adendorf that the halftracks ran into the first enemy resistance. At the outskirts of the town the barking chatter of small-arms fire stopped the spearhead cold and at the same time several deadly mortar shells exploded in a field to one side. Lieutenant Birmingham sped up front in his jeep. There was a roadblock of heavy kerosene drums and paving rock in the town, and automatic weapons were spurting bullets down the road. Even as he scanned it carefully, a whole furrow gouged by steel-jacketed fingers plowed past the wheels of his jeep. His men had leaped from the halftracks and were deploying to right and left of the road. They hit the ground as the mortar fire began searching for them. Kurt Birmingham swung his jeep around and sped back to the tanks. He stood up in his jeep and made a sweeping motion with his arm. The lead Pershing lumbered up the road, skirting the stalled halftracks, and headed straight into town. A few minutes later the big tank cannon was heard in a thunderous blast and the enemy fire ceased. When the halftracks moved up, the big tank had broken through the roadblock and a group of German soldiers were huddled together with hands raised and white cloths were fluttering from the windows all along the street.

It took time, valuable time. The prisoners were sent to the rear, but some of the American infantry were bent on investigating a wineshop whose windows had been shattered by the Pershing's blast. "Keep moving!" shouted Kurt Birmingham. "Mount up and keep moving!" When the tension in fighting men slackened, you had to move fast before they lost their edge. The column had to move. He yelled at them and made that sweeping gesture with his arm and they responded. They started to move again.

He rode in the lead for a while. Men liked that—not too much to be showboating, but enough to show that their commander took some of their risks. He had to think of all those things. He had to pour every bit of leadership he possessed into this spearhead and hope it would be enough. He studied the road ahead through his binoculars as the jeep felt its way along, and, as the wheels turned, he rode out ahead of the American Army and somewhere ahead was the Rhine.

They skirted Arzdorf by a side road. No sense fooling around with a town, if it could be avoided. Birmingham was back in the column nipping at the halftracks in his scurrying jeep when the point platoon ran into a fire fight in Werthoven. He sped forward as a tremendous chatter of machine-gun fire broke out up ahead and his heart was jumping at the thought of an ambush. They were catching fire from the houses around the little town square and the column shot it out with the snipers in clattering crescendo of shattering glass and tile, interspersed with the exploding impact of tank shells. As white cloths again began to appear, they called off their fire and German troops poured from cellars and alleys all along the square, their hands raised, shouting hoarsely for surrender. Again it took time to round them up and send them to the rear under guard. Again he had to pull the slack tight after that brief fierce fire fight and boot the column into motion. They got out on the road to Birresdorf and suddenly everything was graphically, ominously quiet. American P-47s had caught a convoy along here recently and the wreckage of cars and trucks was strewn all along the road and even in adjacent fields. Several guns pointed emptily at the sky and overturned trucks lay in welters of splintered glass and tattered canvas, with packs and canteens and helmets strewn as though scattered by a mighty wind. They gunned their vehicles through the wreckage, all of them strained, alert, listening, suspecting an ambush somewhere, for the woods were again growing thicker and there must be Germans here. Something must be waiting for them.

On the northern edge of Birresdorf they found a deserted roadblock and pulled it apart. Where had the Krauts gone? Farther along a giant Tiger tank, dug in deceptively in the corner of a farmyard and sited to cover a crossroads, brought them to a grinding halt again, until Birmingham saw the little girl standing on top of it. "If that tank hasn't been deserted," he said, "that's the most criminal booby trap you'll ever see." And again he swept his arm. They yelled back at him, "Yeah, yeah, we know. Keep movin'." He grinned tightly. Okay, do it.

They picked up the Birresdorf road and rolled along unchallenged. It worried Birmingham.. They must be heading into something. The Germans must have observation. But there was no reaction. He studied the terrain ahead with his binoculars and his heart sank as he discerned the outline of what looked like a mountain. That was going to be something. And where had it come from? It wasn't marked on his map. The column was grinding through a belt of heavy pine woods now and this was the place where you could get it. Suddenly the lead halftrack halted and the entire column ground to a halt. "Now what?" muttered Lieutenant Kurt Birmingham, and once again gunned his jeep forward.

The road through the woods took a turn and ended in a clearing. The mountain was clearly visible ahead, a blunt forbidding abutment that seemed almost on top of them. Hal Grove, the leader of the point platoon, was kneeling at the farther edge of the clearing. He turned as Birmingham roared up and leaped out of his jeep. "What is it, Hal?"

"Birm," said Hal Grove in a tense voice, "take a look."

Lieutenant Birmingham moved up beside him. The first thing he saw, to his amazement, was that the mountain was on the other side of a river. There was a river down there, a wide gray river flowing between steep slopes. "Why," said Kurt Birmingham numbly, "that must be the Rhine. Why—I didn't realize we were that close—"

"No," said Grove. His voice shook. *"Look down there—"*

He had grabbed Birmingham's sleeve in his excitement and was pointing down to the right. Birmingham followed his gesture and suddenly squatted down on his heels. He rested one hand on the ground and gripped his knee with the other. Down there to the right, still intact across the gray Rhine, was the Ludendorff Bridge.

It had been new then, built the year of the Armistice, and so the American Occupation forces that moved across it made quick use of it. The war was over and another war seemed impossible and what could he have been thinking of as he tramped across the bridge? Had he made up his mind to desert then, as he crossed the Rhine with nothing ahead but garrison duty? Didn't he know how lucky he was? Walking across unchallenged and unhindered, knowing he would be going home to America in one piece, why would he have thrown it away? Sure the war was over, but didn't he know that a lot of men had died so that he could walk across that bridge? That Rhine crossing had been won for him and he had as much as thrown it away. Maybe a lot of people had thrown away that Rhine crossing. Maybe that was why there had been another war. The Germans had remembered that easy unhindered crossing of the bridge and the Americans had forgotten.

Someone had hold of his arm. There was a swift excited voice in his ear. "Birm, look at that traffic on the bridge." It was Hal Grove. "Let's get some mortar fire on it."

Birmingham studied the bridge. It looked to be about a mile away, on the other side of the town.

"Think we can reach it?" said Grove. "Let's give it a try."

"No," said Birmingham. "Hold it, Hal. If that's going to be a target, the artillery should know. Get Colonel Remsen."

"Okay," said Grove. "I'll send a runner. What a target."

"Yeah," muttered Kurt Birmingham, still crouched, studying it. All kinds of traffic going across the Ludendorff. Choked-up traffic, pushing and nudging its way. The Ludendorff Bridge. He still stared at it intact down there. No one could have expected this. No one could have hoped for it. What was going to happen now? He glanced absently at his wrist watch, but the time did not register with him.

Colonel Remsen came driving up fast in a jeep with Major Standlee, the executive officer of the task force. They took a look at the bridge and for a moment were like two men who had walked into a brick wall. Hal Grove was asking about calling down artillery fire.

"They won't give us artillery," said Remsen brusquely. "Don't ask me why."

Birmingham looked up suddenly. Artillery was ordered not to fire on the bridge? Well, then Colonel, don't you see, don't you see, don't you see? If the bridge is up, they want it, Colonel. They want us to try for it. That must be why.

"We've got to get the Old Man!" Remsen shouted suddenly. It was as if the stark fact of that bridge had struck a nerve. "I'll get on the radio to Noon."

He sent off a message to the commanding general of Combat Command B and then rejoined the group gazing down at the town and the bridge beyond. "I've got to find out how we go in there. Birm, you and Packey Hollis get down in there and report me a route."

The two officers descended the slope by a footpath that led in the direction of the town, each with his carbine at the ready, feeling that they could be picked off from somewhere by the sharp *pi-toon* of a sniper's rifle or the flailing lead of a machine gun chattering its death message from a covert. Where was their observation, for the Lord's sake? Binoculars must be sweeping the hills and roads of the town from somewhere.

Kurt Birmingham stopped to study the town through which they would have to advance. It was probably lousy with snipers and roadblocks. The approaches to the bridge must be lethal. The town sprawled down the steep slopes to the railroad tracks that ran along the river. He could see a sort of a castle up there, a big house of yellow brick with a couple of towers, and the church they called the Apollinaris. And not far from the hill where the column had stopped was another big place that looked like a hotel.

They came down on a broad main road. Birmingham took out a map to orient the position. This looked like the main approach to the town and it was joined by a looping road down the hill that must be the Birresdorf road—he felt the danger even as he heard Packey Hollis draw a swift breath and whip up his carbine. A German officer seemed to materialize from a ditch by the side of the road a few yards away, his hands raised. Packey started toward him and suddenly the German's face contorted. He dropped to one knee in the ditch, his hand sweeping up with a revolver, firing point-blank at the two American officers in the road. Hollis immediately emptied his clip, firing from the hip, and the German pitched headlong and rolled over in the ditch. Hollis slid another clip into his carbine and moved slowly to the edge of the ditch. His usual good-humored freckled face was grim. He stood there a moment and then turned away.

"This is the Bonn-Coblenz road, isn't it?" he said sharply. "Well, what more do we want? We have our fix on this place."

It always did something to you when you saw the face of the man you killed, Lieutenant Birmingham put his map away. "Sure, Packey," he said. "We're all set."

They returned to the top of the hill and briefed the task force commander. He studied the map a long time, glancing over at the town from time to time. "Okay," he said finally. "Your company leads, Birm. Clean out the town. Hollis will support. I'll send the tanks in along with you. Hurry up. Let's get going."

Again Birmingham called his platoon leaders into a briefing. Nothing about the bridge yet. Well, it would go any minute now. It would go as soon as his company started to fight its way through town. Hal Grove would take his platoon through the town itself. Tony Gagliardi would fan out on the left along the river and stay low to avoid any observation from the east bank. Joe Czleusniak would be the right flank and would head for the railroad station. By the book, he told them. Get through as fast as possible, but by the book. Work your way through. Don't take anything for granted. Watch for snipers. Okay? Okay. Hal Grove nodded jerkily. Big stolid Czleusniak spat to one side and wiped his lips with the back of his hand. Little Gagliardi moved around restlessly, as though he were shadow-boxing. Okay, okay, okay. Fix bayonets. Get ready to move out.

Remsen waved his hand impatiently toward the town. Sure, Colonel. Kick off. Birmingham took another look at the bridge. Traffic still moving. Still standing. It was going to be an awful shock when it blew, but maybe they could make it close.

A jeep came speeding up with the commanding general of Combat Command B. The wiry figure of Brigadier General Noon sprang quickly from the seat beside the driver. To Noon, this whole operation was late and here they were still standing around. Anything that bogged down was anathema to Noon.

"What's the delay?" he said crisply. "What are you waiting for? This whole operation is speed. You know that damn well. And now when we're getting to the river, you pull a debate. Get that town! Get it quick! Remsen, get those men moving. *Fast!*"

With a sweep of his arm Birmingham started his men down the hill into Remagen. The General was still sounding off in his crisp incisive way. His voice was like a good swift kick in the pants, thought Kurt Birmingham. Get moving. And keep moving. More of the same. But Noon's fierce drive had booted them here and it still was booting them along. Maybe they would be able to rest when they had linked with Patton's tankers, but until then they had Noon on Remsen's neck and Remsen on theirs.

Noon finished his remarks and raised binoculars to his eyes. For a long moment he stood completely motionless. Then he lowered his glasses and when he spoke the anger was out of his voice and he sounded almost gentle. "Be good to get that bridge, too."

He had noticed that black line on the map and he already was testing the chances and consequences in his mind. He had certain definite orders, of course. Establish a bridgehead over the Ahr at Sinzig and clear the Germans out of Kripp. Nothing about trying to capture a bridge. It might cost him his whole task force to try it.

He could hear the rumble of halftracks as Packey Hollis' company started down the Birresdorf road to the main road into Remagen to support Kurt Birmingham. He heard the deeper roar of the Pershing tanks as the drivers gunned their motors and got moving. Remsen was pushing, all right. Noon swept his glasses toward the bridge again. You could not put an outside chance like a bridge into orders, but it was there and they should damn well try to take it. If he had to make up his mind to this before he checked with the division commander, all right, you had to stick your neck out in this kind of trade once in a while.

Noon waited, watching the town, hearing the sudden crackle of M1s. Birmingham was moving into Remagen. Then there was a silence. It was hard to tell whether the infantry was moving slowly or whether there was no resistance. He twisted the binoculars about in his hands and then again raised them to his eyes. No, by God, the infantry was moving along. He could see some white cloths fluttering from windows. There was another burst of spasmodic firing, broken by the exploding detonation of what might be 20 mm shells. The Germans were dropping some stuff in town. Where was it coming from? He shifted his glasses to the east bank. He could not see any firing over there, but several locomotives were getting up steam. He swept his glasses to the top of the Erpeler Ley. There did not seem to be any artillery up on those heights that he could discern, nor even any signs of observation. Strange. An observation post up there could have spotted his column ten miles off.

Now there was the sudden ripping curtain of machine-gun fire coming from the direction of the town, burst after burst. Yes, there was a fire fight somewhere down there. The Germans still had some stuff in town, although, so far, precious little. But your men never knew for sure. They had to go in and find out. Now the tanks were firing. He recognized those 90 mm guns in action.

For some reason Noon became acutely conscious of the ticking of his wrist watch. Slowly he raised the binoculars again and studied the bridge. When would it go? Any minute? Or would they decoy some American troops out there and then blow it? Would he get his task force moving out on the bridge and then see them all blown up and blasted into the river with a crumpled steel structure? Always you realized that your orders were going to cost some men their lives. You hoped there would be as few as possible and you planned it as carefully as you could and you booted them in the pants to keep them moving for their own sweet sakes. But nearly always your orders were simply an implementation of orders received from a higher headquarters. Any orders he gave for the bridge would be his own. And the men that died would be his own. And he would never forget that. Never to the end of his life.

He should be getting back to his CP at Birresdorf, he knew, because the rest of his command was in a fight for Sinzig and the division commander would want to know. But he lingerd on the hill north of Remagen, fascinated by the thought that the infantry and tanks were working through the town toward the bridge and soon they would meet, the American task force and the German bridge, like a crashing impact waiting its moment, and men's lives and his orders and German dynamite and one of the great prizes of the war and the ticking of a wrist watch were all blended into some giant veiled question mark. If the bridge should be blown up in front of his eyes right now, it would be a terrible disappointment, but he could live with it, because the Germans were masters of detail and no one could expect a break like a Rhine bridge. No one could even hope for it. Everything would be simple then. They would have Remagen and they would push on to the link with Patton.

But the bridge still was there. And so were those locomotives and trains on the east bank. It was incredible. It was as though time had ceased, as though the swing of a sweep hand on a watch should bring a blinding detonation, but the sweep hand hung poised in its swing.

Noon's aide came hurrying up to him with a message taken from the radio jeep. "General," he said, "we've taken Sinzig. Here's a flash you'd better see, General."

Noon lowered his binoculars and let them hang by the strap around his neck. He took a look at the scrawled words on the paper. "Prisoner captured in Sinzig says Ludendorff Bridge scheduled to be blown at 1600.

Brigadier General Noon frowned. It did not seem likely to him. It was not like the Germans to set up a fixed time for an operation like this. Far more likely that they would blow the bridge at a time in relation to the tactical situation. Would they blow it at four o'clock, if there was no threat? Would they fail to blow it right this minute, if there was? He crumpled the paper and stuck it in his pocket. Some prisoner in Sinzig talking off the top of his head—but in times like these you took no chances. He looked at his watch. It was not yet three o'clock: 1438. Was the task force bogged down in Remagen? What in thundering hell was holding it up?

He beckoned to his aide and strode to his jeep. It was all clear to Brigadier General Noon now, and this radio message, reliable or not, had helped to make it so. You did not try to outguess the Germans about this bridge, stand on a hill north of town with your fingers in your ears waiting for the big blast. It was the richest prize of the war and you reached for it with all you had, and if you got the east bank you followed through with everything you had, your whole command, the whole damn Combat Command B, and those orders to link with Patton in the south he just had to forget. That was the only way to set this up. If he lost his command while amending Corps orders without proper authority, it might cost him his star. But, as far as Brigadier General Noon was concerned, with a lot of Americans risking annihilation his star was the easiest risk of all and it was up for grabs right here and now.

His jeep barreled back to the Birresdorf road, swung sharply, and sped down to Colonel Remsen's CP at the bend of the road to Remagen past the venerable St. Apollinaris Church. Big Remsen was standing there, trying to cut in his 508 radio, as General Noon swooped down on him. He straightened up as the wiry terrier-like general jumped out of his jeep and waved the Sinzig message at him.

"How about this report that the bridge is to be blown at 1600?"

"I got it, sir—"

"I want action, Remsen. Put some smoke around the bridge, cover your advance with tanks, bring up your engineers. Get your men to that bridge fast."

"I'm doing every damned thing I can to get to the bridge, General—"

There was a sudden shrill whistle from the direction of Remagen, somewhere along the river. It was like a steam whistle, or a factory whistle, and it split the air with a long sustained piercing blast. Down there in the direction of the Ludendorff Bridge—General Noon kicked sharply at the tire of his jeep as though he were trying to drive a tack with the toe of his combat boot.

"That's an alarm signal, Remsen," he said swiftly.

The American tanks and infantry must be getting through the town now. They must be threatening the bridge. There went that whistle again, shrill and piercing between the bluffs along the Rhine, unnerving, with a dread implication in it. Something was brewing at the bridge.

"I'll get right down there, sir," said Colonel Remsen tautly. He saluted quickly and climbed into his own jeep. It sped down the road into town, the driver crouched low over the wheel, gripping it tightly. Colonel Remsen cut in his radio and called Lieutenant Jack Madden, platoon commander of the Pershing tanks. Madden acknowledged through the crackle of static.

Remsen braced himself in the bucking jeep. "Madden get to the bridge. Get there and—"

The voice came crackling back. "Sir, I am *at* the bridge."

And then a terrific detonation shook Remagen. A cloud of black smoke shot up over the Ludendorff Bridge.

14.

THE THREE officers at the Ludendorff Bridge had a very short time to know each other and they all well realized it. Major Hans Scheller looked at his wrist watch and found that he had been in command of the bridge for over two hours and he still could not seem to get arranged in his mind the priorities here.

He had to study two points of view. Captain Friesenhahn, the engineering officer, was interested only in seeing that the bridge was destroyed before the Americans arrived. Captain Bratge, the combat commandant, was interested in defenses that would hold off the attacking Americans. Major Scheller desperately wished that he could define the term "if necessary."

Major Scheller had crossed to the east bank and set up a CP at the end of the bridge. He stood there by one of the squat stone towers, his hands jammed in the pockets of his overcoat, and tried to assimilate the various factors concerned with the defense and the destruction of the bridge. One of them was paramount.

Captain Friesenhahn had tried to explain the complex demolition system. There were three different charges. One was the preliminary demolition that would blow up the ramp on the west bank. The second was the main charge that would collapse the bridge into the river and was controlled by an electric ignition switch at the entrance to the railroad tunnel. To leave nothing to chance, there was an emergency detonator—a primer cord to be lighted by hand, if the electric ignition switch did not work. However, the ignition switch was tested regularly. It had never failed.

Major Scheller nodded. The brisk little Friesenhahn must know his business.

"Major," the engineering officer was saying, "we don't have much time. How long are you going to wait? That artillery battalion hasn't arrived yet?"

"It should be here soon," said Major Scheller.

Captain Friesenhahn restrained himself with an effort. "But how long do we wait?" he demanded, his voice high with nervous anxiety.

"We will wait a bit longer," said Major Scheller, and saw

Friesenhahn go darting on the bridge to where he had a squad waiting near the ramp on the west bank. And then it was Captain Bratge. Captain Bratge was anxious, too.

"How are you going to defend the bridge, Major?" he asked. "There has been a rumor of American tanks at Birresdorf."

Scheller looked at him. Bratge was a small man, too. Well, they were all three of them small men. They were the small men of the great grinding Wehrmacht machine.

"There is no force here," he said. "Your security company—"

"It's on outpost over there," said Captain Bratge. "We must be warned. My Volksturm roadblocks cannot be depended on. And"—his voice shook a little—"those flak batteries are not on the Erpeler Ley."

He would never understand it, Captain Bratge felt. Nothing stayed where it should have been. The flak batteries on top of the Erpeler Ley had been ordered to Coblenz. His defense dispositions at Bodendorf had been abandoned. So had the Volksturm roadblocks. The military police detachment had been ordered elsewhere. He felt as though he were trying to knit streams of water together. But what did Major Scheller intend to do?

A woman came running breathlessly across the bridge, stumbled, and caught at the skirts of Captain Bratge's overcoat to save herself from falling. He helped her to her feet. She was sobbing out something in panting gasps, fending herself off from his hands, and trying to run again. He let her go.

"She saw American tanks," said Captain Bratge. "And American soldiers fixing their bayonets—"

He paused. There had been the unmistakable sound of shots, the sharp crackle of rifle fire in the town. "Did you hear that, Major?" he asked sharply.

"Yes," said Major Scheller calmly.

He glanced around him thoughtfully. All right, he had listened to Friesenhahn and he had listened to Bratge. And there was no way that any real defense could be patched that could successfully hold the Americans away from the bridge. That he would swear to in any court of inquiry. But the greater part of the 15th Army was still west of the Rhine. You knew that, Major? Yes, he knew that. Broken pieces were swimming or taking to the ferries that were still operating, but, yes, the army was still west of the Rhine. How great a force attacked you, Major? One tank? A platoon of infantry? Perhaps a patrol, eh? You ordered demolition of the last bridge across the Rhine without ascertaining whether you were really threatened?

Why was it so easy to imagine himself before a courtmartial? Why did he almost see himself trying to defend himself against some fierce yelling accusations? He had tried to do his best. He hadn't had time to learn the command channels. He did not have time to get a force together. He had not been able to communicate the situation to Hitzfeld, and who else was there? Who was responsible for this bridgehead? Hans Scheller? *Hans Scheller?* Two days ago it had been a general.

A weapons carrier with seven men clinging to its sides rocketed across the bridge and sped past him. Several soldiers came running, stumbling, weaving across to the east bank. Scheller flung out a hand. "Halt!" he shouted. "Stop! I command you!"

They looked at him in a glazed way and ran on past. A young lieutenant rushed up to him. "I am Lieutenant Peters, Herr Major," he blurted. "Commanding a battery of Flakwerfer 44."

Scheller said nothing. They were jostling, elbowing, pushing across the bridge, soldiers manhandling rocket launchers in a thick turgid stream of retreating troops, vehicles, and civilians clutching great bundles. One of Captain Bratge's noncoms was holding a revolver on four men who were trying to abandon a small truck that had broken down. He was forcing them to shove it on across the bridge.

Lieutenant Peters was trying to get his attention. "It is a top secret weapon, Major," he was saying frantically. "Part of my battery is still on the west bank. I must see to the destruction of those pieces, Major, if there is not time to get them across the river—"

Major Scheller looked at him then. "You can hear the firing in town, Lieutenant," he said. "You will have to decide that yourself."

He was very young, Lieutenant Peters, and the boyish face under the snub helmet was pale. Hans Scheller felt a certain kinship with him. Each had to destroy something and each had to decide the right time to destroy it. The young lieutenant attempted to say something. He looked as though any kind of order would be something that would save his life.

Then he turned and started toward the west bank, pushing his way against the crowd plunging toward the east.

The Wehrmacht, thought Major Scheller numbly. How many thousands would be trapped over there? How many thousands of Von Zangen's army were lost to the defense of the Rhine front? And yet these broken, fleeing, panicky remnants could fight again if there was time to give them a rest, regroup and refit them. If only enough of the 15th Army could get across the river, they could still be molded into a new fighting organization. But this beaten mob was not the Wehrmacht. He told himself that again and again. He had to stop thinking of that trapped army.

Who would have commandeered these fleeing men and organized them into a cohesive force that could hold a bridgehead defense? A major? What did a major mean to these men, this running tide of bits and pieces and remnants and shavings? A general with a strong staff might have been able to do something. Perhaps. If a few were shot first and a strong roadblock at the bridge could have been maintained, if some kind of supply line could be organized and some communications established. Hans Scheller was to do this? Hans Scheller was to stop some fleeing staff car and say, "Herr Oberst, I politely command you to direct your troops to join in the bridgehead defense. You have no orders to cross the Rhine, I presume, Herr Oberst?"

Something had been ordered. Order something and then finally someone would be brought to a court-martial. There were so many courts-martial. He found himself thinking of the conference in that yellow brick castle up there above the town, with that atrocious boar's head and the pallid fire and the memory of the Feldmarschall's stand or die orders and the chorus of Heil Hitlers. He had been so upset that he had impulsively picked up a stick of firewood and showed its rigidity and then snapped it in his hands to show that something could break suddenly, anywhere. And Colonel Blum, staring at him with his sharp little eyes, saying, "And if that happens, somebody will be shot."

There was no reason why he should be constantly fighting off thoughts of a court-martial, like shrugging a persistent hand from his shoulder. What was the High Command doing right now? Where was it looking? Where was it sending the flak batteries and the promised battalions and the MP detachments? Was it Bonn, or Cologne, or Coblenz, or Gelsdorf?

The key to the Rhine defense front, Herr Feldmarschall, is here. It is here! It is here! *It is here!*

The thick shoving stream of traffic dried up abruptly, as though some kind of a tourniquet had been applied. Major Scheller saw brisk, determined little Captain Bratge hurrying across the bridge. A noncom and several troops swung along behind him. Captain Bratge approached and saluted correctly.

"I have closed the traffic control point, Herr Major, and withdrawn my men."

"So?" said Major Scheller. He looked toward the western approach of the bridge. Friesenhahn and a squad were down there working at something near the ramp. "There must be many more waiting, Captain Bratge."

"No, Herr Major. There are not many. They have taken to cellars or wherever they can. American tanks have been firing on the Koblenzstrasse." He paused. "I think," he said thinly, "we may expect the Americans soon. Very soon."

Down at the western edge of the bridge a German soldier was painfully making his way toward them, crawling on hands and knees, with one leg dragging painfully. He made his way doggedly, slowly, until suddenly he simply fell forward on his face. Major Scheller looked toward him and then impulsively ran across the bridge toward him. It had been like the last gasp of the 15th Army, that lone, crawling, wounded man. As he ran, Major Scheller heard the unmistakable snapping crackle of rifle and machine-pistol fire, punctuated by the thumping thunder of tank cannon. The Americans were coming closer. He reached the fallen soldier's side and pulled him to his feet. Looping one of the man's arms around his neck, Scheller half-dragged, half-carried him, until a couple of Bratge's men ran out to assist him. They carried the wounded man to the entrance of the tunnel. He was conscious, as they laid him down, and asked weakly for Captain Bratge. The intense little captain bent over him. "What happened, Sergeant?"

"Herr Hauptmann, the tanks cut us off. The whole company." He sighed. "They came so fast—so fast—Herr Hauptmann—"

Bratge patted his shoulder and stood up, signaling for a litter. "He commanded my security company," he said to Major Scheller. "I had these thirty-six men and it was not enough to make a defense, Herr Major. I posted them near the Birresdorf road as a warning outpost—and they were cut off by the speed of the American advance. Only the Sergeant got through."

He made this report in a concise crisp voice. "I will see to my dispositions," he said. First he checked his machine-gun emplacements in the two towers on the east bank, then posted another machine-gun crew in the entrance of the tunnel, commanding a sweep of the bridge. By now the vicious spats of fire were coming from some of Friesenhahn's engineering troops firing from emplacements near the bridge and between the cars of the freight train that had backed in on the tracks near the river. Farther to the north a German 20 mm gun opened up and there was a sudden yellowish flash against one of the houses on the west bank.

Friesenhahn himself was there at the tunnel, checking with his executive officer at the main switch. He nodded and came over to Major Scheller. "We have tested the ignition system for the main charge, Major," he said. "It is in perfect working order. I am going to take station at the ramp."

Major Scheller returned his salute. He stood in the entrance of the tunnel and watched the stocky little engineering captain dash back to his demolition squad at the ramp. Two men knelt with panzerfausts ready in case the American tanks charged the ramp, and two others knelt around the plunger that would detonate the charge under the ramp.

Suddenly a piercing whistle sounded from the nearby plywood factory, a long shrill sustained blast. The Americans were close. Running hard, Captain Friesenhahn heard the sound of roaring tank motors. There was a scorching flash of flame from the German panzerfausts near the ramp. Friesenhahn stumbled and fell on one knee. He could see the big tanks now, with American helmets moving along with them. The men at the plunger looked toward him. Friesenhahn, on one knee, waved a frantic arm at them. "Fire!" he screamed. *"Fire—"*

A terrific detonation blasted the air and a black cloud billowed up from the ramp. Friesenhahn ran forward to take a look. His men were already racing over to the east bank, but he lingered, studying the ramp. As the smoke thinned, he saw a huge crater, thirty feet wide and twelve deep, blown in the approach to the bridge. The ramp had been blasted. No tanks nor any other vehicles would get on this bridge. He turned then and ran hard for the east bank across the planked flooring over the tracks.

He was not young, the little captain, and he was getting

winded. He churned toward the tunnel and then was suddenly knocked flat by the stunning force of a tank shell exploding nearby on the bridge. The American tankers were wheeling into position and covering the bridge by fire. Captain Friesenhahn pulled himself dazedly to his feet, staggered a few steps, and then ran on, panting. There was a steady stream of small-arms fire from the west bank now and he could hear the pinging ricochets among the girders of the bridge. He reached the east bank and leaped into one of the emplacements there for shelter to get his breath. The Americans had some machine guns firing. Chips of stone and dirt flew off the big slope behind the bridge. There was a sudden clanging explosion along the river bank to the north and one of the locomotives shuddered and blew up with a great cloud of steam.

The American tanks across the river were firing smoke shells now. The white phosphorous smoke thickened into a stinging curtain and the men near the tunnel began to cough. Friesenhahn pulled himself out of the emplacement and ran through the phosphorous smoke screen with an arm flung across his face. This bridge had to go. Didn't Major Scheller realize that?

Inside the tunnel a crowd of civilians, soldiers, and slave laborers milled in confusion. Major Scheller stood at one side, near the entrance. The tall young officer stared through the white smoke that drifted across the mouth of the tunnel, his face set and strained, his hands clenched in the pockets of his overcoat. German machine guns were chattering from the stone towers and in deep sandbagged emplacements along the bank, but they were firing through that smoke.

Friesenhahn caught Bratge by the arm near the tunnel. "Get me the order to blow the bridge!" he shouted. "Get me the order quick."

Bratge nodded toward the switch. He bent over, coughing for a moment, then dashed in search of Major Scheller. From somewhere he could hear screams. He found Major Scheller waiting quietly, studying the American tanks across the river.

"Major," Captain Bratge shouted against the noise of the tank cannons, "there is infantry over there. They could charge the bridge—"

Was Major Scheller still waiting for that artillery battalion? The fantastic thought tore at his nerves.

"Major!" he shouted again, his voice cracking. "If you do

not give the order to blow the bridge, I will give the order myself."

Yes, there must be infantry over there. Nothing more of the 15th Army was going to cross this bridge. The thousands of them still there—yes, this was the end. Scheller nodded to Captain Bratge.

"You can go ahead and destroy the bridge," he said.

They were words that had been a long time coming. They were words that had not been imagined in the days when the Wehrmacht had poured like a gray tide from the great citadel of the Reich behind the Rhine and blitzed across France and the Low Countries. They were words that American commanders in the last few days of relentless driving speed had expected and conceded for any time.

They were the words that sealed off the heartland of the Reich into a tough river defense front. They were the words that everyone knew would have to come and they had come none too soon, but there still was time. There was still time to unhinge the bridge and drop it into the river and this was all that mattered in the end.

Still Captain Bratge felt the quiet order like a fist in the stomach. He whirled on the executive officer. "Note that I have received a direct order to blow the bridge," he snapped. "Note the time."

He could not afford to forget things like that. He was a little fish and there was no one to look after him but himself, and the High Command would have him under close scrutiny. Friesenhahn was near the tunnel entrance, coming toward him, his normal self-control cracking. "Blow the bridge!" Bratge shouted at him.

"Can I have that order in writing?" said Friesenhahn mechanically.

Another little fish. "Blow the bridge!" Bratge raged, livid. "Now! That's your order!"

Of course. The competent little engineering officer regained control of himself and ran toward the switch. His special squad of demolition experts were there for the operation. Friesenhahn had tried to think of everything ever since he had been permitted to arm the bridge for demolition. And he had thought of everything and he had tested everything and this, thank God, was the end of his whole racking responsibility.

He arrived at the switch and took the plunger key. And from that moment there were six seconds of life for the Ludendorff Bridge. He twisted the key and mentally began to cout to six.

Six. Five. Four. Three. Two. One. One— One— Friesenhahn froze. He frantically turned the plunger key again. There was no answering detonation. He backed away numbly, completely stupefied. Why, only a few minutes before the system had tested perfectly.

Major Scheller, who had flung himself to the ground to await the blast, leaped to his feet and raced to the switch.

"What is it?" he asked quickly.

"Always it has worked perfectly," said Friesenhahn. "Never has it failed. Never before—" He sounded stunned. "Just now the circuit tested—just a few minutes ago—"

Major Scheller ducked involuntarily as a tank shell exploded against the embankment. That verdammt American armor was shooting at anything that stirred. He pulled Friesenhahn down beside him.

"There is still time," he said hurriedly. "The Americans do not know. All they know is that the bridge is mined. They do not commit suicide, the Americans. They will not know when or how many charges you will explode. Now, think—"

"If there was enough time," said the engineering officer, "my special squad could make a check. But it is better to try the emergency charge now—the primer cord lit by hand—"

"That will be enough to destroy the bridge?"

"Yes," said the engineering officer. "That is sure."

"Then use the emergency charge—"

Friesenhahn leaped to his feet and, beckoning to a sergeant, hand crouching toward a crater near the bridge. Major Scheller returned to the tunnel entrance and knelt there, watching. He saw the sergeant crawling to the edge of the bridge, huddling over something for an interminable minute, then crawling back to the crater where Friesenhahn was waiting. The engineering officer turned and signaled to the officers at the tunnel. The primer cord had been lit.

"Down!" Captain Bratge shouted to the crowd in the tunnel. "The bridge is being exploded. Lie flat—"

Major Scheller again lay down on the ground. He opened his mouth and clasped his hands behind his head. When? When? He felt the ground suddenly reverberate under him and a loud explosion blasted against his eardrums. There it went! They would not need the gift of time from the Americans. It was finished!

15.

IN THE early morning hours of another day Doke Stanton sought out the little room off the downstairs hall and threw himself wearily on the settee. They had sat together most of the night listening to the fearsome young maniacs outside the castle. Several times he had thought they were going to break in, but apparently the big silent shuttered house, dark, lifeless, had provided no flint for the steel of their vicious shenanigans and so, like the jackals Ilse Margraven had called them, they had simply snapped around the fringes of real mischief and gradually tired of it. Suddenly they had gone, but he had not realized it for some time.

Now that he thought about it he could see how she had kept him talking through the whole racking interlude and his preoccupation had carried him to the point where he had realized that for some time there had been deep quiet about the castle.

He tried to review what he had been talking about and, to him, it was like an erratic mosaic, recognizable vaguely as his life in America. He remembered such disjointed topics as the remodeling of a weathered gray barn and a description of an early American farmhouse and the cook-out place in an orchard and the ring-necked pheasants feeding under the kitchen window in winter. These were things that simply came to his mind and he had voiced them, as though they might have symbolized a friendly fire before which he could warm his hands.

He had spoken about America, too, and discovered how hard it was to describe. He had not realized how difficult it would be until he tried to put it into words. So he had talked about the various men he had known in the recon troop. They had come from all over and each had a surprising eloquence in talking about their homes. Buster Gerbig, who was loud and profane, could make you feel the beauty of his Wyoming mountains. Joe d'Alesandro came from a block in the Bronx that had been his entire world and this was matched by Ken Cowley who came off an Arkansas farm, and "Old Man" Sedgwick of Louisville, who talked about "pretty weather," and Pete Filchini, who drove a truck in Jersey City, and Jimmy Naseby, who had bellhopped in the Bangor House in

Maine, and "Rebel" Tremper from the sand flats of South Carolina, and big Nick Halsema, who had worked in the steel industry, reading a letter from his former boss: "He says I'm the best helper he ever had," and repeating it in a reverent reminiscent sort of way, "the best helper he ever had."

The strange thing about it was that the more you tried to weave some sort of pattern, the more impossible it became. Each was like a drop in a small fan of spray flung from a long rolling cresting wave and behind that wave were countless others, so that there was no way to draw a conclusive picture of it for a quiet, listening girl, but just to indicate from a few drops of spray what the ocean might be like. .

So he thought about those things and wondered what it might have cost the girl to keep him talking, to keep his mind occupied under the stimulus of an attentive listener in the world of a small, blacked-out room. She must have withstood not only the physical pain that beset her, but the stabbing poignancy of the smashing German defeat in the Rhineland, which he could take only on faith, but of which she was quietly positive.

He went to sleep with that thought, and, strangely enough, woke with it, so that it was as if he had only closed his eyes momentarily. But he had slept for hours; by his watch it was late in the morning. A head start on another day that he had to get through, that they both had to get through. This one was March 7, if that mattered.

There was one important difference in the day and that was a strange zest and interest. It was inexplicable, but he awoke with it and he took pains with his shaving and he wished he could have had a bath and that he could have somehow laundered his uniform. He wished he could have combed his crew-cut hair. He looked at himself in the small mirror and wished he was still not so marked up. He thought it would be a good day to have a project of some kind, something to do, something to plan, something to fix, or to write, or someplace to go. It was absurd, of course, but it was there and it was not like the old fevered fantasy. It may have been absurd, but it seemed wonderfully natural.

He went upstairs quietly, in order not to awaken Ilse if she should be mercifully sleeping, but hoping that she would be awake. Ilse Margraven was not only awake, but she was sitting up by the window, which had been unfettered of its blinds. Doke Stanton had become so used to the dimness and darkness of the place that the daylight was like some sort of release to the spirits. He wished Ilse a quick good morning and pulled up a chair beside her. Martha had just recently been with her. There was a tray of steaming chocolate, a change from the brew of bitter coffee, and a plate of sliced crusty grayish bread.

"How are you, Ilse?" he asked urgently. "How do you feel?"

Something in his voice made her turn to survey him curiously. "Why, Doke," she said, wondering, "I am all right."

"But your foot," he said. "I mean—"

"It's no worse, Doke." That seemed to be her simple standard reply. Her glance continued to rest on him in that curious, wondering way.

"I talked so much," he said. "I just talked and talked. It must have been hard on you."

"I liked listening, Doke. I liked the way you talked and what you said."

"You did?" said Doke Stanton.

"It meant a great deal that you were able to talk at a time like that. It was so easy for me just to listen."

"Why—" he began, nonplused, and then paused. There was something different about her today, he noticed suddenly. For a moment he was not sure, then he had it. She had banded her ash-blond hair with a blue ribbon. It was a thin ribbon, just a bit faded, but he stared at it as though it were a spectacle. It was the first touch of color he had ever seen about her.

She smiled slightly. "You've actually noticed my poor little ribbon, Doke." She touched it tentatively. "Perhaps it is in honor of your liberation."

He started. "Liberation?" he repeated, savoring the word, like something rare and rich and warming on the tongue.

"Look out the window," she suggested. "Look at the bridge."

Before, when he had watched the bridge, the traffic had been in spurts and trickles, unhurried, easterly but deliberate. Now, immediately, there was a difference that could be discerned even from a distance—a thicker, steadier stream, with an impression of pushing, shouldering haste about it.

"Men," he heard Ilse Margraven say. "That's the retreat. The real retreat."

Yes, that was the long-awaited sight. He had thought about it and yet, now that all the signs were there of defeat, he could not completely grasp it, because it was so impossible that it should be happening. There had been fifty miles of Rhineland and how could the GIs have come across so fast? Where were they now? How far back? How long did the bridge have to live?

"And," said the girl, "also, there is William. He came back this morning. William is an excellent barometer, Doke. He is back here because he feels this is the safest place for him. There is an American here." She gave a soft little sigh. "Oh, yes, Doke, your Americans must be near."

Near? Near! Again he studied the Ludendorff Bridge. Then it would go, of course. Perhaps today? He could not imagine a greater certainty than the destruction of that bridge, and yet he looked at it as though for such a thing to happen would be a terrible defeat. He must be losing his way again, he thought. If the Americans were coming, it would have to go. All along, that had been a firm corollary. Now he was bracing himself against the destruction of that bridge, and yet the Americans simply must come. It was like arguing with the law of gravity or trying to remake the world. How could a moment be both grievous and exhilarating at once?

"Doke," said the girl, "won't you eat this lunch? You must be hungry."

He was glad to turn his attention away from the river. He ate hungrily, the thick sweet chocolate and the crusty bread, while the girl seemed to take up the watch on the town, the river, and the bridge.

"It is an old town," she said meditatively. "They say it once was an old Roman town. I know it has always been a friendly, hospitable place. Something of a resort, really. To think that the American Army is coming here. It is so strange. Remagen has always been so unimportant. Doke, what will they be like, the Americans?"

He considered, the cup poised near his lips. "After the fighting is over," he said, "the GIs are usually friendly. They are naturally friendly. With the Germans, I don't know. They'll like the children, the GIs always do, and it won't make any difference whether they are German or not. They won't be brutal with the people, but they'll probably be suspicious and angry for a while." He smiled. "You still can't imagine what an American is like, can you, Ilse? Not from me, I mean."

She did not answer and he was not surprised, just a little sorry. Instead, preoccupied, she changed the subject.

"What will you do when your people come?"

Again he considered. It was such an unbelievable prospect that he approached it warily, lest he put a jinx on it, lest there be some tremendous unforeseen reversal, a counterattack from Valhalla or something. "Well," he said tentatively, "once the Americans finish up along the river, there'll be a period of rest. That's certain. I'll find my division headquarters and if my orders aren't there by now, then it will be a cinch to wait them out. Once I have those orders, I finish the war in Paris drawing maps for the historians." He mused over his cup about it. This time his angle could not fail him. He felt that he had his luck back.

"That's what I'll do," he said. Then he looked at Ilse Margraven and set his cup down on the tray. "And you," he said. "You will stay here, won't you, Ilse? You'd be safe here. This place might be used for billets, but no one would molest you." He paused, as she seemed to look on past him, and he felt a sudden twinge of anxiety. "The war would be over for both of us," he said. "You know that, Ilse. Wouldn't you stay here?"

Her eyes came back to him again and he was acutely aware of that discerning quality in her even glance.

"Doke," she said, "I suppose I would. But I don't know. I could not be sure."

His anxiety deepened into outright alarm. Now he could realize with immediate clarity why there had seemed an indefinable but cogent zest to the day. There was contact, born of the last few days, continuing with this girl, like a silver chain linking his life and thoughts with hers. The possibility that this might be broken became a thing incredible and that conclusion was there in his mind fully formed, instant.

"I can't lose you, Ilse," he said. "I must know where you are and how you are. I want to be sure that I can reach you. I want to be sure that I can see you."

"That would be very nice, Doke."

"Nice!" said Doke Stanton. "It's crucial for me. Are you in love with someone, Ilse?"

Her eyes widened. "What?" she said uncertainly. "In love? I?—What are you talking about, Doke? You sound wild."

"I know," he admitted. "But in days like these, everything speeds up. A person understands things faster. I understand how much I need you. I wish you felt you needed me. I wish you would realize how important it is for us to find each other after the war. To have the war end for us when the Yanks hit this river and know that it is only a matter of time—" He ran a hand quickly over his hair. He did not think he was reaching her. She did not seem to feel the great urgent importance of one simple fact the way he did. They must not lose each other.

"You thought I was not well at the beginning. But," he went on vehemently, "I was just scared. I'm perfectly well. I may have talked wildly at times, but it was being scared, Ilse. I'll probably get scared again in my life. I can't help that."

"I know, Doke," she said gently. "Neither can I."

"But if we could look after each other," he said urgently. It was so clear, he thought. "We'd always be all right, Ilse. Can't you see how I want to take care of you?"

And then he lost her glance again. He felt a sick little feeling of desperation welling up within him.

"Doke," he heard her say, "listen—"

He looked at her expectantly. She was attentive, but she was concentrating on something else. "Listen—" she said again. Her voice had a breathless quality. "Don't you hear something—in the town—?"

It was a wrench to force himself to listen, but he turned his head toward the window. He was attentive, then. There was a dull roaring sound, with suddenly a few shots. The shots were not anything unusual, but that sound—it was like tanks. He came quickly to his feet and opened the casemented window. Instantly it was apparent, and with the unmistakable raucous roar of tank motors he could hear the sharp, clear, spiteful reports of rifle fire.

He saw the tanks, then. They were moving along a road into the town and with them were moving helmeted men. He squinted toward them, bending forward from the sill. Combat jackets and helmets with netting—

"Ilse!" he said, and nearly strangled. He turned and pointed. "It's the Americans!" he managed, his voice trembling. The obstruction in his throat broke and the words floated and he was nearly shouting. "There are American tanks and infantry in town! Now! Right down there now! They're here—!"

He spun again. It might have been a mirage. He had lost them among the rooftops that closed out the view of the streets. But again there were those bursts of firing among the houses of the town. They had moved into Remagen. And on the other side of Remagen was the bridge.

He knelt at the window sill, staring toward the bridge. Now it was the moment that he had thought of so often. The Americans were here and the sure sign that they were here would be the destruction of the bridge. He could hear the fire fight down in the town— among the gabled gray roofs and chimney pots, somewhere down there like a battle under a cloud, and he felt himself murmuring firecely, "Come on, come on, come on—"

Halftracks crowded with GIs were moving down that looping road toward the town now and behind them were some of the familiar Shermans clanking forward, holding regular interval, buttoned up for action, their guns depressed like probing steel fingers pointing at the town.

Some combat unit, he had no idea which one and it did not make any difference, was fighting the most important battle it would ever fight. He thought about that, straining to catch some idea of where the Americans were. They had penetrated deeper into the town, he judged from the bursts of firing that stabbed out from the welter of roofs, but there was no telling where they were, and he muttered it again between his teeth, "Come on, you guys, come on—" A piece of roof suddenly disappeared in a clatter of slate and a gaping hole jagged with shattered beams appeared. Where had that shell come from? He found himself reporting a running account to the girl near the window, as if he wanted to be sure she realized the enormity of this. There were Americans fighting their way through the town and both time and distance were narrowing between them and the bridge.

The blueprint was explosion and, as the minutes swept by, he waited for it and the fear of it became something that brought the perspiration to his forehead in the teeth of the raw March breeze. It had to come, the shattering, ending, destroying blast, and waiting for it was the worst fear he had ever known. There had always been fear, as far back as he could remember, from the fear of a bully's fist in a grade school playground to the fear of inadequacy and frustration, of dismemberment or death, and this was like all the fear packaged together. And when you met a fear that great, you had to move against it.

The thought came to him and he accepted it quite naturally. He turned from the window, moving rather stiffly, as if he were made of wood. The girl was sitting forward tensely in her chair, looking out at the town.

"Ilse," he said, strained, "I ought to be down there with those guys. I ought to give them what help I can. I ought to be in on this."

She sat back in the chair then and it seemed that she was

breathing rapidly. But she did not speak. "Ilse," he said, "what is the quickest way for me to get down into the town from here?"

She moved her head slightly from side to side against the pillow that propped her. Doke Stanton knelt on one knee beside her chair. "Those men down there are the best thing that could happen for you and me," he said. "How do I get down there, Ilse?"

The girl's lips moved. "At the end of the castle's drive there is a road that curves down to Remagen. But the quickest way is by a flight of steps down into the town square. Then the Koblenzstrasse leads out of the square—past a small hotel on the corner—"

He thought a moment. "Okay," he said.

"It is not the way you planned it, Doke?" Her low voice was unsteady.

"Not exactly," said Doke. "But it amounts to the same. Nothing has changed, except that I'm going down into the town instead of waiting here." He looked at her. "You were listening to me, weren't you, Ilse? Nothing has changed. I want to take care of you. I never want to lose you. You'd like America," he told her, and, for some strange reason, felt the pressure of tears behind his eyelids. "You'd like so much about America. We'll find the right help to heal your foot. You'll meet people who are like the Americans you have thought about—"

She struck him on the shoulder with her fist. "Oh, why," she burst out, "do you talk about yourself so? Do I think Americans are not human beings? Do I not think they struggle and suffer and grow? Do I not think they have so much of heart? You're my America, Doke—" Her voice broke utterly.

"Why," he said softly, blinking rapidly, "then it is all wonderful, Ilse—we have it all in our hands this minute—"

There was a sudden piercing blast of a whistle, a long sustained shrill blast, down near the river.

"It's the emergency alarm, Doke!" she said swiftly, and paused, her lips parted, as again it sounded, like a long banshee wail. He turned quickly to the window. "What does it mean?" he gasped. "Is it the signal—" His words were lost in the blast of a detonation. A thick plume of black smoke billowed up at the Ludendorff Bridge. He pressed a hand across his eyes tightly. "Oh, no!" he said.

The girl pushed forward, looking toward the drifting smoke. Slowly the outlines of the bridge emerged from the thinning black veil. "They seem to have destroyed the ramp," she said quietly. "At least, that's how it looks—"

"Yes," said Doke Stanton. He spun from the window and again knelt beside her chair. "Okay, Ilse," he said. "I'm going. The fight is still on. I don't know for how long, but—"

She clasped her hands around the back of his neck. "Don't go, Doke," she whispered. "Stay here and keep watch with me."

Before, he had felt that he ought to be down there with the Americans in Remagen. Now he felt a driving compulsion to be there.

"It isn't often you get a chance to know what you really want to fight for," he said, "the way I know right now."

She was so close to him and he wondered how he ever could have failed to realize that she was beautiful. That lovely thick mane of ash-blond hair and her fine skin and the delicately modeled bone structure of her face; Ilse Margraven was really beautiful and he appreciated that fact then and there, in a swift fleeting moment. He put an arm around her and drew close to her and kissed her and wished he had time to run his fingers through that hair and brush it back at her temples and again feel the gossamer lightness of her dancer's body in his arms. This girl loved color and music and movement, and, by God, how she would unfold! How she would unfold!

"I have to go," he murmured, and came to his feet. "You know I have to get down there, don't you? I just can't sit this out."

"Please come back right away, Doke," she said brokenly, and those long lashes, he saw, were wet.

"Why, Ilse," said Doke Stanton, "I love you." He reached for the Schmeisser machine pistol and hurried out of the room and down the stairs. Even as he swung open the great front door, he heard the thumping boom of cannon and knew the tanks were firing down at the bridge. He raced through the courtyard and down the paved drive through the avenue of evergreens, bareheaded and gripping the German machine pistol. One man was not going to make much difference, but you did not stand at a window and plead with some GIs to make the fight you wanted. One man might make some difference. There was a real fire fight down at that bridge. One man might make some difference. It certainly was going to make some difference to one man.

He came out of the drive on a broad paved road and looked around for the flight of stone steps Ilse had mentioned. He spotted them a hundred yards farther along and sprinted toward them. They were a long steep flight and he saw the cobbled square below with the gray stone houses around it. He took the steps with reckless speed and paused breathlessly at the foot, looking around him quickly. A little boy taking a drink at a public water fountain peered at him curiously. The remains of a burning roadblock sent up streamers of curling gray smoke. The windows all around the square were hung with white sheets. Several people had emerged from their houses, but, as they saw the bareheaded American, they suddenly ducked back in doors. Two German soldiers, coming up out of a cellar, raised their hands quickly.

Doke saw a street opening off the square, past a half-timbered building with a large sign in gold letters. That must be the hotel and the Koblenzstrasse. It was leading in the right direction, anyhow. He gave one last quick scrutiny at the windows around the square, his machine pistol at the ready. His recon sense warned him that this could be a dangerous town. The American force must have overrun a lot of German stuff that was still floating around. But there was no time to go by the book, when the sound of those tank cannons meant there was still a chance to save a Rhine bridge. He raced across the cobblestones for the Koblenzstrasse.

Lieutenant Colonel Bill Remsen had arrived in the vicinity of the bridge with Noon's crisp orders barking along with him like the brisk staccato exhaust of the jeep. A huge crater blown in the bridge approach fended off anything but men on their own two feet. He saw that immediately, before his jeep stopped. The tanks had maneuvered into position along the river bank and were firing smoke, as ordered. The infantry was staying behind the big Pershings. One man was eating K ration. Some of them always seemed to do that when they were nervous. Gave them something to think about.

Big Remsen picked up Tex Bodman, the leader of the engineer platoon. "Round up some of your boys in a hurry, Tex," he said brusquely. "Get set to cut all the demolition wires you can find. Follow the infantry. We're going across."

The Texan chewed and swallowed, with nothing in his mouth. "Yes, sir," he said.

Remsen glanced toward the bridge. Lord, it looked long. It looked as though there was no end to it. As he studied the structure, it seemed to him it shook a little. He brushed a hand jerkily across his eyes and strode toward Kurt Birmingham.

"Birm," he said. "Birm—"

Lieutenant Kurt Birmingham waited. Remsen shook his big shoulders like a mastiff coming out of the water. "Get your company ready. Get 'em across that bridge. The tanks will give you supporting fire."

Lieutenant Birmingham had to ask it. He had to ask it for the sake of the decimated company of his that had come through to this spot on the edge of the Rhine. "Keep moving!" he had shouted at them and they had yelled back, "Yeah, yeah, we know."

"Suppose," said Kurt Birmingham, "the bridge blows up in our faces."

Remsen said nothing. He gave the young company commander a slight touch on the arm and turned away. Yes, thought Kurt Birmingham, that's it, all right—it's a suicide mission and that kind of thing hasn't come up often on our side of the war, but here's one now. The Krauts were probably just waiting to get some American troops out on that bridge. Well, here it was, here's the bridge you wanted to cross, here's the Ludendorff mined to the teeth and ready to blow. Here it is, boy.

He quickly studied the bridge. White phosphorous smoke was drifting across its eastern end, but he could distinguish Germans moving around near the tunnel. Immediately he set up a CP on the edge of the crater that lay across the ramp approach. His three platoon leaders huddled with him.

"All right," he said calmly, "we're going across. Get your men together quick. We'll—*As you were*—"

A thunderous blast sent them all hurtling to the ground. A great column of smoke rose lazily, hung, and spread. Sergeant Czleusniak lifted his head out of his arms. "That fixes it," he muttered gratefully. "Thank the good Lord."

Birmingham picked himself up off the ground. Yeah, that was it. Must have been. He rested on one knee and saw the smoke eddy off and suddenly gave an involuntary lunge forward, coming to his feet incredulously. The bridge was still standing! The Germans had blown it and yet there it still was! He tried swiftly to get control of himself. Still the suicide orders. Whatever the hell had happened, he could see renewed German activity through the haze. A whole squad had bolted toward the end of the bridge over there, apparently working its way down to the first pier. Another blast coming up.

"Let's go," he said crisply, turning to the platoon leaders. The whole company seemed to have pressed up to the crater in a huddled mass, as though they could not believe they still faced the crossing of that doomed bridge. "Sloosy, your platoon leads, then Tony, then you, Hal. Okay, come on. Move on across."

No one stirred. Birmingham looked at them. Lord, they were a dirty unshaven lot. Tired, too, with the incessant strain of the last few days and it was something they could not grasp—these orders to move up on that bridge. It was something they had never imagined. They had been looking forward to reaching the river, linking with Third Army, and then settling down for some blessed rest. The bridges would all have been in the river. But this one wasn't! This bridge was still intact! It was standing and they had to cross it. They had to get moving to cross the Rhine. *The bridge was there!*

They were men. They were men in uniform, dirty, weathered uniforms. And somewhere in that company there had to be the spark. It had to exist, whatever was in this group of faces under helmets, whatever was in their thinking and their discipline and their answer to a challenge. *There was the bridge!* Where was the spark? It had to be there. Kurt Birmingham scrambled up on the bridge. He turned and cupped his hands and yelled to them. "Get moving! *And keep moving!*"

They stirred. Big Czleusniak spat nervously and wiped his lips with the back of his hand. He hefted his rifle and nudged Private Charlie Boehringer with the butt. "Come on, Charlie. You pick a spot and then I'll leapfrog you."

"I sure as hell don't want to," said Private Boehringer nervously, "But I will."

Czleusniak looked down and made a sweeping gesture with his arm to the rest of his platoon. "Come on, for Christ's sake!" he said. "You want that the two of us should do this by ourself? Like the CO said—get movin'—"

They moved, reluctantly, but the thin platoon scrambled up around the crater and gingerly edged out on the bridge. Boehringer suddenly broke for a gap in the planking, reached it and flung himself headlong. He turned to yell at Czleusniak. "Okay, Sloosy, leapfrog, goddamit."

The big sergeant broke past him and came to a kneeling

stop. "Keep moving!" shouted Kurt Birmingham. "It's a cinch! Keep moving!"

It reached them, that familiar shout. Gagliardi's platoon came up over the lip of the crater. The German machine guns in the towers opened up with their spurting bursts of clattering, chattering fire and the Americans moving out on the bridge went flat. Kurt Birmingham crouched, his breath coming in little gasps. Pinned down. Pinned down and the Germans working up another blast. Oh, great God, he thought, I'll run across this bridge myself, like some officer with a sash and a sword, until I get it. Where is that tank fire? He waved a frantic arm at one of the tanks and pointed to those medieval stone towers across the bridge.

The nearest tank swung its gun slowly, ponderously. The blast of its cannon knocked Kurt Birmingham flat. He rolled over dazed, pieces of dirt between his teeth. Just like home. He came groggily to his feet, spitting. There were men still lying pinned down on the bridge, hugging the planking. Sure, they were just men. They weren't divine. But somewhere within them had to be the divinity that would make them move and attack against the specter of imminent blasting destruction. The tank had knocked a piece out of the right tower and one of those German machine guns had ceased for the moment. But the other machine gun was alive. Holy mackerel, it sure was. Death in the air and death waiting for them under their bellies as they wormed their way over the planking. But it wasn't going to get any better. Get up, get up, get going. Hell, Czleusniak was pinned down for sure. He spun to little Tony Gagliardi. "Take your platoon through, Tony."

"Yeah," said little Gagliardi, and licked his lips. "Move!" he shouted at his men. He came to his feet and started to move out on the bridge in a crouch.

"We're going across!" shouted Kurt Birmingham. "We've started! Keep moving!"

The spark! They were on their feet and starting to move, two, three, four of Gagliardi's platoon. They ran, bending, along the catwalk, and other men saw them up and moving and scrambled to their feet, too. They were moving. They were beginning to go faster. Men were pulling themselves off the planking. They were running in a crouching, weaving, cumbersome way, but they were going. Birmingham pushed Czleusniak's platoon and they moved. They were out on the bridge now with their commanding officer on their tails. They worked clear of the western end and, behind them, the last platoon of the company hit the bridge. The company had moved. They were above the Rhine with a mined bridge under them and machine-gun fire cutting the air around them. The east bank was a long way ahead.

Tex Bodman and two of his engineers raced out on the bridge with cutting pliers, searching for wires, scurrying back and forth from one side to another, looking for the signs of the demolition charges, bending low along the spans to reach with their pliers toward the wires, grab them, twist, and break. Then, on their feet again, they moved forward behind the infantry, searching feverishly, pliers ready to bite, twist, and snap.

Little Tony Gagliardi suddenly started to run. If you ran, you would be all right. It was when you froze you were likely to get it. It was funny the way that worked out. His dark eyes were like black pits in his unshaven grimy face as he thrust his rifle out ahead of him and pushed himself after it. Run like hell. Simple rule of warfare. Keep moving! Yeah, yeah! That damned machine gun. Somehow he had to keep running, keep under its fire.

Sergeant Joe Prinzip had a simple rule of warfare, too. Stay close to his platoon sergeant. Gagliardi had a talent for survival and that was a talent much admired by Sergeant Prinzip. He ran, too, a tall thin GI with the Adam's apple bobbing spasmodically in his long neck, ran after Gagliardi, spraying pleas to some nebulous Authority. "Give us a coupla more minutes. Give us a coupla more. Give us a coupla more—"

The bridge seemed to shake from the blasts of the tanks firing from the west bank. To Lieutenant Kurt Birmingham every blast of tank cannon was like a shove in the back. Moving along with his old platoon, he thought, My God, did people ever walk across this, just walk across—a bullet plowed across the planking just ahead of him. Now they were catching sniper fire.

Private Solly Chergens instinctively started to throw himself flat and Kurt Birmingham swiftly grabbed him by the arm. One man start to do that and they might get pinned down again. He got Chergens to his feet. "Go on, Solly!" he panted. "Get off this bridge." Himself, he looked down through a gap in the planking and saw the gray water down there and his stomach gave a queasy turn. Out in the middle of the bridge now and he could not break into a wild desperate race against the ticking seconds. He had to keep his company moving and he had to get them across as a cohesive fighting unit and not a wild panicked mob. He turned and swept his arm in a wide arc to Hal Grove's platoon. He put everything he had into it, and, if he were to be shot the next minute, they'd maybe remember that sweeping command. Then he turned and ran along the catwalk, crouching, his carbine gripped in both hands. Okay, here's another Birmingham for the Ludendorff Bridge. A long time between crossings, Pop, a long time.

A 20 mm shell hit the top of the middle span of the bridge with a crash that once again sent some of the men lunging to their knees. Kurt Birmingham felt like flinging himself flat, too. That one had hit the bull's-eye and he had felt the impact of it all through his body. Another shell overshot the bridge and landed in the river with a geyser of water. He forged on a few more feet, then crouched as a burst from the stone tower ricocheted among the steel I-beams.

"Keep moving!" he yelled. "Let's get off this bridge. There's other guys want to cross, too, you know."

Someone else yelled "Keep moving," and another and another. They began to forge on again, in a crouching weaving run, digging at the planking as though they were trying to get off a treadmill. The searching engineers following along with them found a cable and blasted at it with their carbines until it parted. Two of them coolly knelt on the planking and swiftly looked for charges among the supporting beams above one of the piers. "There's a damn cute little bundle," one of them grunted, and swung himself down, pliers in hand.

Sergeant Gagliardi came up on the tower near the end of the bridge so fast that he stumbled, trying to check himself. This was the machine-gun nest and he had to clean it out in a hurry. Sergeant Prinzip raced on past him, made a leap and was off the mined bridge and on the east bank of the Rhine. His helmet fell off and he did not bother with it; he was across the Rhine and he simply kept running from sheer surcharged energy down the river road to the south until he finally slowed down.

Tony Gagliardi dashed up the circular stairs of the squat stone tower, panting, but his black eyes hard with a basalt quality and his finger on the trigger of his rifle. He could hear the metallic chatter very near now. He kicked open a door and poised his rifle. A three-man crew was servicing a machine gun at the window. One of them saw the American and there was something about the black eyes beneath that American helmet and the rifle in those hands. He yelled hastily and raised his hands. The machine gun stopped firing. It stopped just in time. There was a tightly wound spring in the mind under that American helmet. The crew quickly abandoned the gun and Gagliardi, keeping those black eyes on them, moved to the emplacement, lifted the gun and shoved it through the window. Then he jerked his head toward the door and fingered his rifle, crouching slightly, balanced on the balls of his feet.

Kurt Birmingham and the second platoon felt the release from that machine gun. They dove headlong for the east bank. Three men dashed into the other tower. Birmingham felt his combat boots hit the end of the bridge and he was running between the tracks on the approach to the tunnel. Then he swerved and looked back at the bridge. It was still there. It did not seem possible, but the Ludendorff was still there. Hal Grove's platoon was piling across fast now. The company commander felt himself quivering all through his thighs. He drew a deep breath and gripped the carbine tightly. If the bridge went now, there was going to be mighty damn few Americans on the east bank. One of Tex Bodman's engineers came racing off the bridge with a carbine in one hand and a pair of pliers in the other. "The main switch," he jerked out. "Got to find it—" He ran down through the emplacements, circling back toward the big stone pier, looking swiftly for the telltale cable.

Kurt Birmingham squinted toward the river, standing there, legs planted far apart, and his chest heaving rapidly. There was a savage exchange of fire out there now. He could spot the tracers like long sprays of crisscrossing steamers. The Germans were firing from positions among the railroad cars along the tracks to the north and American tanks and machine guns were spurting back fire across the gray river. Another engineer came dashing off the bridge and joined in the hunt for the cable. Birmingham spotted Sergeant Tony Gagliardi and waved toward the northern approach of the river road. "Send your prisoners across unescorted, Tony, and get your platoon dug in. We're hanging on by our teeth here and we may get a move."

Yes, they would get a move and they might be left holding on to the eastern edge of a demolished bridge. Lieutenant Birmingham tautly glanced around him, trying to pin down something in his mind that bothered him. There was a teetering balance here, a desperate momentary poising of events and he felt that without being able to see where that little extra edge of decision lay. If the engineers could find the main cable in one hell of a hurry, they would have a bridge and they could hold onto it like a tiny bull pup sinking its teeth into a trouser leg.

His glance was suddenly caught by a lone GI sprinting across the bridge. It might have been a straggler from Hal Grove's platoon, except that for a moment he did not appear like an American and Birmingham watched him narrowly. He wore no helmet and he carried what looked like a German Schmeisser.

He came off the bridge and raced along the tracks and then checked himself near Birmingham, crouching slightly at the knees as though he had alighted from a steep jump, gripping the Schmeisser in both hands. He was lean, with a crew cut, and his chest was heaving rapidly.

"Name's Stanton," he jerked out. "Recon. I've joined you. Where do you want me?"

My God, as if he was a platoon or company commander coming up with re-enforcements. Where do you want me? And yet, suddenly, at this time when the precariously balanced bridgehead teetered in the flying seconds, his question seemed normal. And as suddenly the loose end turned up in Birmingham's mind—*where was that German demolition squad?*—and he had an answer to a question asked at the right time.

"Cover the engineers!" he snapped out, and swung his arm in the direction of the river bank.

Immediately the GI whirled and raced down among the craters that pocked the bridge approach. Birmingham saw him stop suddenly, again crouching slightly, the Schmeisser leveled from his right hip with his left hand gripping the barrel, and at the same instant he saw the three German demolition troops. Two of them were paying out wire from a big steel spool that they were manhandling out of a crater toward a nearby bunker. The third was straightening, a big German, his arm back stiffly with one of those deadly potato masher grenades poised in the direction of the searching American engineers. Those Germans were gambling with the seconds, too, and the Americans must be close to that switch box, and in that frantic moment Birmingham had barely time to yell one word. "Cover—!" he heard himself shouting.

The bareheaded GI, still crouched, fired from the hip. The big German, his grenade still poised, staggered, spun lurching and, even as he fell, heaved it at the American firing off his Schmeisser clip. Birmingham saw the American dive headlong, heard the sudden blast of the grenade, and himself ducked as a cloud of dirt, stones, and smoke shot up in a geyser.

On one knee, he heard immediately afterward a sudden splattering sound of carbine fire and one of the engineers reappeared running, his fingers raised briefly in the V-sign. "Almost got a grenade down our necks," he reported. "But we blasted the main cable. It should be safe now, I think—I hope—"

Kurt Birmingham came to his feet with a breath that shook his shoulders. He ran a few steps in the direction of that new crater, because somewhere around there was a man who had come running across the bridge asking for a place to fill, and there had been a place, a specific and immediate and vital place, and he had filled it, and all in less than thirty seconds.

Then the company commander checked himself. Seconds were still priceless. He picked off one of Czleusniak's platoon and pointed to the spot.

"One of our guys may have been hit. Look after him—tag a medic as soon as you can—"

He gave him a push and then spun and detailed another man to get back across the bridge and inform Lieutenant Colonel Remsen that the Ludendorff was safe. Moving fast to organize the bridgehead, he found Hal Grove. "Take the high ground, Hal," he said tightly, and motioned toward the rugged height that loomed over them and was called the Erpeler Ley. "You know, like at Benning. I'll get support to you quick as I can. Move that platoon."

"Okay," said Grove, still breathing hard, and began rounding up his men.

Kurt Birmingham took another look at the river and his eyes narrowed against the drifting tracery of smoke and dust toward where a GI had disappeared in the geyser of an exploding grenade. It held him for a long moment in spite of the pressing action he needed to take. Whether that GI had survived or not, a bit of this bridgehead belonged to him, a strange soldier with no helmet and a German Schmeisser who had come running across the bridge and asked a strangely logical question for which there had been an acute answer, as if a man and a moment had met out of all the minutes, hours, days, weeks, and months of a whole war. "Where do you want me?"

Birmingham shook his head slightly, wondering, then ran down the river road to post a squad in the bomb craters there. There was no telling when the Germans might make a move. A tank shell exploded against the bluff just above the tunnel entrance and several German engineering troops ran out, their hands raised. Czleusniak's platoon covered them while the big sergeant surveyed the prisoners. "What's in that tunnel?" he demanded. "You got more in there?"

There was no answer. They simply stared with glazed eyes at the unanswerable and stupefying fact that faced them spanning the Rhine. The demolition plan had been carefully and expertly worked out and they had been thorough; everything had been tested and checked regularly and the bridge still stood and the shock of it seemed to freeze their faces into masks. Big Czleusniak sent them on across the bridge unescorted. He had too few men as it was.

He reported to Lieutenant Birmingham. "Looks to me like those guys had enough of war," he said. "But I don't know what else they got back in there."

"Put some men on both ends of the tunnel until we find out," said the company commander briefly. "Sew it up."

"Nobody puts his nose out?" said Czleusniak, fingering the grenades at his belt.

"Not until we get enough men over here to handle them. Get going, Sloosy."

"Got you, Lieutenant," said the big sergeant and lumbered off.

Birmingham walked back up the river road. He had done all he could. Now what was needed were reinforcements and he looked anxiously toward the west bank. It appeared as though Packey Hollis was starting his company across. There was going to be a strong German reaction to this and he hoped that the thin trickle of GIs starting across the bridge would swell into a flood, with tanks and guns. That was up to the brass. The brass had a job to do now, but sometimes the brass was a long way off from the guys holding on.

His eyes swept the Ludendorff Bridge in a long glance and the sight of it sent his leg muscles to quivering again. If he could only thank someone in person, heart to heart. If he could only say thanks. Well, why not?

"Thanks," murmured Kurt Birmingham. "Thanks."

It was strange, but, as he looked at the bridge, it seemed almost as if he were looking at it for the first time and he thought that was probably because of the wonderment that would not leave him. He knew for certain that ten minutes of his life would be forever set apart, as though during that time all percentages had ceased.

Then he turned his attention to the tiny American bridgehead east of the Rhine.

16.

BERKHAM was lying on his cot, reading, when Corps sent word over to him in a note from Lieutenant Colonel Mike Morrow. "Rise and shine. We've grabbed ourselves a Rhine bridge."

Afterward Berkham remembered how he had simply lain there and run the G-3 officer's words over in his mind as though they were in a foreign tongue that needed translation. The Americans had seized a Rhine bridge intact.

"That," he muttered, astounded, "is going to play hell with a couple of Big Pictures. The apples are all over the floor."

He swung his legs over the side of the cot and looked at his watch. It was 5:45 P.M. At 5:45 P.M. on March 7, 1945, what was very likely the biggest story of World War II had hit him. In all his years as a correspondent he could not remember when he had felt anything with an impact like this. Those terse words of Mike Morrow's were like a tag to a big mysterious package.

Over at Corps headquarters he found the G-3 section transfixed with activity. "A bridge!" Mike Morrow howled. "Never in this world, sure—but we have men east of the Rhine right now."

He calmed down long enough to sketch it quickly. One of Noon's spearheads had crossed the Ludendorff Bridge before the Germans could blow it. No, there were no details on that. But Noon had swerved from Corps orders and wanted to pile everything he could across the river as soon as possible and Leonard, the division commander, had backed him up. The Corps commander had backed Leonard and it was now in Army's hands. They were waiting a call from Army.

"But in the meantime we're going ahead with plans to rush all the artillery we can to Remagen," went on Morrow. "That's a light force holding the bridgehead and they haven't been able to get tanks across because of the damaged ramp. We're going to support with artillery from Remagen. We're getting roads and routes set up for a change of missions for the divisions. We're alerting ack ack units to move fast to Remagen. We're motorizing regiments."

He tapped a spot on the map. "That little place, Remagen, could make the First U.S. Army change its whole plan of future operations. All depending on whether Army changes our orders to push south to Patton and supports the bridgehead all out."

"When you get that order from Army," said Berkham, "it will have been all the way up to Ike. He'll call the final signals on that bridgehead."

"Point is," said Morrow, "every responsible commander so far has said to build up that bridgehead fast. When we've got the change in orders from Army, I'll fill you in. See you, Berk."

He dashed off to the big route map in one corner and Berkham studied that spot on the Operations map represented by the Ludendorff Bridge. A doomed country cousin bridge that had survived miraculously and could become the focus of the entire Allied front and, why, hell, it could become the most famous bridge in the world. It all depended—he nodded in his slow precise way—it all depended, not on the thin screen of infantry holding the bridgehead on the east bank, but on how fast and how right the American top commanders thought this one through. He looked at his watch. The decision had come up through Corps mighty quick. Now it would go up from Army to Army Group—to Ike.

The correspondent sat down at the side of the G-3 room and filled his pipe. There was a big lead here. He felt for it in his mind as he tamped down the tobacco absently. What was the thinking here on this side of the Rhine? He stuck his pipe between his teeth and fumbled for his lighter. Wait, he thought he had it now.

"Yeah," he muttered. He stuck his pipe in the breast pocket of his jacket and sought out the duty officers' billet adjoining the War Room and pulled up a folding chair to the field desk. He took out a notebook and pencil. Berkham had some thoughts for his personal war diary. . . .

"Today an obscure bridge was captured," he wrote. "The Ludendorff Bridge over the Rhine at Remagen. Nobody expected it. Nobody had figured out what to do if such an impossible thing were to happen. So how does American thinking move now, when a small force of GIs are holding a shaky bridgehead that the Germans are sure to counterattack with everything they have? It is now 6:20 P.M.

"There are two mighty effects possible from the capture of the Ludendorff. First, it could bust the Germans wide open.

It could break the whole crucial Rhine front. Second, it could bring on the great double envelopment of the Ruhr that the Americans have always wanted. In other words, a second major offensive. That would change the spear carriers into equal billing with Monty. But this isn't part of The Plan. And The Plan has been set since last September."

Berkham paused deliberately and sat there thinking. Then he hunched himself over the field desk again. "So the news of the capture of this obscure bridge will go all the way up to Ike. Then what? An argument with the SHAEF planners? A battle with the British Chiefs of Staff while they thrash it out? Will the decision be maybe to put enough stuff across to button up the bridgehead tight in a limited defense perimeter and then just hold on until The Plan gets underway? What's going to happen? Who," wrote Berkham, "is in charge of the store?" He looked at his watch. "It is now 6:38 P.M.," he noted.

He put down his pencil, closed up his notebook, and took out his pipe. Then he waited, dimly aware of the rush of activity in the War Room, the ring of the phones, the hum of discussions, the orders for draughtsmen, typists, and messengers. They were betting in there that the capture of the Ludendorff Bridge would be exploited with everything First Army could throw into it. Well, maybe. He waited. You had to be patient. This had to go to Army, to Army Group, to the Supreme Commander, and back down again. American generals were thinking about the Ludendorff Bridge now. How fast did generals think? How fast had those GIs gone across that bridge? Berkham simply waited. Tomorrow he would go to Remagen, regardless of the command decision, but he would have liked to go with his lead all set. What was that lead he had always hoped to write: "Here in this one place, at this one time, the whole war can be summed up." A big lead. Had he found the story for that lead? He had never expected to find it. But maybe this was the chance. He would never come any closer.

He made one notation while he waited. "It is now 7:33 P.M. Has Bradley reached Ike yet, I wonder?"

After that he did not look at his watch again. He was sitting there smoking another pipe when Morrow put his head in. "Roll 'em, Berk," he said. "Army just called. Previous Corps orders canceled. Rush everything to defend and enlarge the bridgehead. Five divisions to pile across at Remagen. Supporting tanks and artillery and anti-aircraft. The blue chips are in the pot. We're looking for roads, roads, roads."

"Thanks, Mike," said Berkham. He laid his pipe down on the field desk and looked at his watch. Then he flipped open the notebook and picked up his pencil. "It is 8:17 P.M.," wrote Berkham. "The decision is to bust the Germans wide open. The capture of the Ludendorff Bridge is to be exploited to the utmost. In approximately three hours that decision has gone all the way up to Ike and back. It went up like the snap of a buggy whip and it came back the same way. The brass has kept faith with the men who won that crossing. Seldom has there been a clearer link between the Little Picture and the Big Picture. Like a bridge, itself. And," wrote Berkham, "should there have been any doubts about it anywhere, Ike is the real Supreme Commander in fact as well as in name."

The Correspondent started to sign off there, then paused, thought a moment, and wrote one more line. "I wonder what in the name of heaven happened at Remagen."

That might very well be the last entry he would make in his personal war diary and these notes, for once, he would not destroy. He put his notebook away in his breast pocket, picked up his pipe, and went to check routes to Remagen with Mike Morrow.

"Anything that even looks like a road is going to be jammed tight pretty quick," said the G-3 officer. "You'd better go down tomorrow morning, Berk, and take the route through Gelsdorf."

Berkham checked it on his map. "Right," he said. "I'll go by way of Gelsdorf."

17.

MAJOR CLAY STANTON drove into Remagen in the late evening of March 7. As liaison officer with III Corps, assigned to the 9th Armored Division, he had checked with Noon's CP at Birresdorf to get a sitrep on the electrifying news about the bridge. He was referred to the advance command post that had been set up in Remagen and he drove on into the town with his jeep crew of a driver and radio operator.

He entered Remagen by the same looping road that the American armor had used several hours earlier, and, as his jeep dipped toward the town, there seemed to be lingering reverberations in the air of those first tanks. Then Clay Stanton glimpsed some newly arrived tanks ahead in the dark, moving slowly through town toward the bridgehead, and swift patrol jeeps darting through the streets of Remagen looking for any sign of German observation posts or snipers, and trucks parked on a street called the Koblenzstrasse discharging infantrymen who were quietly swinging off for the river. The build-up of the bridgehead was beginning to gather momentum and in the dark there was a swift tireless purpose about it. It was going to be a round-the-clock operation and he knew he was seeing the beginnings of the race to protect the foothold across the Rhine. There was already some artillery here; it was moving into place back on the hills behind the town.

The advance command post was in a hotel not far from the bridge. Clay Stanton's jeep nosed into a parking square at one side clustered with silhouetted vehicles. "Check with Corps," he told his radio operator, and looked at his watch. It was nearly 10:30.

The lobby of the hotel was already functioning as a message center and the operations section was set up in what had been a billiard room. A colonel was sitting at a big table under a green-shaded light surrounded by maps and the wires of field telephones. Clay Stanton reported to him and sat down somewhat stiffly. Under the light his face looked drawn and tired.

"You look beat," commented the colonel. "Been having it rough?"

Stanton nearly laughed. Within rifle shot of some men who had won the incredible prize of a Rhine bridgehead, and a liaison officer from Corps was asked if he'd had it rough.

"No, Colonel," he said. "I'm concerned about my brother. I haven't had news of him and I can't get him out of my mind—" He paused and grinned wearily. "The Little Picture," he said. "You know how it is, sir. We all have one. Okay, Colonel, what can you tell me? I need a sitrep for Corps. Also I'm supposed to give them a reliable map of the road net."

The colonel snorted. "Road net is inadequate," he said crisply. "And the terrain over across the river is poor. But, by God, this is one of the great breaks of military history and we'll work fast with what we've got. This is a little control center here, Major Stanton. We've got the aid station, a communications set-up, a motor pool, and a traffic control, attached to this command post. We're just trying to get things started."

He lighted a cigarette. "There's a thin screen of men holding that bridgehead over there tonight. We're trying to get some tanks over to help 'em through the night, but we don't have the ramp fixed yet. The Jerries blew it, you know." He looked at his wrist watch. "Maybe another hour. No more, I hope. We're getting three battalions of artillery set up to give interdictory fire through the night to help those Joes." He exhaled a swift nervous stream of smoke. "I don't know how long it's going to take the Germans to pull themselves together and hit us, but we're expecting the Luftwaffe tomorrow. That's going to be some sky. We're rushing antiaircraft battalions here and the Air Force is going to be flying cover. We're getting MP's here in one hell of a hurry, too, so that we don't get tangled up in bottlenecks at the bridge."

He stopped and took another long drag at his cigarette. "Now," he said, picking up a few typewritten pages clipped together, "here's an IPW report on the prisoners taken in the railroad tunnel on the east bank. Nothing much that would interest Corps, I think. Captain Bratge, the bridge commander, and Captain Friesenhahn, the engineering officer, were among those captured. Both of them completely stupefied at the crossing of that bridge. Utterly inexplicable. There was also a Major Scheller, but apparently he escaped from the tunnel before our troops sealed it off."

He looked up at Clay Stanton. "Might have been better for him if he had been captured with the rest. The Führer is going to blow both of his tops about the survival of the Ludendorff. He'll be after somebody." He tossed the papers back on the table. "About your sketch of the road net, there's an engineer CP near the railroad station. That's your best bet, but they'll be busy. We're moving men and traffic over the bridge all through the night."

"Thank you, sir," said Clay Stanton, getting to his feet.

"Drop your bedroll here," offered the colonel. "Mess here, too, if you like. Just get ready for all the noise in the world. This is going to be the hottest place on the whole damn front. The Germans aren't going to like this miracle."

Clay saluted and turned to go. The colonel had sounded almost reverent there, he thought, in a hard-bitten way. Miracle was a word you generally did not throw around. A big break, yes—one of the biggest. Where did an unimaginable break become a miracle? What was he thinking about anyhow? He stepped out into the message center and paused, pinching the bridge of his nose. The colonel was right; he really felt beat.

Standing there, he became conscious of the pressures, the wild racing pressures in the night outside the little Remagen resort hotel. There was the unabashed, swashbuckling roar of truck motors and the shouted profanity of GI's and the intermittent sounds of men moving toward the bridge. It reminded him that he had a job to do for Corps and he had to be about it.

When he came out into the night he could hear the sound of firing from the Erpeler Ley. Clearly, sharply, came the distant firing from across the river where the men guarding the bridgehead must be firing at shadows and wraiths and sounds in the darkness. He twisted his shoulders, as if shaking off a weight, and called to his driver. The night was threaded with tension and he had to feel his way around in it with cat's-eye lights, groping around this town crowded with urgent hurryings toward a showdown battle and, if this unnerved him, he asked himself sardonically how he would like to be holding down a bit of the bridgehead over on the Erpeler Ley tonight. He had been too far back too long.

It was late when he finally returned to the hotel. The duty officer at the command post showed him to a bedroom upstairs and he threw his bedroll on a bed and lay down. But he could sleep only fitfully. The artillery behind the town was in action and every time a gun fired it sounded right on top of him and the solid little hotel shook and the flashes stabbed across the ceiling of the darkened room.

He gave up on sleep as the morning became distinguishable and went downstairs to look for a cup of coffee, his head feeling as though it were stuffed with cotton. A small mess had been set up in a corner of the hotel dining room and he found three officers sitting around a table eating hasty breakfasts. One of them was the Colonel Ponsonby whom he had met last night. The colonel looked up from his coffee, invited him to join the table, and introduced him tersely. "Major Stanton, here from Corps. Captain Luisetti, medical officer, and Captain Stahr, headquarters commandant."

"Coffee, Major Stanton?" asked the medical officer, poising the coffee pot.

Clay nodded thanks and extended his cup. The colonel cocked his head as though listening. He seemed tense and hurried. Then he took a quick swallow from his cup and set it down with a clatter. "Get your road net information Stanton?" he asked.

"Yes, sir," said Clay.

"Going back to Corps today? Well, tell 'em this place is going to be hot beginning as of any time. We got some tanks across last night, but another vehicle got stuck in a hole in the bridge planking and held us up for a hell of a while."

"How about the force across the river sir?" Clay asked.

"They must have had a hell of a night, but they held on to that high ground. We're building up fast. A little more time and we can pull those tired troops out for a rest."

The colonel glanced at his wrist watch and came to his feet. "This is going to be some day!" he muttered. "Today we try to hold on to the big jackpot." He nodded briefly and left the dining room.

The headquarters commandant left shortly afterwards, but the medical officer, Captain Luisetti, lingered as Clay drank his coffee. He sat there with his own empty cup before him and studied Clay Stanton thoughtfully through his glasses.

"Major," he said tentatively, "do I understand you are assigned to Corps? Were you ever assigned to First Army?"

"Yes," said Clay. "I still am. I'm just on temporary duty with Corps. Why?"

"I think you should know that I have a Stanton on the casualty list, Major."

Clay looked at him perplexed. "So?" he said.

"What I mean to say is," the little captain went on steadily, "that in the personal effects of this Stanton is a letter with the return address of Major Clay Stanton, Headquarters First U.S. Army."

Clay Stanton stared at him and, as the words percolated in his mind, he became acutely conscious of the medical officer, as though suddenly he was so important in his life that he had emerged from a shadowy transient entity into clear, sharp, terrible focus. A small, slight man with horn-rimmed glasses and a blue-black shadow along his jaw and a mole high up on the right cheek.

"You do have a brother in the Army, Major? Or some other relative?"

"I have a brother, yes," Clay Stanton managed finally. "But this is impossible. My brother has been reported missing way to hell and gone back at a place called Tettledorf. How could he have been here with a CCB task force? It's impossible, I tell you."

"All I can say, Major, is that you had better look at him. Then there won't be any doubt."

"Yes," said Clay. "Yes." His fingers were stiff as he mechanically pushed away his coffee cup and his knees were stiff as he forced himself to rise from the table. He still wanted to argue the impossibility of this, but, of course, there was only one way to settle whether it was impossible or not and that was to see this casualty, Stanton.

"He's alive?" he asked tensely.

"He was fifteen minutes ago," said Captain Luisetti. "But he's not conscious. I'm sorry, but there's no hope."

Clay Stanton's jaws were stiff, too. "What happened to him?" he asked, as he accompanied the little medical officer from the dining room.

"Fragmentation grenade over across the river during the taking of the bridgehead late yesterday afternoon."

Grenade! First, there had been that mine, and now there had been a grenade for Doke—if it were Doke. He wanted to argue again, he had to fight down the argument that welled up within him. If it were the impossible!—if it were Doke!—

The aid station had been set up in a small building behind the hotel that had evidently once been an annex of some kind. At one side was what looked like a beer garden. Captain Luisetti stopped at a table in his little office and moved his forefinger down a list. He spoke briefly to a medical corpsman and then gestured to Clay Stanton.

"Follow me, please," he said. He was quiet, professional, assured. This was his little bailiwick of competence and authority; this was his own corner in the Army. Major Clay Stanton followed him, that strange stiffness in his knees and his hands clenched deep in the pockets of his trench coat, as he trailed the precise little medical officer through a large room with several litter cases. They were all tagged and two medics were moving among them. Adjoining the room was a spacious alcove. There were three canvas cots here, although only one of them was occupied. A medic came toward Captain Luisetti and said something in a brief low tone.

Captain Luisetti nodded and turned to Clay Stanton. "He has not regained consciousness, Major. Would you look at him—?"

He paused. Clay Stanton stood beside the cot and Captain Luisetti knew by the expression on his face. "I'm sorry," he said in a low voice, and bent over the blanketed form. The casualty, tagged Stanton, Douglas K., had one arm outside the blanket. Captain Luisetti took his wrist gently, held it a moment, then laid it down. He gestured the corpsman out of the alcove and followed him.

Clay Stanton went down on one knee beside the cot. His brother's face was pale, shadowy around the eyes, but relaxed and unmarked by injury.

"Doke—" said Clay Stanton in a low urgent voice. "Doke—" It was simply an involuntary desperate try to let that quiet form know that he was here. He covered his brother's hand with his own. "Oh, God, Doke—"

It was so useless to wonder how this had happened. It was so agonizing to feel this continued argument against facts. This should not have been Doke, there was no comprehensible way it could be Doke, and yet it was Doke. Millions of tons of steel had been flung around in this war and just an infinitesimal bit of all that in someone's hand for a few seconds had ended for Doke what had begun in a Connecticut living room on a wintry Sunday afternoon when the radio talked about a place called Pearl Harbor.

He started perceptibly, suddenly, as he saw his brother's eyelids flicker momentarily, then close again. "Doke," he said swiftly, "can you hear me? It's Clay—"

Again his brother's eyes opened. Clay arose and bent over him, looking down into Doke's face, holding both sides of the cot. Doke's gray eyes came to life suddenly. There was focus and recognition.

"Hi, Clay," he whispered.

"Hold on, boy. We're going to get you fixed up good as new—"

"Sure," murmured Doke, and half closed his eyes. He breathed lightly and slowly for a moment.

"Listen, Doke, how do you feel, boy? Shall I get the doctor—?"

"Clay—" The voice seemed stronger, low, but surprisingly firm. "Do something for me."

"Of course, Doke. What is it?"

His brother rested quietly a long moment, his eyes still half shut. "I'd been hiding out in Remagen," his voice came, then. There was a pause as he seemed to space his words with his light breathing. "Several days before CCB came through. That yellow castle up above the town. Big place with turrets. Can't miss it—"

Clay Stanton bent lower as the words trailed off. "Yes, Doke. Okay. Just take it easy, fella," he added anxiously, as Doke seemed to be forcing himself.

"Wonderful person looked after me. Name is Ilse Margraven. Get it, Clay?—Ilse Margraven. She's crippled. She can't walk. But she's everything—I ever wanted. Clay—"

"Right here, Doke. Don't worry."

"Tell her something. Tell her— there's always a bridge. Tell her. She'll know."

"I will," said Clay. Doke closed his eyes. "Good deal," he breathed, and was quiet.

To Clay it seemed that his brother was slipping away. "Hold on, Doke," he said fervently. "We've got to get you well—"

"Red Rufus," murmured Doke Stanton.

Clay stared down at him. His brother must be wandering in his mind and he did not like that sign. "Who?" he said uncertainly.

"Red Rufus," came Doke's light low voice. "Waste of time."

He opened his eyes again and looked up into his brother's face and yet, in a way, not at him. His mouth flickered briefly, as though he were trying to smile. And then suddenly Clay saw that those gray eyes had lost their focus and recognition.

The medical corpsman had gently drawn the blanket over Doke's face and Clay sat in Captain Luisetti's little office, his mouth tight and an agonizing smart in his eyes. The captain had a square brown envelope on the table before him.

"He talked to me a little," said Clay Stanton. "And then he was gone."

Captain Luisetti's eyes rested on him in a long searching glance behind the owlish horn rims. "Your brother spoke to you?" he repeated. He continued to study Clay Stanton. "Well, it is dangerous to say anything is impossible, I suppose, but Private Stanton was only technically alive. In fact, the corpsman at one time was actually sure that we'd lost him. And for him to come so far back as to regain consciousness, let alone to speak to you, is incredible—" He coughed slightly. "Almost," he added. "I would be most truly grateful, Major."

Clay said nothing. The medical officer proffered the brown envelope and suggested that he might wish to examine his brother's effects. Clay stared at the envelope, started to push it away, then pulled it to him and extracted its contents.

A wrist watch. A soldier's pay book. A crumpled mimeographed copy of Army orders with the paragraph pertaining to Doke encircled in red crayon. A few bills of Army currency issue. A wallet. Clay took a look at that wallet with "D.K.S." stamped in gold. He riffed through several of the pictures Doke carried in the little isinglass cases—Connecticut home scenes, mainly, although there was one of the whole family grouped with Clay Stanton in his dress uniform on Graduation Day at West Point. There was a small address book, too, and a U.K. hospital identification card and town pass to Salisbury. Two old letters to Doke from his mother and one that Clay had written to him while he was in the hospital in England about the chance for assignment with the Historical Division in Paris.

Captain Luisetti had sat quietly, his steady brown eyes still questioning behind the big horn rims. "We can send these to his home, if you wish, Major."

"Yes," said Clay. "That's best."

"Your brother will receive good care. He will be buried temporarily in Keslauf. But later he will be removed to one of the permanent Army cemeteries or sent home to the United States, whichever the family prefers."

"Yes," said Clay again. "I understand." His throat hurt

him when he talked. He stood up. "Thank you," he said. "You have been very kind."

"Major Stanton," said the medical officer, "I believe you when you say your brother recovered consciousness and spoke to you. Believe me, I would not have thought it possible and I say again be grateful for that much."

"Gratitude," said Clay Stanton, "doesn't come easy at a time like this. But thanks again," he said, and left Captain Luisetti's aid station.

He walked blindly back to the hotel. As he crossed the parking area, his driver came to meet him. "Corps says to report back there, sir," he said. "Were you figuring to go pretty soon?" There was a hopeful note in the driver's voice.

"Later," said Clay Stanton, and walked on past the jeep. He made his way along the street toward the bridge. The ramp had been repaired and vehicles were moving across, with lines of infantry using the catwalks at either side. An advance detachment of white-helmeted MPs had arrived and were directing the traffic at the bridge approach. Anti-aircraft units had also arrived during the night and their guns were already probing at the arching gray sky where the sound of planes could be heard high above the overcast. The sound of fighting from the Erpeler Ley had increased in intensity. The Germans were already reaching for the bridgehead. Occasional geysers of water spurted from the Rhine and there was the yellowish flash of an explosion among a row of houses close to the river. The bridge and the high ground to the east seemed caught under a gray bowl that was streaked with tracers and studded by exploding balls of yellowish fire tinged with black smoke streamers.

Clay Stanton crossed the bridge in a long file of infantrymen moving at a rapid swinging disciplined walk. He walked swiftly, matching his stride with theirs, but he had no coherent idea of what he was doing here. Vaguely he felt that this bridge had an association with Doke and he wanted to share it somehow. He felt, he realized, a sense of nebulous dissatisfaction about something, a restless uncertainty of something unsettled in his mind. He came across the Ludendorff Bridge like someone who had been wound up and given a slight shove.

When he reached the east bank he found that the infantry were all swinging left and moving fast along a pockmarked road that ran along the river. He moved out of the stream of combat men and walked slowly toward the entrance of the tunnel, stopping to look up at the Erpeler Ley. Somewhere around here yesterday afternoon Doke had been hit. Well, what difference did that make? He walked on toward the tunnel to get out of the way of a platoon of tank destroyers clanking across the railroad tracks. Then he paused. A chaplain's jeep was parked at the entrance to the tunnel and a chaplain was actually holding a service amid a cluster of GIs. Clay Stanton moved closer and again stopped, listening. Yes, a chaplain had crossed the bridge and was holding a service beneath the forbidding mass of the Erpeler Ley.

He did not know really what the chaplain was saying; he simply was glad that he could stand here and listen, as though he might be doing something for Doke. He was glad that some army chaplain had felt moved to come here so quickly. It deepened that sense of the miracle about this bridgehead. There was that word again and he did not quarrel with it, but it left him detached, as though, whatever it was called, it was not for him.

He mused there, a tall lean officer in helmet and stained trench coat, thinking about Doke's last words—some reference to Red Rufus. And across a span of years he remembered a little red cocker spaniel that had belonged to Doke as a youngster. But that had been so many years ago. Why would Doke have mentioned that? "Red Rufus. Waste of time." What Doke could have meant he had no idea; but his throat tightened so that he could scarcely swallow, and he turned away from the tunnel, grateful to the courageous chaplain, but unable to grasp, unable to cope with the restless searching uncertainty in his mind that he could not explain.

He threaded his way back across the bridge and came down off the approach to the west bank. Enough. He had to leave for Corps and it would be better to leave. No, there was one last thing. He raised his eyes and looked for it. Surely, it had not been in some kind of a dream that Doke had spoken of a yellow castle above the town—yes, now he saw it.

Okay. One last thing in Remagen.

18

HIS DRIVER felt around for it and finally located the drive through the woods. The jeep stopped in a paved courtyard before a massive front door. Clay Stanton swung out of the jeep and raised the big brass knocker. He banged it down two or three times and waited. His driver blew on his chilled hands and exchanged glances over his shoulder with the radio operator. The major was already late getting back to Corps and things were getting rough around here. The Luftwaffe would be going after the bridge pretty quick now.

The big door was opened by a shapeless elderly woman wrapped in a voluminous shawl. Her eyes dilated as she saw the American officer and she shrank back instinctively. Clay Stanton stepped into the house. He was in a vaulted stone hall with a massive dark staircase rising ahead of him and, to the left, a wide arched entrance into a big room. He tried to remember the name Doke had mentioned. He could remember only part of it and he made a tentative try.

"Fräulein Ilse," he said.

The old woman still shrank from him, but motioned toward the big arched doorway at the left and he followed her into a long rectangular stone room with dull wooden beams and woodwork. A girl was sitting before a big fire-blackened hearth on which a few sticks were burning. She had a blanket over her lap and a scarf around her shoulders. Clay Stanton did not wonder. The damp chill of this place hit you right away. He advanced a few strides into the room.

"Fräulein Ilse?" he questioned.

"My name is Ilse Margraven," said the girl.

"Stanton," he said. "Major Clay Stanton, United States Army."

She regarded him for a long moment. "Stanton?" she repeated.

"I'm Doke Stanton's brother," he said.

Again she regarded him intently. Then she made a gesture toward a chair near the fireplace. "Will you not sit down?" she asked.

Clay walked over and sat down. He switched his gloves idly in one hand and regarded Ilse Margraven. She was a slender person, with striking ash-blond hair combed in a curling mane around her shoulders and banded with a faded blue ribbon.

"Doke told me you had been wonderful to him," he said. "He had been hiding out here—I understand—"

"He came here as an escaped prisoner of war," said the girl. Those long blue eyes of hers rested on him in a discerning way that somewhat discomfited him. "Yesterday he left to join in the fight for the bridge. How is he, Major Stanton?"

He stirred restively. He tok off his helmet and scrubbed knuckles in his hair. "Fräulein," he said, "I'm sorry to tell you that my brother has died of wounds."

She continued to look at him as though her glance were something upon which he had strung the words like beads. Then her lashes lowered tightly and she leaned her head back. He waited, tapping his fingers restlessly against the helmet in his lap, feeling the strength of something that she had hidden away to herself. She was Ilse Margraven, a crippled girl who had been kind to his brother. She seemed to have perfect command of English. Her modulated voice was only slightly accented. She was a wonderful person, Doke had said. But she was a German and he felt aloof and constrained.

She lowered her head, but her eyes remained closed a moment longer. Then the lashes flickered and she raised her eyes to him. "I extend you," she said quietly, "my great sympathy."

"Thank you, Fräulein," he said. "I wonder if you would tell me how he came to be here. Please tell me what you can about his days here."

"Yes," she said. "Of course, I will. It is less than a week. It does not seem possible. Less than a week."

He had thought she would dispose of his request in just a few minutes and he would thank her, give her Doke's message, and be on his way to Corps. But apparently she wished to review the past few days of a man's life here. Clay Stanton's restlessness inclined him toward impatience at first and then gradually he found himself caught by the way she was sketching it for him and, as he listened to her soft clear voice, he began to relax and to listen absorbed. Between the time he had seen Doke this morning and the last previous time at the recon troop area there had been barely a week and yet in that period a whole great American attack had broken over the Rhineland and Americans were east of the Rhine and Doke Stanton had come out of hiding to fight for a bridge.

She talked simply, evenly, and he became more and more absorbed, so that when the American artillery shook the tall leaded windows of this room he sat unnoticing. It was like someone gradually rubbing clean a clouded window so that litle by little he began to glimpse the pattern of the last few days and in the pattern was a long slender bridge and a man who had linked his life with it.

Occasionally the girl paused. At times like that he simply waited, saying nothing, until she resumed. Once he automatically arose to take a few more sticks from the basket and replenish the fire. But mainly he sat there quietly. In a way, she spoke about his brother's days here as though they were something she reviewed as she talked, for he had the feeling that she was shaping something for herself with deft expressive hands, unhurriedly, but surely, a figment that grew and broadened and took on form and depth. When she stopped speaking finally, he realized that she had satisfied herself.

For a short while he sat in silence. Then he reached for the words. "Again I sincerely thank you, Fräulein." He hesitated. "Do you—did you love Doke?"

"Yes," said Ilse Margraven. "I learned to love him very much and for always."

He thought about that. "Before he died Doke recovered consciousness briefly. He told me you were everything he wanted in life and he asked me to tell you"—Clay Stanton concentrated to remember the words exactly, whether they made sense or not—"that there is always a bridge. He said you would know."

"Yes," said the girl in a low voice, "I know. And I thank you—so much." For a moment Clay Stanton had the feeling that she was not speaking to him, that she was not even thinking of him, that, fleetingly, he simply did not even exist in this room. His feeling of discomfort increased. He owed this girl something, but he really should not prolong his visit here. "You can be grateful, too," he heard her say. "I promise you, Major Stanton."

"Everyone seems to feel I should be grateful about this,"

said Clay Stanton. "The doctor thought I should be grateful, also."

"Oh?" she said with interest.

"He thought Doke so far gone that it was impossible for him to come back enough to recognize and speak to me."

"You don't agree, Major?"

"I certainly agree Doke was very low when I found him—" He paused. Clay Stanton did not want to talk about that. He clasped his hands on the helmet in his lap. "Doke said one thing at the very end that puzzled me," he said abruptly. "He mentioned the name 'Red Rufus' and then said 'Waste of time.' "

He had not meant to mention this and if the girl had commented he would have hidden it away again. But she remained silent and suddenly he wanted to get the perplexity out of his mind and pin it down with words.

"Red Rufus," he said slowly, "was a little dog that Doke owned years ago when he was just a youngster. He was Doke's special pal. I think at that particular period in Doke's life he had need of something like that devoted pup. He washed and brushed and combed Red Rufus and ran his stubby little legs off in the fields. When Red Rufus was killed by a truck, Doke was grief-stricken."

His fingers beat a restless tattoo on the top of his helmet. "I can remember Doke taking off Red Rufus' harness, giving him his last pat—" Again he broke off. "Well, anyhow, it's likely that Doke may have carried that sharp grief of a youngster tucked away inside him all these years. But why mention Red Rufus with almost his last breath and why or what is a waste of time?"

Well, there it was, and it still did not make any sense, but at least he might not keep going around in circles about it.

"Perhaps," said Ilse Margraven, "it was Doke's good-by to you, something he felt you would understand. Don't you think he meant to tell you that all grief is a useless and unnecessary burden?"

"Fräulein," said Clay Stanton bluntly, "I doubt if I could ever imagine any such meaning as that."

"I think it simply had not occurred to you," the girl said in her even way. "But when you think about it, perhaps you can see it is Doke's way of telling you there is no end."

He shook his head. "This is beyond me."

She looked past his shoulder thoughtfully and he saw that

there were traces of tears in her eyes. "I remember a beautiful little American poem. By your Emily Dickinson. I have always liked it and it comes to my mind now. Perhaps you know it, Major Stanton. It has these lines—

"These are the days when birds come back
A very few, a bird or two,
To take a backward look—"

There was a silence. The sturdy little fire popped violently in the great blackened cave of the fireplace. Clay Stanton rubbed a hand slowly along his jaw.

"I don't understand you, Fräulein," he said, somewhat sharply.

"I really think you do," she said gently. "Doke had glimpsed the truth that there is always a bridge."

He was baffled and uncertain and his voice came brusquely. "Are you a mystic?"

"No," said Ilse Margraven. "I love facts and law and clarity and reason."

He found himself anxious to challenge this girl who could afford such serenity when he could not, who could put aside all the facts that he himself must live by. She was entitled to draw comfort wherever possible at a time like this, but not by leaving him with the feeling that something genuine lay beyond his grasp.

"Listen, Fräulein," he said directly, "Doke surprised the doctor by rallying briefly when it was thought he was too far gone. That's all."

"At this precise moment you were there," reminded the girl. "He came back a long way, you told me the doctor said."

"That's just a medical phrasing. Are you basing your beliefs on that?"

"No, Major. It would not have changed my thinking, if Doke had never regained consciousness. I am simply grateful that occasionally there is the possibility that we may be given—to know a little—of what we believe—"

"I've heard a lot about miracles lately." Clay Stanton was still crisp. "But, unless I've completely misunderstood you, I'm afraid this is something beyond any reason."

"I do not know why you cannot accept miracles," said the girl. "It seems to me that a miracle is an expression of the highest law and sometimes through the upward reaching human spirit it sets aside what limits or threatens us."

She bent forward slightly in her chair. "Major," she said

seriously, "the people who serve the cause of freedom have great resources they know nothing of. Who can tell what enters into a miracle? Think of the people who have been praying for your success, ready to risk and sacrifice if they have a chance, the enslaved people, the little people, the remote people. Think of the resilience and strength in any cause that has such deep roots."

She was genuine. He was sure of that. At the moment she was like some mountain stream of clear fresh water bursting from a fissure in the great monolithic rock that was Hitler's Germany.

"It is not easy," she mused, "to match great risks with great courage and great sacrifice. But every so often it is done and those resources materialize—unplanned, unexpected—like the Ludendorff Bridge. Those heroic men proved that yesterday. Why can you not accept Doke as the symbol of what happened at Remagen?"

"Well, perhaps," said Clay Stanton uncertainly. "But—"

"If you object to the thought of a miracle, Major, call it what you will. But when you think of your brother, think of Remagen. Oh," she said shakily, "I shall miss Doke so. But I'm sure he knows"—she made an expanding gesture with her hands—"that there is always continuity and progress—there is always," she repeated, "a bridge."

He listened to her and knew that he would never make any headway against her convictions. They were quiet, but unshakable. Strangely enough, he did not want to. His intransigence was gone. If he could not agree with her, at least he found he could be grateful that someone in the world felt as she did. That, he reflected, was like sitting tight while someone else fought a cause for you.

He tried to speak, cleared his throat, and said nothing. He had come closer to losing his moorings than he had suspected, he discovered with some shock. He had better go. But he knew that he would never forget that last rally Doke had made. And those last words about Red Rufus were no longer senseless, but had a certain depth of feeling; they connoted a relationship deep in childhood and sealed that relationship through the future.

He looked at his watch and was astounded to find he had been here nearly two hours.

"Fräulein," he said, "I must report back to my headquarters. Is there anything I can do for you? I know Doke would like me to do anything for you I possibly can."

"There is nothing, thank you," said Ilse Margraven. "You have already done for me all I could ask."

He did not understand that, either, but he did not pursue it. "You are going to stay here? There's a big fight coming up around Remagen."

"No, I am not going to remain here. I am going," she said steadily, "to join my family in eastern Germany."

He stared at her thunderstrck. "You're going to try to cross that river out there?" he managed.

She smiled. "Oh, it can still be done, Major. There are still a few ferry points operating here and there. The river has not been sealed yet and a few of the little fish will be getting across for a while. I shall go tonight. I have two people here who will help me."

He shook his head, dazed. "As you think best, Fräulein. You know what you want to do. And," he said, rising and extending his hand, "I wish you good luck always."

She took his hand, then suddenly swept aside the blanket over her lap and came to her feet. "Of course!" she said in an eager whisper. "Of course—" Again he was struck by the tears in her eyes. She was really, he thought, a beautiful girl the more one looked at her.

For a moment she stood motionless, as if poising herself. "All right, Major," she said in a low voice. "Let us go."

He found himself walking toward the door with the girl at his side. She seemed to limp slightly, but he did not notice that her right foot was heavily bandaged until he turned to say good-by at the arched entrance to the great stone room.

"Well," he said, touching his gloves to the brim of his helmet in a soft salute, "once again, good-by, and thank you for taking care of Doke."

She rested one hand on the side of the archway and with the other gently drew his head down and kissed him lightly on the cheek.

"Good-by," she whispered. "Be happy."

"Good-by," he said again, and turned away from her. The elderly woman servant swung open the massive front door for him and he nodded briefly and stepped out in the courtyard. The big door closed behind him and he stood there, drawing on his gloves, his dark brows knit in a frown. Wasn't that girl supposed to be a cripple? Doke had said she could not walk. What was all this? Nothing seemed to fall in place.

His driver had thrown away his cigarette and straightened up expectantly behind the wheel of the jeep, but Clay Stanton still lingered there on the steps of the yellow castle above the Rhine.

Maybe all these things had an answer. Maybe it was possible that in this place the ordered world, as he knew it, had been turned upside down. Maybe a person should accept a miracle, whether he understood it or not, whether he believed in such things or not, because then there was truly peace of mind. Even if there was only about one chance in a million that she was right, there had been only about one chance in a million for the Ludendorff Bridge, too.

These are the days when birds come back
A very few, a bird or two,
To take a backward look—

He swept a gloved hand tightly across his face. Suddenly he was reluctant to leave here. At least, he should try not to let her vanish.

The driver of his jeep looked at the radio operator and then at the tall officer. "You ready to go now, Maior?" he called.

Clay Stanton took his hand from his face. No, he simply must go and go immediately. "Ready," he said, and swung into the front seat.

"Figure the quickest way back to Corps is through Gelsdorf, sir."

"What?" said Clay Stanton absently. "Oh. Yes, go by way of Gelsdorf."